Fourteen Stories from One Plot

BASED ON
"MR. FOTHERGILL'S PLOT"

The Authors

STORM JAMESON ⸱ REBECCA WEST

SHEILA KAYE-SMITH ⸱ G. K. CHESTERTON

GERALD BULLETT ⸱ FRANK SWINNERTON

MARGARET KENNEDY ⸱ EDWARD SHANKS

J. C. SQUIRE ⸱ H. R. BARBOR ⸱ A. E. COPPARD

HELEN SIMPSON ⸱ THOMAS BURKE

L. P. HARTLEY

The Editor

JOHN MILTON BERDAN

Professor of English in Yale University

NEW YORK
Oxford University Press

PREFACE

THAT the short story is an easy form in which to write is a delusion as wide-spread as your acquaintance, and it is usually believed fervently by the particular person talking to you. Encouraged by cheap advertisements that suggest writing short stories as a means to increase his income, he apparently assumes that the only requisites are time and inclination. And he is perfectly willing to outline several for your edification and delight. It then becomes your unpleasant duty to suggest doubts. Actually, of course, the short story is the most sophisticated form of writing. To evolve the form has taken the world from the earliest times almost to the present age. It is the latest to appear of the great types of writing. Naturally narration goes back until lost in the mists of the ages. Before the use of artificial light, although men rose with the sun, they did not wish to go to bed with the chickens. And in the gathering dusk and by the fire-light they amused themselves by the telling of tales. But these " tales " are not short stories. If the short story be defined as a single dramatic episode, rendered credible, the line of demarcation between the " tale " and the " short story " becomes at once evident. The best known collection of the former is that called generally the *Arabian Nights*. The scheme of this, as outlined in the prologue, requires such a construction of the individual " tale " that Sheherazade may cease narrating at day-break with the comfortable assurance that the Caliph will postpone her execution in order to hear the continuation. So one yarn with its episodes may wander on for weeks; a " short story " consisting of a *single* dramatic episode would have been literally fatal. To illustrate this distinction, think of the wealth of material in the one tale of *Ali Baba and the Forty*

Thieves. First Ali Baba up in the tree watches the thieves reveal the whereabouts of their ill-gotten treasure. For contrast, turn to the twenty-sixth chapter of *Tom Sawyer,* the chapter dealing with the haunted house. Whereas the Arabian author dismisses the episode in a few words, Mark Twain carefully brings his boys to the place, elaborately stresses their fear of discovery, emphasizes their delight, and reaches a pitch of excitement when Indian Joe crashes on the staircase. In outline both are the same; the treatment renders them completely dissimilar. But the same condition is true with the following episodes, the story of the jealous sister-in-law and her trick upon Ali Baba's wife, the story of the brother who dies in finding the treasure, the story of Ali Baba's saving the family reputation by disguising the corpse, etc., etc. Today each of these incidents would be developed separately until the last ounce of interest had been extracted. So the word " single " in the definition has a very real place. It differentiates the " tale " from the " short story " as a form of literary art. And it is a comparatively modern discovery. Although it may be found in the Italian *novellieri,* such as Boccaccio, it was accidental; Edgar Allan Poe is the first to employ it consistently. In his work you find careful subordination of the detail so that the reader interest will be focussed upon the one culminating scene.

The question of interest is, therefore, an all important one. The orator, the preacher, the lecturer and the conversationalist may hold you by the glittering eye of the Ancient Mariner, but the unfortunate writer is dependent upon his writing alone. If you are not at this moment interested in what I am saying, it is pathetically easy to close the book. You are not even restrained by the laws of common politeness. Consequently the author, to persuade you to continue reading, relies upon dramatic appeal. The essence of all drama lies in conflict, the struggle of one man with another man, or a man in struggle with natural forces. The reader is unwilling to stop because he wishes to find out what happens next. The simplest form of drama is a fight, and you will notice that in every fight you, observer, take sides. Instinctively you hope that A, or B, will win, and your interest is in proportion to your desire. From this human weakness arises the necessity of a hero; the story must be told from the point of view of one person. One character has, in theatrical parlance, the " lime-light." In the crucial scene it is what he will do and say that arouses your interest and it is his fate that evokes your sympathy.

But before you, as reader, sympathize with the character, you must be willing to play the game; for the time being you must believe the story. After the basic assumptions have been made, no matter how intrinsically improbable may be the course of action, that action must proceed logically. To accomplish this each step must be carefully prepared. This means that the short story is written backwards, that the reader takes it in the reverse order that the writer conceived it. The author starts mentally with the climax. But to appreciate that, the reader must be in possession of certain facts, — a condition that entails a series of preparatory scenes. These are so arranged that before the culmination the reader has received progressively and unobtrusively all the necessary information. These preliminary scenes are presented as attractively as is possible, but the interest must lie in the dramatic episode; what can be done with that is the determining factor in the value of the story. So the author is torn two ways. If the reader has not been given sufficient information, at the critical moment his mind will be distracted because he does not understand; on the other hand, if these scenes are long, his interest will flag and he will close the book. The aim of every writer is, then, to give as much space to the first and to condense as much as is practical the second. It is a question of proportion. A common fault of the young writer is to become so involved with his explanatory material that both he and his reader are worn out. The question of elimination is the difficult one, and, in Pater's phrase, the artist is known by what he omits.

With these general considerations in mind, we may now turn to a discussion of *Mr. Fothergill's Plot*. Mr. John Fothergill, the genial landlord of an inn near Oxford, evolved the following plot:

> A man gets into correspondence with a woman whom he doesn't know and he finds romance in it. Then he sees a girl, falls in love with her in the ordinary way, marries her and drops the academic correspondence. Happiness, then friction. He writes again to the unknown woman and finds consolation till by an accident it is discovered that the married couple are writing to one another.

That Mr. Fothergill is the landlord of an inn is a fact; that he is genial is a safe deduction because he persuaded a number of well-known writers each to write a story based upon this plot. Whatever may be the opinion of the general reader of the interest of the book, there can be no question of its appeal to the student wishing to learn the difficult art of the short story. Certainly it is the sort of book every instructor has desired. Here are to be found all the forms of the short story, with the exception of the detective story, and here are to be found all varieties of treatment. And as the plot was not original, each story represents that particular author's attempt in solving a common problem. The book then gives a series of studies in the technique of the short story.

The first comment to be made is that the various stories, although all written on approximately the same plot, are yet so surprisingly different. It is an illustration of the fact that it is not the plot but the treatment of that plot which is important. The usual experience of an instructor is that the student comes to him with a really novel idea, an idea so good that in spite of past experience his heart warms. Then the story is written, — and the result is appalling. The idea was so good that the student expected it to carry the story. But he must learn that there is no plot that cannot be spoiled by inartistic treatment. The original conception was good only in that it gave opportunity; if advantage is not taken of that opportunity, the result is valueless. So when the student has his first idea, he has a long, long road to travel before he turns out the finished product. Many questions must have been answered and there will have been much groaning and travail by the way.

And it cannot be said that there is only one answer to any question, that there is any definite right or wrong. Every type of treatment has its assets, but those assets are balanced by equally great liabilities. For illustration, suppose the story is told in the first person, as an occurrence that has happened to the narrator. Here the asset is a feeling of actuality. If I, John Jones, tell you something that happened to me, presumably you, as reader, are in touch with first-hand authority. But the liabilities are equally obvious. If the plot is one involving a question of life or death, clearly there is no uncertainty if the narrator tells it. He must have survived. Therefore the interest can lie, not in the uncertainty, but only in the manner of escape. A more subtle objection is that it is a cumbersome device. Nothing can be told the reader that the hero does not know, and no scene can be described at which he is not present. It requires considerable ingenuity to maintain the suspense and at the same time to impart the required information. A modification of this is to have the narrator not the main actor, but a subordinate figure in the drama, a Watson to the Sherlock Holmes. This gives increased freedom. He now can tell the reader the essential facts about the hero and his actions, he can be present at scenes where the hero is absent, and he can compliment the hero for the reader's benefit, when, if the story had been told in the first person, it would have sounded arrant boasting. But there is naturally a diminution of interest; the tale is at best only second hand. The last method is to tell the story in the third person. Here the author is everywhere and anywhere. He knows what the hero is doing and what he is thinking. And he knows what all the other characters think and feel. The interest given by the personal touch is necessarily lacking and the sense of actuality must be given by other means.

The most obvious means of acquiring conviction is by the setting of the story. You can treat it realistically by flooding it with the multiplicity of humble detail. You can enumerate all the articles of furniture in the room and can specify all the odors in the house; you can quote all the documents in evidence; you can retail all the original conversations; and you can call spades spades, until the wearied reader is willing to be convinced. In recent years such documentation has been carried to extremes. Its adherents call it artistic truth, but as a matter of fact it is only one of a number of ways of giving the conviction of actuality. There is no reason why, if it seem best, the story should be told as taking place in the present. Any plot can be put at any time or any place. There is no logical reason why I should not locate Mr. Fothergill's plot in ancient Babylon and have the correspondence written on bricks in cuneiform, or in modern Hungary, or in the South Sea islands, or in an entirely fictitious locality. The gain lies in the possible charm of the unfamiliar setting, and the still greater advantage that the reader cannot be certain of the probability of the events; he knows perfectly well that under given conditions a Bill Jones would not have done so-and-so and said so-and-so, but he is not at all sure that Ashtar, or Count Sobieski, or Ahulalula might not have acted in such a way. Yet whereas he probably would feel a fellow sympathy for the Bill, it is quite possible that he may not care at all for your esoteric hero. Moreover a great deal of effort and space is required to describe the foreign conditions, and, with all your care, you may make fatal mistakes. Or again, you can have the place familiar, but the time distant; London, but London in the eighteenth century, or New York at the time of the Civil War. If here the setting is easy to work up, the difficulty lies in rendering the mental states of the characters. The Civil War hero, for example, may use the telegraph, but he cannot use the telephone, — that is easy. But while clearly he would not believe in the doctrine of evolution, the harder part is to be sure in what he would believe. And you, as author, must know.

The same line of reasoning applies also to the question of the characters. Unless the author while writing cheats himself into believing in his people, the reader is apt to lose faith. This does not mean that the character must have been drawn from real life, but it does mean that the character must have had an existence in the mind of his creator. Unless you, as author, believe in Bill's existence, I, as reader, will not because you cannot give me what you have not yourself. The story is told that a gentleman, on hearing Dumas roar with laughter, hesitated to disturb him when he had company; whereupon he was told by the servant that it was only Monsieur D'Artagnan that was there. Dumas was writing *The Three Musketeers*. And because D'Artagnan was present to Dumas when he was composing, he is present to us while we read. The character is emotionally realized. But it is possible to substitute for this emotional realization an intellectual comprehension of the motives of the character and an understanding of his situation. A large number of modern stories are analytical studies of individuals. As the unusual is more interesting than the usual, there is a tendency toward the presentation of abnormal personalities. The proper study of mankind is man and many stories read like the case-book of a physician. The author tries to make you sympathetic with weakness, or even with crime, by making understandable the human motives that underlie the actions. " To know all is to forgive all " might be adopted as the motto of much of our modern work. So even the writers of the short story may be divided into the two classes, those that write to amuse and those that write to instruct.

Naturally both types of writers use dialogue. One of the most revealing factors about any man is his speech, the words he chooses and the way he pronounces them. In the extreme form this is called dialect, but the important fact to remember is that we, every one of us, have each his own dialect. No man has the same vocabulary and the same pronunciation as any other man. In the words we use we betray our social status, our education, our geographical environment, and our past history. It is clearly the part of the writer to make the character thus reveal himself. And at the same time the necessary information may be given the reader. The use of dialogue is, therefore, a labor-saving device.

From what has just been said, it may be inferred that much more than hasty inspiration goes to make a good short story. It is a test of the intellect and requires hard work. To expect that you can sit down and rattle off a piece that will win approval is comically at variance with the facts. Otherwise stories would not command the prices that hard-headed editors are prepared to pay. In the present conditions of the market, it is easy enough to hire the services of innumerable college graduates for a six day week of eight hours a day for twenty dollars. If an editor will pay you fifty dollars for a single story, that is equivalent to two weeks and a half of solid work. This is a brutal way of expressing the situation, but much of the failure in short story writing is due to plain laziness. The student expects the reward without the necessary work. Until he is willing to think and think again, to write and re-write, to study and plan, he will continue to receive the little slip of rejection. And it is in the belief that the various solutions of the same problem may aid him to find his own that this book is given him.

CONTENTS

VARIATION

By

A. E. COPPARD

NOTE

Mr. Coppard's story is an example of straight narration, without the devices that are employed in the following series. It is the normal presentation of the plot, of which it is only an amplification, told from the point of view of the man. Arthur Hart, a manufacturer of lavatory basins, is, in spite of his occupation, romantic and diffident. This explains why, on receiving an anonymous letter, in spite of his doubts he replied. The ensuing correspondence is broken by the war, in which he lost two fingers and part of an ear, but from which he gains a wife. As his wife seems unresponsive, he himself cools. When therefore in the agony column the former woman re-opens the correspondence, he gladly replies telling the facts in the case. But her letter has crossed his, a letter in which she has identified him by the two fingers and the ear. The result is that they find their true selves for the first time. From this outline it is apparent that all the questions have been answered. You ask why she wrote him, and you are told that, since she was never attractive, she had had several epistolary love affairs, and that this was merely the continuation of a surprising habit. You ask, why did he marry her, and Mr. Coppard replies that owing to her having been his nurse, he was attracted. And equally obvious is it that such a marriage would not be a success. Theoretically, then, this is a perfect story. Unfortunately it lacks interest. Neither character appeals strongly enough to the reader to make an impression on his memory. And the story remains little more than an amplification of the given plot.

VARIATION

By A. E. COPPARD

AS a rule, Arthur Hart was a lucky man, but there were times when fortune, without really failing him, did not seem to be helping him very much, and then he was baffled. But he was never baffled for long at any one time, being a lucky man. Physically, mentally, and socially Hart was a good average sort of person, with pink cheeks, coal-black curly moustache, a romantic disposition, and a habit of clothing himself in suits so very dull that they verged on the vulgarly unimpressive. Yet he must not be unkindly blamed for this, having been orphaned early in life. At thirty he was still a bachelor, with a prosperous factory for making lavatory basins and such-like ware on the outskirts of North London, left him by his father; in other words, he was in a position to be envied by orphans of many degrees and a fair number of other bachelors.

Arthur and his prosperity were also in a position of some exposure to women, eligible and ineligible alike, but a shy man who blenches before his own desires helplessly assumes an armour he detests and longs to discard. Romantic though he was, he had never been able to conquer his graceless inhibition and meet the desiring challenge of any pretty creature. It was, therefore, in a state of extreme excitement that one day he read a rather intimate letter addressed to him from an unknown lady, a Mrs. Wright. The circumstances which brought this unusual letter into his hands were themselves by no means unusual; one of those controversies was raging in the columns of the *Daily Signet* upon the topic (or topics) of Love and Marriage, in which it seemed to Arthur Hart that both pros and cons were understating their experiences, and,

3

conceiving this to be due to popular regard for the delicate nature of the theme, he composed a letter embodying views of more than ordinary candour, derived mainly from his browsing in the published case-books of various psychoanalysts. He signed his letter *Pro Bono Publico,* with the honourable addition, " I enclose my card," and the letter duly appeared. The controversy continued its raging career; but Arthur did not write again, because he had received this letter from Mrs. Wright, and straightway embarked upon a private correspondence with her.

Her letter to *Pro Bono Publico* was transmitted to Hart by the *Daily Signet,* and it stated that Mrs. Wright was in profound sympathy with the views expressed in his letter, and would like to correspond directly with him upon the matter. The letter was typewritten on a quarto sheet, faintly pink and perfumed. It bore no date, address, or name, but pinned to it was a stamped envelope, addressed to *Mrs. Wright, Poste Restante,* at some office in the district of Ealing.

Arthur Hart turned the letter over and over in his mind. Never in his life before had he received a personal private letter from a woman, and it excited him as much as her presence would have embarrassed him: an unknown creature; pink and perfumed, like her letter, he was certain. For an hour or two his imagination played with all the romantic possibilities offered by the piece of pink paper, until some tiny shoots of doubt began to burgeon in his mind. Why had she not given her real address? Why was she hiding under cover of a suburban post-office? Well, for one thing, she was married. And then, of course, she had no idea who or what sort of person *he* was; it was only natural that she should want to assure herself of his *bona fides* at the outset, to know who he was before giving the clue to herself. Besides, there was her husband, who, presumably, was not to know about the matter. But why had she not, at least, *signed* the letter? There was not a scrap of handwriting, not a "Yours truly," not even a name upon it; all was typewritten, even the envelope, and that was stamped as if she very much desired an instant reply.

It was truly romantic, mysterious, and inviting — thought Arthur Hart — but soon he had a further misgiving: it might be a joke. By God! yes, it was a practical joke. Some ass was trying to play the fool with him, some man, perhaps, who would get him to commit himself and then hawk the letter round his club: " Ho, ho! D'ye see this! My dear Mrs. Wright. Love and marriage. Won't you, will you; will you, won't you? Ha, ha! Look, look! That fellow Hart! What a dog! "

Yet there was something veridical in that pink and perfumed invitation, the sort of truth that Arthur was eager to put to the test. Already, to his fancy, Mrs. Wright (if this letter *was* genuine) would be dark and beautiful; the letter itself was a witness to her romantic intelligence; it might be a crass blunder to ignore her because of his fear of being victimised by a joker. Nothing venture, nothing win. So he replied that very day, declaring his willingness to continue the discussion with her, in the hope of arriving at some sincere conclusion about these questions through their mutual sympathy. But, in order to safeguard himself against that possible joker, he adopted the same means as Mrs. Wright, and typed his letter and did not sign it. Moreover, he attached a stamped envelope, addressed *Alaric Delmaine, Poste Restante,* at some post-office in North London.

By such crude courses do people like Hart embark upon their clumsy adventures. He took a false name and a post-office as defence against a practical joker; on the other hand, it would intimate to Mrs. Wright that what is proper for goose must be good for gander.

Mrs. Wright answered his letter in the same form again, with pink perfumed paper and stamped envelope, addressed to her *Poste Restante*. She intimated in a graceful way that, while she preferred them both to remain impersonal, she wished the correspondence to be as personal as the subject demanded and circumstances allowed.

Hart still feared the joker's heavy hand, but, having begun, he would not withdraw, and trusted to his own wariness to escape ridicule; so they continued to write to each other anonymously until all his suspicions were allayed, and he, too, became as frank in his attitude as the lady had been from the beginning. He wanted to know her Christian name; Mrs. Wright, he pleaded, was a mere abstraction that gave him no image of her. Also he wanted to meet her; could they not do this now, and realise all the joy of their letters?

She told him her name was Charmian, but that she was a wedded wife and never could they meet; that his letters were the great solace of her life so tinged with darkness; that it was impossible for her to step beyond the barrier of their letters. Within these limits she would do anything for him; it was a delicious intimacy, a marriage of minds. Never would she forget how thrilled she had been by his own beautiful name in the first letter; he was always Alaric to her.

From now onwards the letters were cumulatively love letters. Hers were almost always written in exalted tones, and, if her language was somewhat extravagant, it must be remembered that this is the common issue of vivid emotion. Mrs. Wright was undeniably a woman of good-will and generous tendencies. Her knowledge of human nature was perhaps not very profound; she seemed to think that the machinery of life could be run by mere kindness and that every complication could be resolved by simple treatment. It was a sort of spiritual arithmetic, her two and two always making four. When that sum refused, as it often did, to compose itself so readily, she attributed it to the evil disposition of the factors and not to her faulty arithmetic. There were things in the human heart, she admitted, that *could* not be accounted for. At such times Hart felt ashamed of having assumed a false name, but he could not bring himself to confess it to her, and, anyway, if they were never to meet, it was a harmless subterfuge, and did not matter. At other times Charmian's letters were the outpourings of an amorous woman revealing her tempting self to a man from a safe distance; she was thus free because he could not observe her; in his presence she would have been restrained.

For over a year they exchanged their inflaming notes, and Hart did not again press her to meet him. Save for an occasional tantalising desire to meet this beloved woman in the flesh, he was content with the anonymous relationship. Confronted by her, he, too, would certainly have been confused, possibly ashamed; he could not have faced with equanimity this ruthless partner in illicit intercourse. There was, too, the obstacle of her husband; for, although Mrs. Wright never referred to him again, he remained an insurmountable and dangerous problem. By this scheme of theirs they had made their position safe; their fantasy of love had bloomed like a flowering tree; it was most beautiful, but a touch of reality would blight it. Charmian was a woman of rare free spirit, but not, oh, most certainly not, one to be flattered, fluttered, and flirted with.

They might have gone on thus until in another year or so, maybe, their devotion had wilted and dried in its own sterile husk, but the Great War crashed upon them, and Arthur Hart went for a soldier. Both agreed it would be impossible to correspond when he went off to the war.

"Let us say good-bye," wrote Charmian, "and keep only

the memory of what we have been to each other. We are strangers in the flesh, and I could not bear to hear of the dangers you will meet. But always remember you are in my heart, and when war is over we may come together again. A hundred unexpected things may happen before then, and so, if you *do* care, put a line in the personal column of the *Daily Signet* (it brought us to each other!). I shall surely see it and reply."

Hart the more readily agreed to this, because it absolved him from the embarrassment of confessing his real name. He tried to persuade her to meet him just once before he left for the front, but she answered that it was impossible, that even if it had not been impossible she could not think of breaking the frail romantic thread they had woven around themselves.

Hart thought vaguely that this was a little callous, but he soon found out that human slaughter, filth, horror, starvation, and wounds were more tremendous things than pink notes from unknown women, and at length he ceased to think of Mrs. Wright.

Three times he was wounded, and on the last occasion he stayed pleasantly through the end of summer and autumn in a Brighton hospital, where they had amputated two fingers of his left hand and repaired the remnants of an ear that had been torn away. In consequence, he did not return to the front, and the Armistice found him sufficiently in love with a V.A.D. nurse to propose marriage. Edith Stone had shown a tender interest in his case, had treated him with singular kindness, and behaved devotedly, but in the end she married him.

At breakfast on the first honeymoon morning they sat facing each other in the hotel over the question of what to eat, and Arthur was enchanted to learn that his wife shared his predilections for coffee and haddock.

"Now I know one thing!" he cried, picking up his knife and pretending to sharpen it on his fork.

"What?" asked Edith.

"I think we shall get on well together."

"Do you?" said Edith, whose finery made her look almost pretty. "Do you really?"

"Of course we shall," answered her husband.

It is perhaps beyond human power to maintain any relationship at an ideal level, least of all marriage. Arthur and Edith were married a month after the cessation of war, and they went to live in a sweet little house at Kew, with a cook-general named Mackerel, whose jobbing-gardener of a cousin came and forced rhubarb for them and produced anæmic lettuces three times a week. The Harts had not known a great deal about each other except that they wanted to get married. Edith was an orphan, without any relations; her father had been an artist; she had undoubtedly made the best of her situation by marrying Arthur, but she was fond of him, and they were happy for quite a while. But as time went on and the minor disillusionments ensued, he could not help sometimes comparing the rather dutiful response of Edith with the ardour of Charmian's love. One was fire and the other, if not ice, was cool. And her coolness made him cool, just as Charmian's fire had inflamed him. He did not tell his wife of that episode, and the letters he still cherished were kept under lock and key. He did not complain to Edith, he was not a complaining man, but whenever he re-read the letters, and he began to do so rather often, he could not help but see Edith in her rather meagre properties. And it seemed to him she was less like a woman than a corset-bust in a woman's shop window. There was the curve of a bosom — made of wax — the fall of hips that served no sensible office. In her

eyes there was more drought than dew, in her speech more
vanity than understanding, in her love more function than
emotion. Edith was not at all handsome, nor endowed with
any special graces. Once she had been tender and devoted,
now she was dutiful and efficient, though occasionally he was
aware of strange moods in her which were hostile to him, and
warned him to keep at arm's length for days on end. At such
times her brown hair seemed coarse and harsh, her grey eyes
smouldered in the pale face with gleams of unuttered ill-will,
her face grew more emphatic in its plainness, and her touch
chilled him. There were headaches then, and little ills which
she imagined to be the preludes to some fatal sickness, appre-
hensions of a decay which she sought to arrest by resorting to
patent medicines. Edith never criticised *him,* or quarrelled
with him, not even about his common respect for omens, a
failing which undoubtedly annoyed her. She had no super-
stitions, absolutely none, and reduced every omen to its farcical
ineptitude. But still, when a strange cat crossed her path, she
was pleased if it was a black cat and disturbed when it was
not. That was merely because, although she did not like cats
at all, she preferred cats to be black. It would never do to walk
under a ladder, anything might drop on you; and if salt were
spilt at table she cleared it up at once because she disliked
untidiness.

Frankness and pride, she declared, were the noblest qualities
in life, and begged Arthur never to stoop to artifice or descend
to pity; he was to speak freely to her about everything that
concerned themselves, with truth, the whole truth, and nothing but truth. Yet once, when moved by the lack of warmth
in their relationship he ventured to speak about this, she declared she had never been so insulted in her life, that he had
a vulgar mind and a disagreeable temper, that he imagined
. . . Oh, depths!

"Ah, you don't understand," muttered Arthur huskily.

"But I *do* understand. Quite well I do. What *is* there to understand?"

"I was merely saying . . ."

"What? Oh, Arthur, why are you so weak, so silly?"

Baffled, he interrupted her denying tirade by handing her a pair of nail scissors and saying:

"I wish you'd just clip my sideboards for me."

So it was inevitable that his comparison of bleak Edith with the passionate Charmian nourished a sense of loss; but after a year of wedded fortune he recognised resignedly that women are as variable, unstable, and incalculable as the waves of the sea. Fashioned of wind and water, all alike hurrying to the shore, these resemble each other though changing from moment to moment. But the shore they break upon does not know in what mood or shape they come, and before it can know this they are gone. And yet, there are others, waves that have yet to break, pink and perfumed waves!

One morning at breakfast, on opening his *Daily Signet,* he was astonished and agitated to see a notice in the personal column:

"CHARMIAN TO ALARIC: Where are you?"

For minutes his blood seemed to do nothing but swarm into his breast and then discharge in frightful showers to every limb. He shot a stealthy glance at Edith, who was rather blithe this morning and did not notice his perturbation. Putting aside the newspaper, he made an effort to consume his food, but all appetite was gone.

"Aren't you feeling well?" Edith asked.

"Oh yes," he brightly replied.

"But you've not eaten anything."

"Just don't fancy it this morning."

"Is it your liver? Have one of my tabloids?"

"No, no. I'm all right. It's nothing."

"I wish you would."

"I'd take one if I wanted it," said Arthur. "I'd absolutely love to, *but* I don't want it. I do not, really."

"Are you going? Already?" she asked, as he got up from the table.

"Yes, I want to get off to the office early. Got to leave the car somewhere for the brakes to be overhauled, they're slipping a bit. Bye, bye."

As he bent and kissed her, her hand casually picked up the newspaper, and she asked:

"Do you want this?"

"I might as well take it," he said. But before handing it to him Edith glanced up and down the columns, and it seemed to his guilty fancy that her gaze hesitated upon that invitation from Charmian! Just that very one thing! He was horrified.

"Here you are," she said, folding it up for him. "Don't be late this evening."

"No," he answered. "No, I won't." And off he drove to his office and factory, chanting absurdly to himself. There is nothing more remarkable than a lavatory basin manufacturer in the transports of a mystical passion. The cool, glazed commonplace exterior seethes and becomes magniloquent, rhetorical, melodramatic, and fatuous, and our friend kept murmuring:

"Alaric, where are you?"

"Beloved, I am here!"

"Beloved, where are you?"

"Alaric, I am here!"

and so on, until he came to the office of the *Daily Signet,* and there he left an advertisement for its personal column on the following day.

The succeeding twenty-four hours were spent in a discordant, distracted state, and the throes he experienced were those of a scoundrel, a victor, a coward, a god; he was all these rolled into one, loyalty to Edith contending with the reawakened passion for Charmian. The issue was never in doubt, and it may be suspected that his sense of loyalty was little more than fear of the consequences of discovery.

When the *Daily Signet* came at breakfast-time he saw his own advertisement in the personal column:

"ALARIC TO CHARMIAN: Write to old address. Enchanted."

Immediately above it her own announcement was repeated, with an addition:

"CHARMIAN TO ALARIC: Where are you? Write to old address."

Away his thoughts whirled in wild-cat imaginings, until he heard his wife petulantly call:

"Do put that paper down, Arthur. Your breakfast!"

"Good!" he cried. "By Jove! it's getting late, I must hurry."

"You're not to," she admonished. "Are you feeling better this morning?"

"I could eat a horse," he declared.

"Are you sure?"

"Not about the horse, but I'm all right."

That evening he posted a long letter to Mrs. Wright, *Poste Restante,* at the old office in the Ealing district. It began by announcing — he wanted to be perfectly straightforward — that he was now married, and then it continued, in the traditional way of such letters, that his marriage was an unhappy one, his wife was cold and unresponsive and did not understand him. She was an Edith Stone; it had been a momentary attraction due to his weak state in hospital where she was nursing him. He had lost two fingers of his left hand in the war and a part of his ear was shot away, otherwise no damage but a few scars.

" She told me her father was an artist; but, do you know, I found out since that he only designed umbrella handles. But enough of such troubles, we have found each other once more. Your last letter said to me, *Always remember you are in my heart.* I want to hear from your lips if that is true now. You must meet me; you must; I insist! It is stupid to waste our love on mere letters."

That and more like it was the kind of thing he wrote. He was grown-up now. Having been to the war and lost some of his fears, he recklessly plunged.

Next morning on his way to business he popped into the North London post-office he had designated.

" Any letters for Hart? " he enquired of a pretty girl behind the counter. After searching in the rack she told him " No."

Disappointed, he turned away, and then it flashed upon him that he had made a stupid mistake. The name he should have asked for was Alaric Delmaine, not Arthur Hart! It was impossible to ask the girl again for a different letter; she would think him an impostor. Blast it he would have to wait. Twice again during the day he peeped in at the post-office, and each time the same girl was in attendance; he dared not go in, and it was not until he was driving homewards that evening that he found a different official there, and secured the letter for Alaric Delmaine. He slipped it into his inner breast pocket; he could not bear to open it there, it would keep until he had a few calm moments alone.

At home he was soon able to obtain them, for Edith had a headache, wanted no dinner, and so, after bustling about tenderly for her, her indisposition having made him feel something of a villain again, he left her lying on the couch in the drawing-room with a tube of aspirins and a cup of tea. Then he went in to his dinner, and, alone in the dining-room, he opened Charmian's letter.

Oh, it was a strange upheaving revelation, written by hand, not typed, and the paper was neither pink nor perfumed. Yet it was full of the old passion.

"I am a widow now. Perhaps if you still care for me it will be possible for us to meet somewhere. My husband is dead, but you know how unhappy I have always been with him, so I cannot pretend any sorrow."

But then came a passage that turned his heart, blood, and brains into buttermilk and cheese.

"He did not understand me, no one has ever done that except you; he had none of the fine feelings and the glow of my Alaric. But what could you expect of a man who made lavatory basins and things like that? He was a well-meaning man, a good man, and did his duty in the war; he was wounded several times, and lost two fingers and the part of an ear."

And the handwriting was Edith's! Yes, it was that guilty thing lying in the other room, that piece of dry pumice, who had fooled him with monstrous balderdash. She was Charmian! And she had got his letter, too, by now. Sure! Jesus, Joseph, and Mary, they were properly bowled out! Oh, the hell, the hell! Edith was Charmian, Charmian Edith! Oh, marvellous! Olympus had been in labour and produced this — this — pincushion! It was stuffed full of poisonous pins.

Half an hour later he went into the drawing-room; it was impossible to postpone the discussion any longer; they were in it, up to their necks, together. Edith sat on a hassock, staring into the fire, her face huddled in her hands. Hart went and stood looking down at the top of her head.

" Well," he said casually, " I got your letter. Did you get mine? "

Silently she nodded her head.

" So I'm dead, am I? " he cried angrily. " And you're a widow, eh? "

" You've done just the same as I have," she answered dully, " and perhaps for the same reason."

" What do you mean? "

" You take assumed names and make love to girls you think are married. Have I done worse? "

" That's what I want to know."

" I have not."

" You wished me dead. Dammit, you *make* me dead."

" I'm sorry, Alaric, I did not know you."

" Who the devil was Wright? You never told me you had been married before. Did you kill *him?* "

" No," she said sullenly. " I was never married before. There is no Mr. Wright, there never was any Mr. Wright, he's a fiction — like Alaric Delmaine."

" And like Charmian! "

" No " — the answer was sharp — " she's not a fiction."

" Oh, I'm all wrong, and you're all right, I suppose. Well, for God's sake explain it all to me."

But Edith remained as quiet as the wall in that teeming silence, until he blared out:

" Well, what have you to say? "

Wearily she rose and confronted him:

" What *can* I say? "

" That's what I want to know."

" I'll try to tell you," she said, " if you'll sit down and be patient."

There was such a deprecating humbleness about her appeal

that he dropped into an armchair, while she sat down on the hassock again and faced him.

"Think of me as Charmian, will you? You know *her* well enough. There are all our letters, yours and mine; you know me only too well. Perhaps I am a romantic fool who thinks passionately but never feels passion; but I can't believe it, even yet. I was never attractive to men, but I yearned to be loved, and a good many years ago I got into correspondence with a man I did not know, and we wrote letters without seeing each other. They were not very nice letters, his to me, but he persuaded me to meet him, and when we met I was repelled. I never saw him again, nor wrote him, but I missed the letters terribly. That was what I wanted, to pour our my intimate thoughts and feelings to a sympathetic man in a way I dared not do face to face with him. I suppose I was a very virginal type of creature, who feared the realities of love and was satisfied with the romance. I did not want a real love affair; I wanted a fantasy. This kind of thing happened half a dozen times, I think. I wrote to men, and they responded, and though they never gave me in their letters the fine thing I dreamed of, I was fairly content until they wanted to meet me. That always proved fatal, the glow and charm faded immediately on seeing them, I could not write to them any more. So at last I determined I would never meet a man in such circumstances again; never, never, it spoiled it all. It sounds so simple to me, all this, but I suppose you find it hard to believe."

Arthur Hart shrugged his shoulders vaguely.

"But it is true," she continued. "It *is* true. Then I wrote to you, and your letters gave me all I had ever craved. All, all. And I was so afraid of spoiling it that I would not meet you, and I did not."

"Not as Mrs. Wright," he said, half laughing.

"I called myself that, and pretended that I was married, to give it as an excuse for our never meeting. I am glad somehow that you respected that and did not insist on seeing me, and yet you were the only one I ever longed to meet. That is all."

Her husband sat staring into the fire; then he said, turning to her and fidgeting in his chair:

"Well, it has cleared up things a bit, but it leaves matters pretty hopeless."

"I suppose it does," she admitted.

They were silent for a long time, and then she said:

"I shall write no more letters."

"Why not?"

"To no one now," she said sadly.

"Not even to me?"

She leaned forward and scratched at his knee reflectively with her finger-nail. "Would you like that? Would you care? Would you care as much as before?"

"Would you?" queried Hart. It was a fascinating enigma still. She replied:

"Would letters be necessary now?"

Strange excitements were stirring him, incredible blisses.

"Ah, but you've killed me off," he said brusquely.

"That was only symbolic. I wanted to put out of my heart anything that interfered with my feeling for Alaric. That has been so perfect. I felt your letters were more than words, just as mine were really me."

"Six men," he grumbled.

"You were the last. I never wrote to another. You were perfect to me, something I'd been trying all my life to find."

"As Alaric?"

"Yes."

"But not as myself?"

"I did not know your real self. It was hidden. I only knew an Arthur Hart, and he never loved me as Alaric."

"Nor you me as Charmian. I only knew you as Edith."

"Don't you think," said Edith slowly, "that we have found each other now?"

"I wish," he said, "you had not sneered at my lavatory basins."

"You sneered at my father's umbrella handles."

"Did you really wish me dead?"

"No, no, Alaric, no!" She eagerly clasped his knees with both her hands. "Don't you see that I've found all I've been striving to get, and I'm no longer afraid? I was frightened this morning when I got the letter and realised all, but oh, my dear — do you really think I am cold and unresponsive?"

"Depends on whether you are Edith or Mrs. Wright," deliberated he.

"Then doubt no more," she whispered, rocking his knees fondly. "Alaric, where *are* you?"

Bending down, he caressed her flushed cheeks between his hands, murmuring:

"Charmian, I am here!"

MR. JOHN ARNOLD

By

SHEILA KAYE-SMITH

NOTE

Like Mr. Coppard's *Variation, John Arnold* of Miss Kaye-Smith is an example of straight narration. It is divided into three sharply marked sections. Section I is explanatory, giving the motives that led to the marriage and ends with the statement of its failure. Of that all but the last page is simple statement of fact. Section II explains his psychology towards the unknown correspondent. Then the dramatic scene is staged in Section III. The scheme is thus clearly outlined. For this reason it should be compared, point by point, with Mr. Coppard's work. Miss Kaye-Smith focuses entirely upon Arnold. His psychology is given in detail, showing his reactions and his motives. In contrast to him his wife is a nameless shadow. Even at the end she never knows that her husband was the anonymous correspondent. Mr. Coppard's scene between the husband and wife is naturally lacking. In place of that, the drama is entirely in Arnold's head. Curiously enough the ending in both stories is the same, a reconciliation and a willingness to begin life anew. But Mr. Coppard explains it emotionally. Miss Kaye-Smith argues that he was disgusted with romance, and that he was caught on the rebound. "After all, there might be something in Frances to explore . . ." and that is the only time when the wife's name is mentioned. She has been bitterly hurt by his letter. So romance for neither has proved satisfactory. Compared with the sentimentality of Mr. Coppard's "Charmian, I am here," this is hard and cold. The two stories are so much the same, and yet are diametrically opposite in the mood given to the reader.

MR. JOHN ARNOLD

By Sheila Kaye-Smith

I

THROUGHOUT four chequered years of married life Mr. John Arnold had managed to conceal from his neighbours the fact that he had met his wife through a matrimonial newspaper. By slow-growing processes he had come to regard the circumstance as disgraceful, though at the time it had struck him as highly romantic. The war had given him a taste for Unknown Woman. Enlisting in 1914, he had been in the very first batch of Lonely Soldiers whose advertisements, hung like flags in the agony columns of the newspapers, signalled their need of " cheery letters." The cheery letters had come by the bagful, many of them accompanied by photographs, and Mr. Arnold, then aged nineteen and a half, had had the luxury of choosing the six prettiest patriots out of an offering of fifty-eight.

For four years, in and out of the trenches, in and out of hospital, he had carried on the game. It had been a good game, even when he had lost. For, of course, he had lost sometimes. The story of Anne of Cleves is of universal significance — as he found when he met the office girl who had sent him the photograph of her sister who was on the films, hoping forlornly that if they ever met he would not notice the difference. But what did it matter? There were plenty more where she came from, and it was not always or often the plainest girls who plied the Lonely Soldier trade. As he told his less enterprising comrades-in-arms, he never went on leave without a choice of half a dozen peaches.

His leaves became a phantasmagoria of London streets and

crowds, of Lyons' Corner Houses, of *The Bing Boys, Bubbly, Nightie-Night,* and half a hundred cinemas. He grew to glory in his power — he emphasised his choice of peaches by ordering a fresh supply on every leave; and once he had the whole basket of them to see him off at Waterloo. What fun it had been to watch their surprise and disgust when they met each other, to wonder afterwards how they had left the station, together or separately, united in grief or sundered in jealousy! By the end of the war he thought he knew a lot about women.

Peace robbed him of his glory. It would not be true to say that he was sorry it had come, but he realised that with his khaki tunic — and it had been an officer's tunic for the last two years — he shed his pasha-hood, his power to pluck, enjoy, and finally discard the peaches of his country. Not only was his appearance considerably impaired by a ready-made suit of civilian clothes, but he no longer had the time or the money required for his old gaieties. He was lucky in being able to find a job — a clerical job with a shipping firm — but his salary would not rise to war-time standards of entertainment. He must be content with a dull life of lodgings and high tea and an occasional gallery visit to the theatre or cheap seat at the cinema.

It was a bitter change, and sometimes in his more dejected moments he thought that he would willingly endure three months in the trenches if they could purchase three delirious days in the West End. Lice, cold, mud, hunger, terror, were better than the grinding safety of his present life, bereft equally of danger and delight. His new limitations made him self-conscious, and, being no longer able to take girls to the Dress Circle and the Corner House, he would not take them anywhere; in fact, he would not know any girls. The memory of his past splendid spendings would not allow him to enjoy their company cheaply, so he would not have it at all.

The result was that at thirty-five he was a lonely, rather diffi-cult man, more prosperous than he had been, but with no idea of spending his money on anyone except himself.

Then the unexpected, the fantastic, happened. An almost unknown aunt died possessed of quite unknown riches. For years she had lived meanly and solitarily, having quarrelled with all her relations except Arnold, whom she had never seen, and to whom, therefore, she left all that she had. There was only one condition — that he should take her name, and his pride had no scruples about this — he had long used it as a Christian name; all he had to do was to push it into the place of the undistinguished Taylor his father had given him and revive a buried John. As John Arnold he bought a new house, moved into a new suburb, and started a new life.

It was then that for the first time he thought of getting mar-ried. He had not thought of it when he went swaggering as a war-time pasha — why bother with the pains of matrimony when he could have its pleasures in such certain variety? He had not thought of it when he was poor and lonely. He had told himself that a wife would only complicate his poverty and embitter his loneliness. But now, when he was rich and lonely . . . it was another matter.

He did not by this time know any girls or women, there-fore it was practical as well as natural for him to return to his old methods and advertise in the newspapers. " Well-to-do bachelor would like to meet young lady with a view to matri-mony. Must be under thirty, good looking, and good house-keeper." One or two matrimonial papers immediately wrote urging him to advertise in their columns, and in course of time his notice reappeared worded more attractively. But even in its original form it brought him many replies. Once more he had the female world to choose from.

He chose carefully, and finally selected a widow living in

Sheffield. He thought that it would be as well to have a wife with a previous experience of married life to sober her and teach her wisdom. She had not been very happy with her husband, so there would be no distressing comparisons. She had sixty pounds a year of her own, which would spare him the trouble of making her a personal allowance, and yet at the same time would leave her dependent on him for all the necessities of life. She was satisfyingly pretty, and yet aloof and shy in manner, so there was not much fear of her bestowing her charms save where they were due. Altogether it ought to have been an ideal marriage — and yet it wasn't.

He couldn't understand why. All the auguries had been right, all the precautions had been observed. Here was no hasty war wedding, the trap he had so wholesomely feared as he had watched it snap his friends; here was no raw young bridegroom or inexperienced bride. Yet from the first there had been uneasiness, conflict, dissatisfaction, distrust. They did not apparently care for the same things — their desires were sundered from the foundations to the superficies of life. He had thought from preliminary enquiries that they had tastes in common, but, though they might both like the same sort of home, the same sort of holiday, the same sort of amusement, their liking was of a different quality, arousing more conflict than like and dislike. They quarrelled about everything they did — her queer abstracted listlessness provoking his attack, intensifying under it, and goading it to frenzied renewals, as a stone will strike sparks out of iron.

" I see what it is," he cried on one of these occasions, " you don't love me."

" Love you."

She stared at him strangely. What had he said that was so startling?

" Well, do you? "

" Why should you have ever thought I did? "

It was his turn to stare strangely.

" But why did you marry me, then, if you didn't love me? "

" Why should I have gone to a matrimonial agency if I had wanted to marry for love? "

" Don't talk about that."

" But it's the point of the whole thing. Neither of us wanted to marry for love, so we decided to put the matter on a business foundation. It's been a failure — up to the present — but don't let's drag love into it now we're examining the causes. I did not want to marry for love — I had done it once, and the misery had been awful, so I thought that next time I would arrange the whole thing differently."

" It's unnatural for a woman to want to marry without love — cold-blooded. If you'd had such an awful experience, why did you want to marry again? "

" I told you at the time. I found I couldn't manage alone. I'd only sixty pounds a year, and no training."

" You'd worked in an office."

" That was only during the war — I was sacked immediately the market became crowded. I hadn't a dog's chance in the scramble, so I decided to get married, and, like you, I thought I'd do better if I didn't lose my head over the business. I can't think why you should suddenly start talking as if the whole thing were a romance."

" It could have been a romance if you weren't so damned cold and superior."

" A romance — after meeting like that? "

" We met as I've met dozens of girls before — first a correspondence and then an appointment. I've told you some of my war adventures, and I think even you agree that they were romantic."

" They weren't quite the same as this."

" No, but the beginnings were similar."

" Not at all. A muddy pencilled scribble from the trenches thanking Miss Jones for her interesting letter and charming photograph, isn't quite the same as a typewritten communication *re* her advertisement in the *Matrimonial Mail*."

" For Heaven's sake stop casting that up at me! "

She walked out of the room, leaving his rage to short-circuit in his heart.

II

It was after that or some similar quarrel that he went to the locked drawer where he kept his war-time letters and read them over again. There was a huge quantity, for he had never been able to make up his mind to destroy one of them, even those he had not answered. He read them now with a curious sense of pathos and regret. These girls had understood him, even those who had never seen him. . . . There were all those Clarice Brown letters. How they had poured out their souls to each other! They had been perfect pals, and yet whenever he had fixed up a meeting with her something had happened to prevent it, and then she had suddenly got married and had stopped writing — he had been quite upset. . . . There was that Phillida girl, too. She would not meet him, nor would she tell him her name, because she was engaged to a chap in the Durhams. But she had written, she said, because she felt romantic. War, and living in London on her own, and being engaged, had made her feel romantic, and the chap in the Durhams apparently was not. Romantic — he would like to show Frances her letters; they were full of talk about romance. . . . She had not written many, only about half a dozen; she had apparently become conscience-stricken about her rightful young man, and had left three of his unanswered. Yes, he had written to her three times without an answer, beseeching her to let him see her, even to see her photograph. For some unexplained reason she had captured his imagination as it had never been captured by women he had met and handled. Ten years ago now . . . just at the end of the war, just before his poverty began. He wondered if she remembered.

Then suddenly a mad idea came into his head — rushing in with a fanfare of excitement. Why shouldn't he write to them again? — all those whose addresses he had here. No, it could not be quite all, for he had quarrelled with some and had seen more than enough of others; but suppose he wrote to a score or so — asked them if they remembered. . . . Perhaps he might even meet one or two of them again. . . .

At first he played with the scheme, not definitely committing himself to any details of its performance. But as the day passed his play became more serious — it hardened into planning. And that night he dreamed of himself in uniform, jostling his way down the Strand with a girl on his arm, a girl who was sometimes Lucy and sometimes Molly and sometimes Gertie or Doris or Gwen or Dora, and sometimes provokingly unknown Clarice or unknown Phillida. . . . If I were the only boy in the world and you were the only girl, which girl would you be?

He did not care. He would write to them all. Dear old thing, how goes it? His war-time phraseology came back to him, and he did not notice that it was war-worn. As he wrote he found himself humming: " You called me baby doll a year ago."

He wrote the letters at his club, and asked for the replies to be sent there. He was now a member of the Automobile Club, and those vastly glimmering premises would do well for any entertainment that might result. He would have the girls there to luncheon and to tea and to dinner. He would take them to theatres, to the more palatial talkies. Why had he not thought of doing this before?

His eighteen letters brought him just a dozen replies. Six damsels either were dead or had decided that the past was best forgotten. One or two wrote, " Fancy hearing again from *you,*" told him that they were married and lived in such inaccessible places as Fife or Mountain Ash, and were ever so happy. Certain others were equally remote, though still unmarried — " The war took all the best boys." From only one did a second letter bring any reply, and that, humiliatingly, was the only one who had never seen him. Clarice was among the completely vanished; it was Phillida who seemed inclined to let the correspondence ripen.

He could not help feeling disappointed. All those gallant girls and not one wanted to renew an acquaintance which his memory painted as hectic, dazzling, and glamorous. Oh, it was all very well to slang the war, and paint it in mud, and write of it in blood — there had been a lot in it that wasn't mud or blood, that was better than anything that was going on now. Those were the days! His lost youth called him from the war, mud-spattered and bloodstained, but Imperial. As he'd often said before, he'd go back into the trenches if he could also go back to that splendid war-time Piccadilly, which seemed to him a different thoroughfare from the crudely banal post-war Piccadilly that he sometimes trod.

However, he continued his correspondence with Phillida. He told himself ruefully that he must be thankful for what he could get, and after a while he came to the conclusion that he was not getting such an utterly bad thing. Phillida still chose to remain anonymous — she was no longer at the office where she had worked during the war, but she asked him to write to her at what she confessed was an accommodation address. She evidently liked mystery, thought it romantic, and he found himself, to please her, growing more and more mysterious. He, of course, used the name that had been his during the war, and felt a certain satisfaction in being again Arnold Taylor for a few minutes every week.

Phillida was married, not to her young man in the Durhams, but to a man as unromantic as that young man — moreover, to a man who did not love her, as the chap in the Durhams had certainly loved her before his bullet found him. They lived in a suburb (though her accommodation address was in Chelsea), and her husband was out all day, not at work, but either up in town or playing golf. No, she did not think he was unfaithful — he was too dull for that; she did not expect any other girl would look at him. But he just couldn't be happy at home like an ordinary, rational man. She was neglected and she was lonely — and if ever by any chance he spent a day at home she was bored. She could not make friends easily with other women (a number of his girls had said that, implying somehow thereby their superiority to those who could). Yes, their friendship of years ago had been Romantic — so Romantic, indeed, that she had taken fright and refused to answer any more of his letters. Thus his vanity was soothed and his self-confidence restored. Would she be afraid this time? he asked her. No, she did not think so. She was older — she realised that you must Take what you Want, for it won't be given you.

" After all," she wrote, " our first duty is to Live. I do not believe that such things as Right and Wrong matter at all, do you? Life comes first, and when I die I shall want to feel that I have Lived. As Hugh Walpole so truly says: 'It is not life that matters, but the courage you bring to it.' I think that when the time comes you will find that I am ready to Dare."

Thus encouraged, Arnold wrote and suggested a meeting. This, he told himself, was a woman in a thousand. His wife could never have written a letter like that, so full of originality and daring. Oh, that he had met Phillida before he had met

Frances! He would not then have let her go so easily — he
would have compelled her to give up that wretched chap
in the Durhams, who, after all, had proved a phantom. . . .
He would have married her himself. The reason why he had
married none of those other girls was that none had ever given
such proofs of a generous and original mind. He had never
been the sort of man whom the flesh alone can satisfy. . . .
No, he would certainly have married Phillida, and that hasty,
reckless war wedding would have justified itself as his
marriage of calculation and inspection had altogether failed
to do.

Then it suddenly occurred to him — Was Phillida herself as
beautiful as her thoughts? There was his former experience
with the typist to remember. . . . He had better not commit
himself too far before they met. Indeed, inspired by this new
doubt, he begged her for a photograph: " Or how am I to
know you when we meet? It might be extremely awkward —
I might miss you altogether."

But Phillida preferred to remain Mysterious. The more ro-
mantically complicated and baffling their first encounter, the
more, he gathered, she would be pleased.

" For years now I've had too much of things I know, and I've
known everything too well. I want our meeting to be sudden,
rapturous, artistically satisfying. I feel sure I shall know you,
even though I have never seen your face. But, to allay any
doubts that you may feel — I have none — let us each wear a
white flower and carry a copy of Swinburne's poems."

These signals seemed to Arnold highly unsatisfactory, especially as their meeting was to take place " under the clock "
at Charing Cross. But her firmness forced him to agree. She
had refused to come to his club, saying that her husband was
a member, and as, according to her, he was often there, that
seemed a pretty good reason. He would have liked her to come

to him in some quiet restaurant, where the first shock of their encounter could have been hid in a corner, but, remembering how easily this pretty bird was frightened, he would not argue or oppose. She should choose whatever was for her, even if incomprehensibly, the smoothest way.

III

Once the meeting had been fixed a strange elation took possession of him. He felt himself already back in the glamorous past — young and free, with life and romance before him instead of behind. A sunshine of warmth and gaiety poured over his life — even Frances seemed lit up by it, she no longer struck cold. If he had not known that the change must be in him, he might have said that she, too, had changed, had become warmer, happier, more animated in her manner. She certainly seemed to talk more than she used, and he detected her in sudden little airs of gaiety. . . . But it was his reflected happiness, of course; she was the moon of his sun. She was lit up because he burned so brightly with hope and expectation. Poor Frances! She was not so bad, in her way, but how different from Phillida! They were two opposites — one all unimaginative constraint and cold reserve, the other all romantic impulse and warm imagination. Even Phillida's insistence on the due observance of the mysteries, which at one time had irritated him, now seemed to him a part of her attraction, of her glamorous antithesis to all he knew and disliked in Frances.

But, sitting in the train, on his way to meet her, he had a sudden reaction — a sudden fear of meeting anything so disembodied as Phillida. After all, he had of her no physical image whatever. The body with which he perforce had clothed her was nothing but his own creation. Actually he had nothing physical of her at all — not even such slight physical indications as are conveyed by handwriting, for her letters to him were all typewritten, as the first had been. His heart suddenly armed itself against her. She had no right to treat him like this. She might at least have sent him her photograph, given him some indication of her air. She had said that she was young — but what are young and old? Forty is youth to sixty and age to seventeen.

He forgot most of his qualms in active preparations for her arrival. He had planned gorgeously for her entertainment. No Corner House was adequate now, and he went to the place which had always shone like a beacon above his war-time revels, the Carlton Grill. Here he ordered a special luncheon and special flowers for the table. At a florist's he bought a white gardenia for his buttonhole, and at a bookseller's a pocket edition of Swinburne's poems. The latter purchase revived some of his irritation. First of all, he should not have had to make it, as there ought to have been a pocket Swinburne in the shelves at home, and its disappearance at this crisis was gratuitously inopportune; secondly, he thought this was a silly stunt of Phillida's — surely a white flower would have been enough; there weren't so many men likely to be wearing them under the clock at Charing Cross on a foggy day. But Phillida had seemed to think there might be, and had insisted on the supplementary Swinburne.

He felt an idiot standing there with the volume clasped in his hand. Why not a copy of the *Strand Magazine?* He ought to have insisted on it. He hoped she would not keep him waiting long, and comforted himself with the thought that a suburban train was not likely to be unpunctual at this time of day. The normal crowd of a station platform moved about him without seeming to notice him, and after a time he began to feel more at ease. But she was late. Looking up at the great clock face behind him, he saw that the hands pointed to twenty minutes to one. Had her train, after all, been delayed? He would ask a porter. . . . Damn it all, he didn't know where she was coming from! This was preposterous. Thank Heaven it would all come to an end today! He would insist on these tinsel wrappings of "mystery" being torn off the gingerbread of love, leaving it clean and wholesome. Meanwhile, the situ-ation infuriated him. He felt helpless and foolish, waiting there for the unknown from the unknown. What fools women are when they try to be romantic! There was something to be said for Frances after all.

Then suddenly he saw his wife standing quite close to him, looking away from him towards the crowds that were begin-ning to stream from some suburban platform. He moved back instinctively, but there was no use thinking he could hope to hide himself. He could not go far, and directly she turned round she would see him. But it was some time before she turned round — she gave him the impression that she, too, was waiting for somebody who did not appear. She stood there, gazing anxiously, first at the suburban arrivals, then towards the entrance from the Strand. She was certainly expecting someone, and it seemed to him the last cruel stroke of Fate that her tryst should be the same as his.

The minutes passed, and at last she turned and saw him. He went towards her, thrusting the Swinburne into his pocket as he did so, but painfully conscious of the white flower. Then, as he approached her, he saw that she was wearing flowers, too — a bunch of marguerites pinned to the collar of her coat. A ri-diculous thought crossed his mind that she, too, might have made an appointment with an unknown lover.

"Hullo!" he said. "What are you doing here?"

"I'm waiting for a friend. She's late. What are you doing here, John?"

" The same. I'm expecting a man up from Orpington to lunch at the club."

For a while they stood facing each other. How could he get her away?

" I don't think I'll wait any longer," she said suddenly. " I've a lot of shopping to do. It's her own fault if she doesn't find me —— " And she walked off towards the Strand.

Arnold stayed fuming under the clock. The hand moved from the three-quarters to the hour, from the hour to the quarter past. It now seemed obvious that Phillida was not coming. At the last moment she had betrayed him. Or perhaps she had never meant to come, but had been fooling him all along . . . miserable little devil! He cursed her, standing there with his white buttonhole. This was the last time he would have anything to do with a romantic woman.

Ten minutes more, and he would leave the spot. He could not possibly have missed her; from where he stood he could see anyone loitering at the bookstall or tobacco kiosk. There could be no mistake. She had failed him — failed him or fooled him; perhaps both. The clock hands were at the half-hour. He tore out his buttonhole and threw it away for others to tread on. Then he walked out of the station.

Turning into the exit, he nearly ran into his wife. She was standing just inside the arch, either spying on him or still waiting for her friend. If the latter were the case, then that friend must certainly be a lover, for she had lied to her husband, telling him that she was off shopping, whereas she was still hanging about the place. From where she lurked she had a good view of the platform.

" Hullo! " he cried. " I thought you had gone out shopping."

" Yes, but I came back. It struck me that Mrs. Smith might come by a later train. Your friend hasn't come, either? "

" No, he hasn't."

He stared at her. She was certainly a beautiful woman, and she had a new gown on today. That proved it, of course — she had an assignation, and hers had failed her even as his had. Serve her right!

"Why are you waiting here?" he asked her maliciously. "You'll see your friend more easily if you wait on the platform."

"It's so draughty there, and I hate waiting in a crowd."

He admired the readiness of her lying. Here, he told himself, was a practical and resourceful woman. He looked at her again, and a faint trickle of jealousy made her suddenly desirable.

"What are you going to do now?" he asked her.

"I shall wait a bit longer, and then, if Mrs. Smith doesn't come, I shall go home."

"Why not come with me and have a bit of lunch."

He was surprised to find himself asking her.

She shook her head.

"No, I'd rather give her a chance."

She was more tenacious than he — perhaps he was a fool to have been so easily discouraged; and yet after an hour . . . Then he found himself wondering: What if Frances's man came after all? He found himself astonishingly provoked by the idea. She must not meet him. He would see that she did not — he would insist on her taking the next train home; he would put her into it himself.

"Look here," he said, "there's a train goes at one forty-five; if you're quick you'll catch it."

"I don't want to hurry off like this, without giving my friend another chance."

"You've already waited for her an hour," said he, "and no woman on earth is worth it."

He looked at her meaningly as he spoke, and it seemed to

him that she quailed. He took her by the arm and led her without further protest to the suburban departure platform. The train was waiting, and, feeling suddenly magnanimous towards her, he paid the extra first-class fare on her third-class ticket and bought her a copy of the *Strand Magazine*. A few minutes later the train glided out, with her rather stricken face at the window, and he walked out of the station surprisingly more pleased with himself than at any time since the days of his war glory.

He went to his club and ate a solitary lunch, which he enjoyed more than he could have thought possible. He still felt pleased with himself, and, in a different way, he felt pleased with Frances. His new jealousy was a stimulant rather than a goad, for if Frances had an admirer, that admirer had certainly failed her; his rival was no more formidable to him than Phillida was to her. Ah, that little cat! She had cured him for ever of his romantic cravings, and, though he cursed her for it, he felt that henceforth his life would be better balanced and happier without them. After all, there might be something in Frances to explore. . . .

But he did not forgive Phillida. On the contrary, directly after lunch he sat down to write her a truly formidable letter. He told her how he had waited for her in vain, and, even if it were a mistake and not treachery on her part, the whole thing was due to her romantic stupidity, wrapping up their friendship in mystery so that it was impossible to make anything sensible or practical out of it. He was through with it, anyway; this was the last letter of his that she would ever receive from him. "It's all very well to talk of feminine mystery. I don't believe there's any mystery about women except what they make. Personally, I prefer women who don't make it. After all, I think I'm better off with my wife than I at first imagined.

You've done me this much good in that you've shown me, etc., etc."

He thought it was a good letter, and posted it with great satisfaction. Owing to her absurd love of complication, she would not receive it till the next morning, since it would have to be forwarded from the Chelsea address; therefore he could not expect a reply for a day or two. He forgot that he had imposed a similar complication on her, and wondered if the next morning's post would bring him her explanation; in which case he might feel sorry.

But no explanation came, and he had settled down to the fact (more comforting than he would have thought possible two days ago) that there was none, when the evening brought a familiar envelope forwarded from his club. He generally collected the letters himself from the hall, but today he had for some reason chosen to have tea with Frances in the drawing-room instead of having it brought him in his study. She seemed to him still very dispirited, and his magnanimous goodwill towards her grew rather than shrank as he watched her.

There were letters for her, too, and he was glad that her evident eagerness to read her correspondence gave him an excuse for examining his. Phillida could not have had time to answer his letter. This must be an explanation, after all. In spite of himself, his hand trembled a little as he tore the envelope. For some moments he read in utter amazement.

Phillida had been at the tryst. She had not failed him. On the contrary, she had waited for him an hour. It was he who had not been there. "Half-past twelve, under the clock at Charing Cross Station." She had made no mistake either as to time or place. "And I wore a bunch of white marguerites. I confess that I accidentally left my copy of Swinburne behind me in the train, but you always said that Swinburne was unnecessary, that the flower would be enough. Besides, if you had been there with a white buttonhole and carrying Swinburne's poems, I should have gone up and spoken at once, but there was no one at all with a white buttonhole except my husband, who . . . "

Arnold dropped the letter and stared across at his wife. She was holding a letter close up to her eyes, and her hands were trembling. He looked intently, and recognized the notepaper of the Automobile Club — his own signature trailed across the sheet. . . .

Suddenly she threw her hands down into her lap, her eyes screwed up, and her face contorted like a crying child's.

" The brute! " she sobbed. " The cruel, selfish brute! Oh, the brute! The brute! "

The violence of her anger and misery frightened him, and for some moments he stared at her in silence. It was not till much later that he found relief in telling her all that he thought about romantic women.

THE IVORY TOWER

By

Thomas Burke

NOTE

The great advantage of telling the story in the first person is that it at once solves the problem of conviction. When a man tells you that such and such experiences happened to himself, you are forced to the alternative of either believing them or calling him a liar. Therefore the use of the first person in fiction is very common. There are, however, two disadvantages. The first is that the reader naturally knows that no matter what may happen the story cannot end fatally. At the best, the reader can anticipate the end so that he tends to lose interest. When Mr. Burke tells us "I attained the substantial bone, and lost the precious nourishing shadow," he has told the story. If the plot had been one involving violent action the interest would have been sustained; the reader knows that eventually the hero must survive to tell the story, but he is curious to learn how he escapes from his difficulties. But, as in this case the action is slight, the interest must lie in the psychology of the first person, and if you don't care whether or not he is irritable, you will not continue reading. The second difficulty with the use of the first person lies in the fact that nothing can be reported that he does not know, and no scene described, except by hearsay, in which he does not participate. So he cannot explain Madeline's point of view; she necessarily remains a shadow. How great a loss this implies in dramatic values becomes obvious in comparing *The Ivory Tower* with *Fanny Baines*. To compensate for this lack we are given at the beginning a series of details, an umbrella-stand with a bowl of sweet williams, Welsh miners and, as a culmination, the smell of boiled fish. Such details are used to bring out by contrast the romantic longings of the hero. The story ends with the so-called "surprise ending." Here, of course, the surprise can only technically exist, since the reader of this book already knows the plot. This ending, which is very common, consists in holding the whole plot in solution until the last sentence which completely reverses the situation. It is a mechanical but effective construction. "It was Madeline's handwriting" is the keystone of the arch.

THE IVORY TOWER

By Thomas Burke

LA FONTAINE'S dog has my sympathy. We are in different cases, but I can share his dismay. He opened his mouth to clutch the shadow of a bone, and lost the (to him) precious substantial bone. I attained the substantial bone, and lost the precious nourishing shadow. It's a queer story: the more queer because I am one of those commonplace creatures to whom queer things don't happen.

At the time it happened I had been married nine years; long enough to have reached the stage where I was no longer sharply aware of man and wife, but had accepted the fact that I and a familiar human creature were sharing a home. It was during this ninth year that I began to be aware, month by month, of a slowly growing irritation with everything. Virtue seemed to have gone out of life; the very air of it seemed to have no more zest than flannel. I don't think this irritation had anything to do with the materials of my life, shabby as these were; it was rather a symptom, common in nervous people of my kind, of some chemical process — a sort of middle-age growing-pains. Most of my life had been set among shabby materials, and many of these had evoked my active dislike. But in earlier days I had simply registered dislike; they did not drive me, as they did at this time, to exasperation. They did not make me feel that I must do anything — no matter how reckless or cruel — to escape them. They were then merely isolated facts; later, they came to fill my landscape. Boiled fish, for instance. Boiled fish was the climax of that year's irritation.

One hot evening of July I had come home worn, but not

really tired. Restless, and wanting rest, but not down to the point where I could peacefully take it. We were living as well as things permitted while I was making my way — I often forgot how long I had been making my way, but Madeline's eyes sometimes reminded me — and the best that things permitted was a standard villa at Kilburn, with one incompetent but willingly overworked maid. I hated coming home to it, and it was a daily distress to me that Madeline had to live in it. She hated it as much as I did. Well, that evening, the first thing I saw was the umbrella-stand, which held a bowl of sweet williams. I discovered at that moment how much I had always hated sweet williams. When I had settled myself with the paper in the sitting-room, the maid, three times in five minutes, bustled in and bustled out. I discovered how much I hated people who bustled in and out of rooms. In the street a group of unemployed Welsh miners were singing Welsh airs. I discovered how much I hated Welsh airs. Then, from the kitchen, came the smell of boiled fish; and I discovered that in all my memory of odious things nothing remained so odious as the smell of boiled fish.

But this time it was not merely a horrible smell; it was a persecution. All these tiny matters had for years been part of my daily life, but I had been no more aware of them than of the pattern of my boot-laces. It was only then, at the point of accumulated distresses, that I perceived them and realised how I hated them, and why I hated them. I hated them because they were a part of my life, and because I had come to hate everything about my life. That smell, creeping like a mist under the door, filled me with long-forgotten oaths. It so infuriated me that I could not get up to do anything to stop it; the mere speaking of it would only have increased its effect upon me. So that when Madeline came in I continued glumly to read the paper.

She said something — some complaint or other — I didn't catch what. The tone was tart. I said " Oh," and went on reading, and she snapped. Through the cloud of boiled-fish-smell I could feel a tart atmosphere about the house — an atmosphere that was often there — and when I asked " What's the matter now? " she snapped again: " Oh, don't listen if it interferes with your reading."

And then I snapped: " Well, if you'll tell me what it is instead of mumbling, I'll listen."

" Oh, it doesn't matter. You don't want to be bothered with it."

" Well, don't snap at me."

" Oh, it's all very well for you. You're not in the beastly house all day."

" I'm not much better off. I'm in a beastly office, and a lot of other things."

" Yes, but they're interesting things. Not petty, sordid things like tradesmen's books."

" Business is just as petty as suburban life, and more sordid."

" Yes, but you're out and seeing people all day."

" Well, you get out, too. To more amusing places than I see."

" Oh, I know, but . . . And then when you do come home you flump down like a dumb-bell."

It was the usual fatuous and ungainly married-life bicker, and as it went on I realised that we had been bickering like this every day for some months. It did not smooth my temper, and if at first I had wanted to be sympathetic with her nerviness the smell of boiled fish wouldn't let me. " It's the end of the day," I snapped. " Not the beginning. If you're tired in one way, I'm tired in another. Going out might refresh you. It'd only make me more tired. You expect a man to run two businesses — his own in the city and a lover-business at home. I can't do it. If you want somebody who's bright at the end of the day you should have married a private income."

"Yes, I should."

I was expecting that, but on top of all the other prickings it stung. "Perhaps if you had he might have made your complaint. Because you're not particularly bright to come home to. All I come home to is snaps and the damnable smell of boiled fish."

"The what?"

"*Boiled — fish!*" I'm sorry to say I shouted the word. "Boiled fish. The foulest smell there is. You know how I hate it. Why the devil can't you keep the kitchen door shut?"

"Oh, *damn* the kitchen!"

The quiet, gentle girl of nine years ago turned on me a bitter mouth and angry eyes, and all our accumulated disgust with life and dissatisfaction with each other came out.

It was over in half an hour, but its clouds hung about the whole evening, soggy and exhausted, discolouring the atmosphere and pressing upon every thought. Under this cloud, which nothing warm could penetrate, we began to talk rationally, and by bed-time we had mutually reached the spiritless decision (which some married couple reaches every hour) that it was useless going on like that.

We were starting our holiday the following week, and had arranged to spend about twenty days along the Rhine. I had not been looking forward to it; indeed, at the prospect of it I was conscious only of my persisting itch to Get Away From Everything — from Madeline, Kilburn, my wretched business, and everything that impinged upon them. But I hadn't enough resolution to say so. When Madeline, then, in this cold moment of mutual examination, said that she didn't want to come, I was relieved. She thought it better, since we were only getting

on each other's nerves, that we should go away separately; and
to this I agreed with spirit. It would clear the air, I said, and
in three weeks, apart from each other, we might be able to discover where the essence of our disagreement lay, and find some
way of treating it. Upon this we decided that we should make
our own arrangements, without further consultation; and
when Madeline had gone to bed I looked forward, with something as near to pleasure as I knew, to the prospect of three
weeks of solitude; and took my jangling nerves into what I
called my ivory tower.

I must explain this bit of sentimental nonsense. All my life
I have been shy, reserved, and cut off from the plain, blunt
things in which the majority find both zest and satisfaction. I
hate games. I hate parties. I hate dances. I hate the theatre. I
hate dinners of more than four. I hate crowds. Indeed, I think
I turn from all fact. From childhood I have always recoiled
from the abundance of life, and its rough beauty, and have
sought my happiness (foolishly) in an imagined world where
bliss was static and creatures never veered from the magnetic
point of charm. Seeing that I had to live in the world, this was
something more than foolish, but without that shadow-world
behind me I could not face the real world.

The ivory tower was built in my schooldays. These were
spent at a cheap boarding-school at Ramsgate, where I was as
melancholy as a naturally lonely boy is in a crowd. But when
I was fourteen something happened to stir the melancholy, and
colour it. One of the boys in my house had a sister who was
at a boarding-school in London, and this sister, in her brother's
words, was a goer. This, of course, was before the war had
brought wider horizons to women, to schoolgirls, and to the
nursery; and the favourite reading at the sister's school was the
romantic novelette. The whole school, by the sister's reports,

was clotted with "romance." So much so that the boy, Esmond, told a group of his friends one day that if any of us wanted a girl, his sister knew heaps who would just love to write to a boy and have letters from him.

This at once appealed to me. I could find little to interest me in the actual girls I saw. They were not as pretty as I wanted them to be, and their manners fell far short of my ideal of girlish manners, gathered, I suppose, from early Victorian novels that I had found at home. But a distant and unknown girl was another matter, and the clandestine element gave the thing a touch of real "romance." I begged Esmond to count me in; and he did, and a fortnight later the first stone of my ivory tower was laid.

Twelve of us were in it, and when a fat letter arrived one morning for Esmond we gathered about him in crude excitement. Besides his sister's letter, the packet contained twelve folded notes from his sister's friends, addressed into the air to some unknown boy, as, years later, socks and cigarettes were addressed to Lonely Soldiers. He took us to a sheltered corner of the grounds, and there, with the aid of a football case, he made an impartial distribution of the missives. He put them into the football case, shook them up, and then commanded the twelve, in alphabetical order, to take a dip.

I had the fourth dip, and I can feel today the thrill of that moment when I unfolded the first note I had ever received from a girl. An unknown girl, too. But though she had been only a vague idea before I received the note, once I had the note in my hand she became (for me) definite. In the first glimpse of the handwriting, in one second, I built and visualized her in form and face and dress so clearly that for ever after she lived in my mind to the pattern of that moment. I took the note to the most secret place I knew, and there I read it and reread it. It was a short note that probably thought it was a long letter because it had been written in a large clear hand. It was childish and giggly, but to me it was charged with poetry. It went like this:

" Hullo, Whoever-you-are. I wonder what sort of boy you are. I hope your dark and got big eyes. Will you write to me and tell me what your doing and I will write back and tell you what I am doing. Do write soon. Doris' brother will send it on to her. She isnt half a rip. Do you have exciting times. It is so dull here you wouldnt believe, but sometimes we manege to have a flare. Tell me what your like. I have got yellow hair Doris says it is carrots but dont you believe it and grey eyes, and I am in our hockey team what ho. Do write soon but dont tell me your name. I am not going to tell you mine and I dont want to know yours. I think it makes it more thrilling that way dont you?

" Well, good-bye and lots of x x x x x

" From

" LITTLE NOBODY."

So began a shadowy friendship, the memory of which remained with me long after the thing itself had ceased. I fell in at once with her suggestion of anonymity, and was so delighted at having found a kindred spirit in the cause of " romance " that Esmond rejected my first letter (ten pages) for fear of suspicion being aroused by his despatching a crate to a girls' school. It made a blissful background to the heavy monotony of school. Every ten days or so the mysterious Little Nobody came out of the air with confidences and jokes, and at every available opportunity I unloosed my most secret thoughts to her. After a year of this I knew her better than I knew any of the boys about me — better, indeed, than I have since known any human creature. About the only things I did not know were her name and where she lived. I had no desire that she should have a name, and made no attempt to learn it, but I did want to know where she lived, so that some spot of the map of England should have a meaning for me. But she would not tell. All I could get from her was that she lived in Almond Rock Cottage, near the Charcoal burner's hut, what ho. When, in my first letter, I told her that I was, as she had hoped, dark, that I had completely black hair, I became throughout the correspondence, " Dear Inky."

It went on for four years, and although, since I was living in it and growing up with it, I was not then able to perceive any inner significance to the correspondence, I could see later that it marked, at different stages, the gradual development of character, and, at its end, the emergence of a very fine, generous, and sensible nature. Her letters, which I still have, make a graph of a young girl's growth from giggling fourteen to an unusually gracious and intelligent eighteen. She became, for me, the essence of the ideal girl, the test to which I put all the girls I met and before which they all failed. Yet even then, deeply engrossed as I was with her who had become the background of my young life, I had no desire to meet her. I had sufficient knowledge of myself, and sufficient experience of the actual, to know that a friendship of actual contact could never satisfy me as this remote and shadowy adventure in friendship did. In this we were at one; indeed, in many ways she was my complete double. She, too, felt as I did, and found our correspondence far more stimulating and satisfying than any of her real friendships. We were each other's confessor, and things that we could never tell to people we knew we could pour out to the unknown. Our pseudonyms, " Inky " and " Little Nobody," gave us a sense of exquisite disembodiment, as though we belonged to a land of legend where we could be wholly ourselves without any recognition of the restrictions and inhibitions of the dull world we live in. We could take our delights and our bruises to the secret chamber of this correspondence, and be sure of finding solace and understanding. For each of us there was one creature in the world, in complete agreement with ourself, with whom we could be entirely free. The fear of the penalty of ridicule or exploitation, which is the basis of all discretion and reserve, was in this affair non-existent; neither would ever know who that creature was.

But at eighteen it ended. I don't remember how. I suppose Esmond left the school, or his sister left her school, and thus its channel was stopped. I only remember that it did end. Most school friendships come to an end when the world begins to call, and this particular affair, with its childish origin and furtive basis, would easily go under at a time when we were both putting away childish things and preparing to become citizens. No doubt we could have found means of continuing it, but it may have been that each of us, faced with the world, began to see its ridiculous side; not to be ashamed of it, but to realise that it was a phase which we had passed. It ended, anyway, but it never left me; and from her latest letters I carried ever after a picture of one beautiful personality to set against the crude and commonplace beings among whom I had to pass my days. That secret correspondence with an unknown girl was to become the one clear spot in my muddled life. For me it had been more than a friendship. It had been the perfect love affair, and I guessed then, as I know now, that, although love might later revisit me, it would never hold the colour or the accent of that affair.

Love did revisit me. At thirty I met Madeline, and I thought that at last I had met a woman beyond all other women. At our first meeting at a friend's house, in the first moments of that meeting, we seemed to move to each other and to slip into easy talk as though we had been meeting frequently. Our ideas seemed to be companions, and, shy as each of us was with others, we found no difficulty in silence or in talk. When we parted I casually suggested meeting the next day, and she as casually accepted. It seemed, with both of us, to be a pre-arranged thing which scarcely needed saying. We had but three meetings, and then, without words, we passed to marriage.

There was one year of something as near to delight as I could ever extract from the actual world, and then I began to realise that Madeline was just one more woman. I wondered how I had been so bemused as to see her as anything else. Possibly, from my foolish habit of never seeing the thing as it is, but as I wished it to be, I had seen qualities in her that were not there, but were reflected by her, hypnotically, from my own desire. Certainly they were not there after the first year, and the ensuing eight years of our life were like a muggy London winter. I had married a woman where I had thought I was marrying a fellow-spirit, and, as time went on, the memory of Little Nobody, which had grown very faint, became stronger and stronger as I fancied her as she would be then, and compared with her sweet nature the characterless woman I had chosen. If only . . . Every man, it is said, is looking in all women for one particular woman, and his ideal woman is not Venus or Cleopatra or Rosalind or Helen; it is the pinafored girl he fell in love with when he was fourteen or fifteen. I think that is true. It is certainly true of myself, and after long experience of Madeline I realised my folly (and unfairness) in marrying at all. I knew that it should have been Little Nobody or nothing, for every day the memory of her lived with me and grew, adding one more stone to the wall that was rising between Madeline and me, and making our already fretful life almost unbearable.

This, then, was the " ivory tower " to which I retired after every quarrel. There Little Nobody lived, and there I could pass imagined hours of amicable life. Everything else might go; indeed, a great deal had gone. I had no particular place in the world; friends had failed me; marriage had failed me; religion might fail me; but, whatever else might fail, she could not fail. I could lose everything else, but I could not lose her. She remained; serene from all assaults of this world's fortune or the malice of this world's friends, she remained; and I could turn to her in any place at any hour for comfort or delight. All things might die, but she was immortal.

So, at least (like a fool), I thought. And I was wrong. I *have* lost her. There is now no ivory tower and no Little Nobody. This was the way she went.

Madeline went off the day after the boiled-fish quarrel, and I went off on the Saturday. She was not certain where she would go, nor had I made any plans. Frankly, I was not concerned with where she went so long as she went, and I think the feeling was mutual. We parted with a considerate courtesy to each other that was almost horrible.

On the Saturday morning I took a suitcase aimlessly to Paddington, and managed, on the way, to make a decision. I had no mind for the irritations of European travel, and had thought vaguely of the west or south-west. By the time I arrived at the station I had chosen a country which I had not visited for some years, but which I had always remembered with affection — the Glastonbury part of Somerset. The Vale of Avalon is not beautiful, but I had always found refreshment there. It is essential England, charged with a spirit that is at once serene and vital, and I know no other corner where one is so readily tranquillised.

Within three days I had forgotten all about boiled fish, and was beginning to make practical plans that would give both Madeline and myself a more sensible life. Separation seemed the obvious thing, and I was quite ready to go through the ugly formalities necessary to a divorce; but there was still the possibility that, by some rigorous adjustments of ourselves, we might be able to pull some sort of happiness out of the wreck. I considered this, too, and examined carefully every collision of our life so that I might see just where I had been at fault. I was discovering, one morning, that seven-tenths of the fault was on my side, when the post put an end to all examination. It brought me a letter marked " Personal," and forwarded from my office. I was expecting no private letters, as we had sent the maid off for three weeks; but I had given the office my address in case anything urgent should arise that required a word from me. I had no friends who wrote to me at my office, and for some seconds I behaved as people do behave with strange letters — turning it over and trying to discover its sender and its purpose instead of opening it. At last I opened it, and a queer little thrill went through me, and years slipped off me, and I caught the perfume of the flowers of the inn garden as though I were smelling flowers for the first time. The letter was signed " Cyril Esmond," and this was its message:

" DEAR COLWILL,

" If you're the Colwill I knew you will remember my name, and Ramsgate. I think you must be, because in trying to trace you I made the first obvious shot of the London telephone book, and there can't possibly be another Colwill with your stack of initials — A. P. K. Assuming I'm right, do you re-member in the Ramsgate days, when we were kids, the letters that I used to send my sister? And do you remember that you were in it — very thick — with an unknown goddess called Little Nobody? It's going back a bit, but my own memory of those days is very clear. If you make an effort, it may come back to you. Anyway, the reason for troubling you with this is that Little Nobody's memory is as clear as mine, and she's suddenly dropped out of the air on to my sister. My sister hasn't seen or heard of her since those days — had forgotten all about her — but she's just written to Doris to ask if her brother is still in touch with a school friend of his to whom he used to pass letters for 'Inky.' (That was you, if you remember.) Well, she wants to know if I know whether you're still alive, and where you are, because she'd like to write to you. She's always remembered the correspondence you two had, and, as she's not at all happy just now, she's got a sort of sentimental notion that she'd like to write to someone she doesn't know, and who doesn't know her, as she did in the past, and the obvious thought was the far-away ' Inky,' because he understood her in those days better than anybody else.

" I don't for a moment imagine that you want to be bothered with childish nonsense of this sort, but don't blame me. In passing on the story I'm simply performing a duty. You know what women are — treasuring sentimental memories, and all that — and you see my position. If it doesn't interest you, just ignore this. If it does, a letter for ' Inky ' is waiting here, and will be forwarded. But if I may venture a word of advice — Beware. Sentimental letters between kids is one thing, but to revive a kid thing with a middle-aged woman. . . . What? It sounds to me like incipient idiocy, but I promised to try to get in touch with you, and I've done it, and that's that.

" How are you these days, and what are you doing? Prospering, I hope. I've often thought of you. I see that your office is in Holborn. Mine's in Kingsway. We might possibly have a drink one evening. I wonder if we'd recognise each other?

" Yours sincerely,
" CYRIL ESMOND."

I need not, of course, say that my answer to this letter was a wire to Esmond: " Thanks for yours. Please forward letter. Writing." And I began to watch the posts. Concentration on my immediate personal affairs became impossible; I could think only of Little Nobody, visualising her, balancing her essential nature, and the little traits that I had known, against the flight of years; wondering which had been obliterated by time and which had been developed. But however much she might have changed in detail, the essential nature, I knew, would be the same. For what we are at twelve we always are. The blows of life may thrust our real self down and down, and bury it under a crocodile hide of self-protection, studded with accretions of worldly mannerisms, but it is always there, ready to reappear at any time at the bidding of quiet eyes and a sympathetic mind.

It reappeared in Little Nobody. By the afternoon post of the second day her letter came, and I took it to the garden with a revival of the old sense of sweet conspiracy. As I opened it, and read the first sentences — there were six typewritten pages — I was again eighteen, filled again with the spirit of morning fields. Here were the very accents of the Little Nobody I had known but never seen; here was the same gentle, laughing, warm character; the same odd twist of phrase; the same almost foolish outpouring of secrets; the same ——

And then I dropped the letter to the grass. " . . . things not very bright with me . . . married poor man . . . usual humdrum life . . . husband ceased even to pretend to care . . . living in makeshift style in rickety villa at Kilburn. . . ." To make certain, I picked it up and looked at the last page for the signature — "Little Nobody." It was Madeline's handwriting.

BY THE LAST POST

By

H. R. Barbor

NOTE

The setting here is a dramatic conversation. The scene is laid in the Cairo Turf Club, a group of four officers of the English Army are talking casually, between drinks, of the tragedy of a mutual acquaintance. There is some suggestion of dramatic characterization. Reynolds, who leaves early, sees merely the obvious; Bayes, the airman, is positive and definite; Domremy is the sympathetic listener, and Prescott, who has been connected with the events from start to finish, tells the tale. This device gives an air of actuality. Prescott knew Bretherton intimately from "prep" school days, he had known him in college, in the Army and had been the best man at his wedding. The reader, consequently, overhears the interpretation of the tragedy from the one man best able to interpret it. The skill in presentation consists in making the conversation flow naturally; therefore you have quotations within quotations, and you are given conversations which had taken place years before. But a man that would commit suicide because he had married his ideal is confessedly peculiar. Your interest is at once aroused by Reynolds's confession, " I never could stand the chap. Too damn morbid." On the other hand, Reynolds is not a good judge. It is the reader's privilege to decide. The interest is, then, in the character study. Lady Bretherton is very lightly sketched in. And the incidents themselves are of minor importance. An idealist brusquely confronted with reality, would he commit suicide? His best friend thinks that he would. But by thus shifting the stress from incident to character Mr. Barbor has solved many of the problems involved in the plot, — by simply ignoring them. This, he tells us, is what happened, and let it go at that.

BY THE LAST POST

By H. R. Barbor

"IF for 'gustibus' you care to read 'the other fellow's taste in women,' I'll admit the classic tag runs in Bretherton's case. For Humphrey Bretherton — poor devil! I never thought he'd do this — certainly had taste, for the pick of the feminine bunch, to boot."

"Seems to me he had the pick of every bunch," growled Reynolds, drawing his great length ruler-wise up from the *chaise-longue* — a leisured process of human triangulation. "Spoilt child of luck, and this is the end." He threw the evening paper aside and drank up his peg, shivering in the evening air that oddly seemed to accumulate around him in the usually stuffy lounge of the Cairo Turf Club. Then he made signs of a departure not altogether unwelcome to the other three men. "I never could stand the chap. Too damn morbid." Reynolds went.

"Morbid?" Prescott muttered the word speculatively.

"M'm. Something to be said for that." Bayes pondered. "Not morbid. Reynolds doesn't choose his words — possibly because the words aren't his to choose. When he says 'morbid' he means thoughtful. The psychological factor. 'Cogito ergo sum.' Reynolds doesn't."

PRESCOTT. "What?"

BAYES. "Think."

PRESCOTT (*drinking inattentively*). "He does. Not about people."

BAYES (*imitating hospitably*). "Not about persons."

PRESCOTT. "Precisely. Bretherton was a person."

BAYES. "A dramatis persona."

PRESCOTT. "Of his own drama."

BAYES. "You mean?"

PRESCOTT. "Of the drama we've read of tonight, anyway."

BAYES. "Go on."

PRESCOTT. "Why? Anyhow, it's after hours. You fellows ought to be in bed. And I've an early parade."

DOMREMY (*as if awakening from Nirvana, though his cigar had glowed from moment to moment throughout*). "If you have a story, Prescott, it won't keep. Nothing keeps in Cairo this time of year, unless you run to ice-chests — and a story off the ice is worse than a . . . dammit, anything. Your soldiering can stand the strain of another hour; my curiosity can't. I liked Bretherton, and if he's . . . Well, let's have it. . . . *Abbas!*"

The Sudanese waiter enters, serves drinks, exit.

PRESCOTT. "If you're not tired, then. Well, I knew Bretherton in the old days, before we chaps knew one another. His father had a little place near us in Norfolk. We went to the same prep school — old Ashenden's, Folkestone, you know. In the holidays I used to see a lot of him. Even then he was always writing letters, I remember."

"What's that got to do with it?" Wing-Commander Bayes, R.A.F., liked to read his map before a flight. But Domremy warned him to stillness with a flick of his cigar.

"He wrote to everybody. Had an amazing number of interests. We only had an hour for letter-writing before chapel on Sunday evenings. But young Bretherton used to drop a line to one of the gardeners about his bugs and grubs — you remember he collected out here? — and to the keeper about his particular pets — a hedgehog, ferrets, and so on. He'd write to all his aunts and cousins and to the old man. Not the usual schoolboy letters: 'Dear Pater, I hope you are quite fit. My cricket pads are worn out. Can you send me half a sov?' You know the sort of thing. No, real letters, brand new from the mint. Of course, the women loved it. I remember my mater thought him no end of a *walad*. He came to stay with us at the sea one summer; he was about ten then, but he kept up a correspondence with my mother for years and years. Told her all my doings and his own. She held him up to me as an imp of perfection for ever afterwards. 'I wish you were like Humphrey,' and all that sort of thing. Gad, I took it out of him for that, too, I recall. It made us strangers till I met him at the Eton and Harrow match years after — he went to Eton. Handled a nice bat, but dandified.

"I said: 'Still letter-writing, Hump?' He said: 'Yes, like some?' I said: 'Rather.' Not that I cared. But he had made sixty on a tricky wicket. And he kept it up, too — the letter-writing, I mean — right till he was married, and after, except, of course, when he was with his regiment out here."

"You were always together then," Bayes remarked.

"Yes, I saw a lot of him, naturally. Used to go bugging with him in the Delta. At least, I shot while he bugged. Mind you, he handled a gun prettily. One day he got fifty-seven *bécassines* against my thirty odd. 'That was for a bet,' he said. 'I don't care to shoot birds. I'd rather watch 'em through a pair of Zeiss any day.' He was like that. It was that day he really confessed to me all about his correspondent. He was still in love with her then, but I'm sure he thought it was all finished by that time."

"What correspondent?" enquired Bayes, inquisitive as ever.

"The girl he had been writing to."

"You haven't mentioned her," Bayes remarked.

"He will," suggested Domremy.

"Who was she, anyhow?" asked Bayes, unperturbed.

"Bretherton didn't know. When he left Eton he went up to Magdalen, read history, and rowed. One boat-race night he was in the West End on the usual batter — you know, too good dining and wining, too leggy musical show, too long intervals. Anyhow, he and his companions in the box were asked to leave, and did so. More fizz, more fun — this was before the war. Ended up at Fulham or Balham or Camberwell, with a taxi back to his hotel ak-emma. With an umbrella."

" An umbrella? "

" Oh, shut up, Bayes." Domremy showed claws, bear's claws.

" She had left it in the cab. The unknown she. She who came to be desired." Prescott took a long gulp of his Amer Picon and squash. He lit a cigarette with all the enviable complacency of a story-teller who knows the night is his.

" Was she a lady from Balham or Fulham? "

" No, my dear Bayes. There are no ladies in Balham or Fulham. At least, there had not been that night — not for Bretherton, anyhow. She had left it in the cab by mistake."

" Her umbrella? "

" Exactly. Her umbrella — or sunshade. It may have been a sunshade."

" Well, what did Bretherton do? "

" What would you have done? No, he didn't do that. To begin with, he opened it and solemnly paid off the taxi and entered his hotel — an ultra-respectable Mayfair pub — under the shade of the contraption. He was still tight, remember. In the morning he found it. By that time he was thoroughly aware that (*a*) unlawful possession of a lady's umbrella or sunshade did not, as Mrs. Malaprop might have remarked under similar circumstances, become a young man, and also (*b*) there was nothing intrinsically funny in parading under the said umbrella through the streets of London. So Bretherton took the only logical course — got the valet to pack it carefully, and despatched it to Scotland Yard Lost Property Office. Unfortunately, as the event and tonight's copy of the *Egyptian Mail* prove, he did not leave it at that. For Bretherton was a confirmed correspondent. He enclosed a letter with his *trouvaille*. And I defy any woman, as my mother is witness, to resist falling into a correspondence with a man who wrote letters like our friend."

    *   *   *   *   *

"The girl apparently lived in the country. Maiden aunts: parties: garden: horses: dairy: was Dostoievski a better novelist than Thackeray?: it was cold at Mentone in November: her first complete cycle of *The Ring* at Covent Garden and the superiority of Boche over wop musical shows: did he sing?: she didn't really, but loved it: bees (Auntie Belle kept them): Maeterlinck *versus* Fabre: on his advice she had read Darwin on earthworms. . . . That led to archæology, classicism *versus* modernism — you know the sort of thing that can develop between people who have the epistolary urge, the most objectionable and soul-destroying form of the *cacoëthes scribendi.*"

"Were they anonymous?" asked Domremy, as Prescott paused to light a cigar.

"Sorry. I didn't make that point, did I? They were. It was accidental in a way, to begin with, at any rate. He had written his first letter to her — an impudent scrawl really, diagnosing her from her umbrella. But he had written on hotel paper. She had replied, care of the hall porter, who, remembering the episode of Bretherton's dippy return on boat-race night, had no difficulty in forwarding the girl's letter. He had written to *La Belle Dame Sans Merci,* and she took up the conceit by writing to say *merci.* Two romantics — you get the idea? — rather scornful of romanticism.

"Afterwards, as I say, the correspondence between these two unknowns developed. They preserved their incog. but that was the danger. They took advantage of their mutual invisibility to strip themselves stark naked. You know what a difficult hound Bretherton could be. Perhaps you don't know how self-revelatory he could be. I was his friend, but I never knew him in the flesh — only by post. When we met he would hedge on his letter-writing personality in a perfectly maddening way. He wouldn't even gossip by word of mouth — only on notepaper. With a pen in his hand the man became alive — or, rather, became another man. That, perhaps, illustrates how some great authors have been cads, and fine humourists misanthropic swine in the family circle.

"The first inkling I had had of a woman in the case was when he wrote me just after I had come out here first in 1914 and was stationed at Kasr-en-Nil Barracks. He hadn't written for months, and, by way of apology, explained that he had absorbed all his leisure in scribbling to his Fair Lady of Thanks. They fixed their aliases as Mr. and Miss Thankful, and arranged accommodation addresses, taking pains and pleasure in these overt mutual deceptions. It seems they carried this correspondence right along from 1913 through the war. Of course, Humphrey Bretherton had his own particular reactions to that business, and he worked his early pacificism out of his system in letters to Miss Thankful. She helped him through that intellectual stickiness, too."

Domremy stirred, hotched, reached for his drink. "You've read her letters?"

"And his, some of 'em. Hump was a methodical oaf — typed, and kept duplicates of most of his screeds. And she showed me some."

"Gad, did you know her?" Bayes asked, recreated interest vibrant in the question.

"Oh, it's no triangle. I know them both. You'll hear — if you aren't too tired?"

"Fire away!"

"Well, Bretherton joined up. King Edward's Horse, a couple of months in France, and then was detailed for special duty in the Balkans owing to his knowledge of the comic opera dialects they talk down there. Someone put a bullet into him, and before he was well he got on board a French boat for Marseilles and was torped in the Mediterranean, picked up nearer dead than ever, and bunged back home. They put him in charge of prisoners in Scotland, for he wouldn't clear out of the Service like a sensible chap. He had little to do in Caledonia stern and wild but write letters, a whole spate of 'em. The girl was nursing and reciprocated. They psychologised war, society, and themselves. The Thankfuls approximated.

"In '17 he was on the Somme, had got his company, and I ran across him on a leave train bound for Paris, where he was to meet a Swiss geologist with whom he had been having an acrimonious discussion in some learned journal on the velocity of Pleistocene glacial movement in Northern Europe. What a way to spend leave — eh? That was Bretherton. It was in that train that he first mentioned *La Belle Dame*. Without having the faintest idea of it himself, he was in love with her head-over-heels. One could see that with half an eye."

Bayes ejaculated the obvious: "But he'd never seen her?"

"No. Not even a photo. Didn't know whether she was married, single, widowed, or in any of the intermediate states. Didn't even know whether she was white or black, yellow or brown, rich man, poor man, beggar-man, thief. But he loved her, like hell. Of course he could have found her if he'd had the inclination. He hadn't. Just let love of her blaze away and burn right into him."

Bayes sniggered.

"As bad as that?" from Domremy.

"Not bad — no. It just took him that way. He became much more human too — less abstracted. His imagination flourished.

He said she made the war bearable. Perhaps it was because of battle and the need of creating another life alongside the squalid farce and incessant shock of trench existence that he had let his emotion rip for what must have been the first time.

" Well, it's getting late; I must cut the cackle. Humphrey stopped a few bits of shrapnel in Jerry's '18 push. While in hospital in London he wrote his ' Speculations on the Psychology and Culture of Megalithic Man,' in the intervals of composing love-letters to Miss Thankful. He got about again just before the Armistice, and the book appeared with the spring crop of '19. By a fluke *The Times* Book Club sent a copy to the hospital where she was recuperating from a bad bout of 'flu. She wrote to Bretherton about it — not knowing his authorship, of course.

" That was the beginning of the end of their correspondence. Bretherton, as you know, was one of those damned abstracted people, and the very threat of personal contact drove him into his shell. Their letters had been a thing apart. The book belonged to his ordinary life. It belonged to Major Humphrey Bretherton, D.S.O., M.C., F.R.S. The letters were Mr. Thankful's. In his turbid, half-ashamed way he let me into that while he was stationed here in Cairo. During his stay in Egypt and Palestine both he and she eased off gradually, and there's no doubt that the changed tone of his epistles after her reading of his ' Speculations ' was the cause of this."

" And his love? " Domremy grunted.

" I don't know. Probably it just faded. Anyhow, he certainly loved his wife, there was no mistaking that."

" Oh yes, of course — he married, didn't he? " commented Bayes.

" Yes."

" Why, that was just after he left the Service? "

" He succeeded to the title the following spring and married soon after. I was his best man, and I saw a lot of him that autumn and whenever I was home. She was a glorious girl, old Sir Michael Enderby's daughter."

"The Yorkshire half of the Enderby clan of which that old rip, the Marquis of Repham, is King Pippin," Bayes, a double first in country-house genealogies, supplemented.

"You've read the stud-book all right. They met at Repham's house at Newmarket. Bretherton taught that shooting party what whirlwind courtship really was. Diana fell like a plum. But for the fact that her old guardian aunt took and died at Christmas, he'd have married her out of hand, I imagine.

"They settled in to the life domestic. Society never had meant anything to him; she had had its luxuries and excitements piled about her till, like Freya under the Nibelung treasure, she had been pretty well stifled. Satiety and indifference make comfortable bedfellows. So he farmed with genius and she housekept *par excellence*. They were a model couple redolent of the outmoded pre-war admirabilities. Some of her set smiled, some of his wondered, but all envied the Brethertons' luck. Kittle cattle, women."

DOMREMY. "Why?"

PRESCOTT. "She had a thorn in the flesh all the while. She 'fessed up to me, after much dilly-dallying with conscience and confidence, that she had stalked Hump and was in an eternal twitter of apprehension in case he should find her out, discover that she had deliberately hunted him down. She had enough sense to know his queer hunch by this time. The change in him after the affair of the 'Speculations'—for, of course, Lady Bretherton was, as the story-books say, none other than the *cidevant* Miss Thankful—had broken her up. She had scoured his letters through and through for the reason, spotted it by inspiration, enquired about the author of the book, got him invited to Repham Court, and—so to the

altar. . . . Should she tell him? I plugged in an emphatic
'You must not,' backed by all the evidence I could muster
relative to Hump's intangible mentality.

"Like a damfool bachelor, I couldn't understand why this
fly in the ointment should buzz to beat the band. She knew,
though. Women do. And, though it took years to outbuzz
love's melody, the symphony went phut.

"One leave she told me that Mr. Thankful had started
writing to *La Belle Dame* again. Judge how she felt. But she
played up. Diana is game all through."

"Even if her tactics are bad," sighed Domremy.

"Not tactics. Strategy. This was the big action of her life.
She worked out the movements, in a woman's way. 'He loved
me — he loved me not. He loved me — he's loving me less.
He'll love me — and third time pays for all.' She meant to
confess when volume two of 'The Letters of the Thankfuls'
had reached the crisis of confession. Rather pathetic, isn't it, in
the light of tonight's *Egyptian Mail?* "

Bayes gulped his drink. "Damned rough luck," he said.
"But how did they keep up the deception? "

"Same old way, until the third payment fell due. She was
happy — in a devastated sort of way. 'At least he still loves
me,' she kept on trying to assure herself and me. But it was
wearing her out. Perhaps that's how she came to make the
fatal slip. You see, as a kid she had practised writing with
both hands. She wasn't one of those ambidextrous monstrosi-
ties, of course, but she had acquired what we may call a certain sinister dexterity. And her left hand knew not how her
right hand wrote.

"One night he interrupted her in her dressing-room as she
was despatching a letter to Mr. Thankful, and, in her haste
to get it out of sight, she unwittingly addressed it to him in
her right-hand caligraphy and to their own house instead of

to his bank. She had, of course, no suspicion of what she had done.

"Next morning at breakfast it happened. They were alone —— "

Prescott paused. His hands unfolded and reclenched. Then he continued steadily:

"Poor Diana. Poor old Hump. She has tried to tell me all about it over and over again. He tried once too. That was worse. The hell of it was that they both wanted to play up, went on living together, entertaining, instead of breaking away for a time to get it worked out, each one alone. When it got quite unbearable he joined that Tibetan expedition, and — you know the rest."

Bayes took up the evening paper and read aloud slowly:

"BARONET EXPLORER'S FATE

" Sir Humphrey Bretherton's Body Found

" The Cairo public will learn with regret of the tragic accident to Sir Humphrey Bretherton, Bt., D.S.O., M.C., F.R.S., F.R.G.S., whose body, according to Reuter, has been found in a crevasse of the northern Himalayas near the Tibetan village of Akgong. Akgong is the summer base of the Indian Exploration Society's expedition, of which Sir Humphrey was a distinguished member.

" He left camp on Friday last to climb a rocky eminence on the sides of which grew some rare Himalayan plants. Though he failed to return that night, no concern was felt by his brother scientists until Sunday, when a search party went out but was unable to trace the missing baronet. Yesterday a native came into camp bringing word of his tragic discovery. It appears that the intrepid explorer had slipped and fallen over the cliff. An experienced rock-climber, Sir Humphrey had taken no rope or tackle with him, and his death is probably ascribable to this negligence and to his collector's zeal for rare flora and fauna.

"Before his accession to the title, of which he was the eleventh holder, Sir Humphrey, as Major of the West Worcestershire Regiment, was well known in Egyptian circles. A student of archæology, he contributed distinguished papers on Egyptian and Palestinian excavations to the transactions of various learned societies. He was also a keen naturalist.

"Sir Humphrey married Diana Mary Enderby, of Repham Lodge. Of well-known West Riding stock, Lady Bretherton is a connection of the Marquis of Repham. She is the sole survivor, there being no children of the marriage. A nephew, Lieutenant Charles Mortimer Bretherton, R.N., succeeds to the baronetcy. A personal biography contributed by the late gentleman's friend and brother-in-arms, Colonel B. L. Prescott, will appear in tomorrow's issue of this journal."

Bayes laid aside the paper. "I don't see anything in that. Accident, of course."

"Unless Prescott is disposed to put two and two, or three and four together, and make a newspaper splash," suggested Domremy.

"I shan't do that. But, between ourselves, this is how I see it: Diana loves Hump. Hump bolts for Tibet and stays there. He's been out there now three years, for he waited on over there after the first till the second expedition was fitted out.

"Six months ago she wrote me that she was going all out for him — restitution suit, don't you know. She thought that would bring him to heel — calculated on his hatred of fuss, I suppose.

"I tried to dissuade her all I knew, but I'm a rotten letter-writer. She thought if she could only see him again it would be 'He loves me.' You see, they were both old-fashioned, belonging to the kind that hates the sight of dirty linen on the lawn. She thought a lawyer's threat of a suit for conjugal rights would bring him back to her post-haste. I'll bet he got that lawyer's letter in Akgong just before he went out to that cliff — and over it."

" But he may have fallen," argued Bayes.

" I've done a spot of rock-climbing with Hump several times in Wales, Westmorland, the Alps. He couldn't fall — unless he tried."

" M'm." Domremy unloaded his chair of his bulk solemnly. " 'Fraid he did try."

"MR. RIGHT"

By

Helen Simpson

NOTE

" *Mr. Right* " of Miss Simpson should be compared with Mr. Barbor's *By the Last Post*. In each case the " story " is the man's; in each case he is the victim of his environment, and in each case he ends it by suicide. But the interesting fact is, not the similarity, but the difference. Mr. Barbor asks the reader's sympathy for Bretherton; granted that he is almost a pathological case, yet it is a case of hard luck, and his suicide is at least comprehensible. " 'Fraid he did try " is therefore the logical conclusion. Humphrey Bretherton is a tragic figure. Miss Simpson has no such feeling about Edward Phipps. From the intentionally stressed vulgarity of the first scene to the futile dramatics of the last he is a weakling and a poseur; Miss Simpson makes it quite clear that in no period of his career was he worth discussing. She studies him with scientific detachment as though he were a kind of disgusting insect. First his mistress cannot stand him, and, after the revelation, he cannot even stand himself. In the first case, Bretherton marries because he is manœuvred into it; in the second, Phipps in his emotional lack of control has no one to blame but himself. Certainly, in contrast to Edward, the butcher's daughter is honest with herself, with her " he-man " ideals. If *By the Last Post* vaguely suggests the type of story written by Mr. Kipling in the nineties, Miss Simpson strikes the post-war note of disillusionment. We are puppets at the mercy of our environment, so that the real culprit was " that unknown undergraduate who started the low-brow fashion in Oxford with a bowl of goldfish and two pink silk garters bought at Woolworth's Stores." And each sentence leads with grim inevitability to this rather disheartening conclusion. And Edward's death was " what he needed even more; a gesture."

" MR. RIGHT "

By Helen Simpson

I

IT was during that period which everybody remembers, when a passionate enthusiasm for all that was recognisable as commonplace, lowbrow, and hearty came upon Oxford. Not upon all Oxford; only those were caught up in it who in 1840 would have been leaders of Tractarianism, and in 1890 leaders of lobsters upon silver chains; in short, the impressionables. These, defrauded of God, and unable to discover a standard of beauty to which they might be faithful, took up the anti-highbrow pose to cover their nakedness. It must be said for them that of all the poses which Oxford has adopted since her foundation, this was probably the least expensive.

Indeed, it began with the opening of a Woolworth's Stores on the site of a delightful but unprogressive old building in the Corn Market. To this cathedral of cheapness devotees came every day, buying diamond cuff-links, ice-cream cornets, gold-fish, and pink silk garters with which they adorned their rooms to the admiration of contemporaries. Commonness set in like a heat-wave. Young men in the rarer colleges sent each other vulgar postcards of fat women paddling, drunkards enveloping lamp-posts:

("'Scuse me, sir, is that light up there the shun, or the moon?"
"Shorry, sir (*hic*); I'm a stranger here myshelf.")

There seemed to be no single activity or possession or phrase which could not be reduced to a lowest common denominator; and thus it was strange that the possibilities of the Press should have remained unexplored, until, one November afternoon, Edward Phipps had his brain-wave. He arrived during teatime at 400, St. Giles — high tea, naturally — waving above his head in triumph a copy of *Marriage*.

It was not the book, that treaclish birth-control affair, but the journal; something quite new, and tremendously sympathetic to the prevailing pose; a kind of Exchange and Mart for the unmarried. There, at so much a paragraph, persons over twenty-one described their appearance, height, religion, temperament, savings, and hopes. The Editor, to cheer readers on, had interspersed the paragraphs with rhymes that were like nudges in the ribs:

". Hearts " (sang the Editor) " are here for them that seek,
 And found ofttimes within the week."

Or again:

" The homeliest girl is fair, I ween,
 When Mr. Right comes on the scene."

Edward Phipps, who from this hour became a man of weight, read out amid hysterical laughter descriptions of some of the Editor's bargains.

" Lady, single, good needlewoman, C. of E., fond of motoring, refinement, etc., wishes to meet widower aged about 50, who would be proud of a wife ten years younger than self with full shapely figure."

Then there was " Gentleman, divorcee, almost an abstainer," and the widow, " sensible, would accept any white nationality."

" God, Edward," said one of his hearers, exhausted, " one must do something about this, you know."

" We're going to," responded Edward instantly. " I'll answer one of 'em. And send photo. Where's your typewriter, Charles? Come on! "

It was admitted by all that Edward was in excellent form that afternoon. But an objection was raised by one, a trifle envious of Edward's inspiration.

" Whose photo? " enquired this carping spirit. " She'll switch off at once if you send your own."

" Josser's," responded Edward without an instant's hesitation. " There's a marvellous one of him in Bagot's window."

(Josser was that year's President of the O.U.B.C., a dark Adonis.)

The carping objector was silenced. It was Edward's hour.

" The only question," Edward swept on, " is which one to answer? "

There was a chorus of suggestion, in the course of which the journal was nearly dismembered.

" Shut up! " commanded Edward, with a voice of power.

They shut, recognising authority, and looked towards him.

" We've got to give them all a chance," Edward declared, " and since we can't put the lot into a hat, I suggest that the page should be fastened to the wall with tacks. Then one of us will stand ten paces off and take aim with his eyes shut —— "

" How the hell can anyone aim with his eyes shut? "

" What with, anyhow? "

" A fountain pen," responded Edward coolly. " First spinster it drops a blob of ink on wins. Widows are barred."

There was discussion, but on the whole the plan was acclaimed. The thrower was selected on account of his short sight, which, when his glasses were removed, rendered the target no more than a pallid rectangle, thus ensuring that the trial should be perfectly fair. He took the weapon, discarded his glasses, aimed and flung. There was a yell and a forward rush as the pen hit the wall and fell.

"Spinster," read Edward Phipps aloud, smearing away the blot with his hand, "aged 21, height 5 feet 6 inches, fair, lonely, would like correspondence with a view to marriage. Box 108."

There was a tiny silence.

"Sounds dull," said Charles, voicing everybody's first thought. "Why don't you do the nice juicy widow with the full figure?"

But Edward was on to this rebellion at once.

"I'm going to do what I said. Ink-blob wins. If you want to write to the lousy widow with the shape, write; but I'm going to stick to this one. No more. Finish. Charles, where's that typewriter?"

Even seated before the instrument inspiration did not desert him.

"I am," tapped out Edward, never pausing, "an Oxford undergrad., affectionate, shy, ill at ease among the coarse fellowship of my college companions. I have no sister to introduce me to nice girls. Besides, I am shy; all I can do is dream. I am also slightly psychic. When I read your advert. in *Marriage* a kind of shiver ran through me, and I thought, ' This is the only girl in the world for me.' I cannot confide in any of my friends, they are too coarse-fibred to understand this kind of longing for the Dream-Girl which I have had all my life. How glorious if you were to be She! I enclose photo. This address will always find me —— "

He broke off.

"College paper," the carper pointed out. "She'll be turning up one day and asking for you. Give a wrong address."

"Not much," rejoined Edward; "I want to get her answer. How much simpler to give a wrong name! What shall it be? Think of something romantic."

They obliged.

"Lancelot Lop-Ear."

"Rudolf Vaselino."

"Shut up!" interrupted Edward, beginning once more to tap. Over his shoulder they watched the name grow, letter by letter.

"Orlando Vane," they read aloud. "Grand, Edward! Damn good! How do you do it? Strangers might conclude that you had an intellect."

"We've only got to warn them at the Lodge," said Edward, "that all Orlando letters are mine."

"Right!" they agreed. "Dear Edward exudes intelligence today."

And the band departed, to warn the college porter and purchase a portrait of Josser for enclosure.

After that for a week Edward had no peace from his friends. Had Box 108 written? Would she write? What would she say? Josser's picture ought to have done the trick. The psychic touch was a mistake. She would go to a medium, who would trickle ectoplasm and find out that Edward was a fraud. Thus the conspirators, until after ten days they got tired of the joke and began instead to collect pub notices — "Please Do Not Spit," "Betting Prohibited," and so on — to hang above their mantel-pieces. By the end of term they had forgotten Box 108, and returned to their homes perfectly unaware, thanks to Edward's duplicity, that the joke had come off after all.

For the fact was that Box 108 had replied almost at once, and her letter, catching Edward in sentimental mood after an evening with a highbrow friend who drank vintage wines, had made the whole conspiracy seem rather shabby, rather callow.

"Dear Mr. Vane" (she wrote),

"Your letter was the only answer that came to my advert. I wonder what made you answer. When I read that week's

Marriage and saw all the others I didn't expect to get any at all. It must have been like you say, psychic.

" Thank you also for the photo. I think I ought to say my father has a small business, family butcher's, and Mum and I help in the shop. I don't mind the work, some of the customers are ever so nice. But Mum is very religious, and does not like me to make friends, so I put that advert. in the paper.

" I saw in a paper that the Prince of Wales was at your college and I ought to have said more details in the advert. So if you don't reply I shall quite understand, and remain

" Your sincere friend,

" ELLA HAWKER."

Something in that humble but not ill-written letter got under Edward's armour of pose. He read it, and hated himself, and walked up and down half the night almost in tears. Family Butcher's. Good Lord! Steaks, and livers, and skinned sheep's heads, all raw, all bloody — Christ, what a life! And Mum not allowing friends. No friends; then, by God, Ella Hawker should have a Prince Charming! It should be a romance, conducted entirely by post. She should have something to live for, and he would have an odd little experience, half a love affair, all the more enchanting because it could never turn real.

At midnight he sat down to his typewriter.

" CHILD " (wrote Edward, aged twenty years),

" How could you think I wouldn't answer? I told you that I had a feeling about you; well, that was true. I want you to be the one person in the world I can talk to about anything, and everything. I shall talk a lot; do you mind?

" I suppose this is the thing we're all looking for, someone we can be completely ourselves to. Hardly any of us find it. Men are all right, but they always want to do the talking. That's why these fellows here are no use to me, though they're a good lot, and I adore being up. But we don't any of us dare say what we really think about — oh, well, God, I suppose, and finding complete happiness with a woman, and wanting to do things, enormous things, with one's life. We just don't dare, except to laugh uproariously at the idea of believing in anything, or falling in love. Let me talk to you, Ella; say what I think without any of this silly protective guffawing for once.

" You mayn't want to listen. In that case, just say, and I won't write again. But if you would let me, it would be divine. I want, oh, how I want to be real for once! "

He hesitated, then signed his fictitious initials. " O. V.," and went out to find a pillar-box.

II

And so the letters began. Having begun they went on in spate for over two years. Edward talked about himself with the joyous freedom of a slightly intoxicated traveller who opens his heart to a fellow-passenger in a railway carriage. He never would meet Ella, never wanted to meet her. He was not cowed to reticence by the thought that one day his puerilities and unbuttonings might be brought up against him; he was free, in this black-and-white shadow of companionship, to be himself, Edward Phipps, who found himself the most interesting person in the world, and could say so freely to an audience which admired and understood.

For Ella, during this time, allowed hardly a hint of her own personality to show through her answering letters. Yet she managed, somehow, to get hold of a little of Edward's Oxfordism, to use the right silly words, even to copy the turn of his sentences now and then. As to her own life and movements, she was secretive as a cat. Possibly someone less self-engrossed than Edward might have perceived that she was trying to

educate herself, to climb up to his level out of the slough of
Family Butchering. She spoke vaguely, more than once, of
making a change, and eventually her letters bore another address, somewhere in Isleworth. But Edward did not notice.
He was practising his temperament on her, lashing out into
preposterous rages over nothing, philosophising over her head,
enjoying himself intensely, being real.

" I'm sick of this," he wrote, after some difference of opinion with college authorities, " s'welp me Satan, I am. I'm going
to raise hell, with a book, a million books. Up the rebels! A
new toast — to the unchaining of all evil passions! *À la lan-
terne* with eunuchs such as preside here over youth, gowned
like women instead of trousered like men and brothers! Down
with everything!
    " I wish I could write.
    " Could I?
    " Not original stuff, blast it! It would be a medley of all I've
ever read, plus a few blasphemies.
    " What could I call it?
    " What would it be about?
    " What drivel it would be! But I've a damned good mind
to try. Difficult —— "
    " Oh, bloody difficult! "

To which Ella would reply:

" Things do seem to be awful with you just now. I'm so
sorry; wish I could help. I have been reading that book by Sir
Thomas Browne, it was marvellous, what I could understand
of it. I really am so sorry you're so upset. I like to hear what
you feel about things, then I feel I really am being a help. I
have had a lot of worry this last week too."

Neither of them ever made reference to the advertisement
which had brought them together, and which had ended with

the words, "correspondence with a view to marriage." Edward, of course, had never had the faintest intention of marrying. Ella — but it was not possible from her letters to tell what Ella thought. Nothing of her personality came through, which was as well. If Edward had ever considered her for one moment as a real person, the curious exchange would not have gone on. She sent him no photograph, nor did he ask for one. He used her as a vaulting-horse for his talent of self-expression, and put some really good stuff into his letters, more especially when he was slightly drunk.

Nevertheless, at the end of two years the correspondence was beginning to tail off. Edward was obliged by his *amour propre* to work during his last two terms; it was to be a First for him, or nothing. He was busy, besides, with an undergraduate journal which he edited, and where he could blow off steam. Thus during his last summer term he wrote to Ella a single letter; she answered, and refrained in the most unfeminine way from prodding him or demanding explanation. He thought gratefully of her more than once, but there really was not time. Life had become suddenly real, suddenly earnest for Edward. He worked furiously, got his First, and went down; from October till January he was abroad. The correspondence flickered up in a postcard or two, and at the New Year finally expired.

III

Like many another brilliant young man, Edward was faced with a choice of career; and — again like many another brilliant young man — without hesitation he plumped for the films. He had a little courtesy title which helped, and he had looks, though not of the burly Josser's variety. Edward was willowy, with a rather featureless face which took make-up admirably. He obtained jobs. His salary mounted. Within six months directors were able to remember his name, and he was halfway to the stars. Six months more and the Hon. Edward Phipps found himself, indignantly and unwillingly, and for the first time in his life, in love.

She was a little creature, graceful and slender as a fawn. She played small parts, and might have played big ones but for her voice, which was of a timbre hateful to the microphone, neither rich Cockney nor skin-tight stage-English; it was refined, and that was the best and worst thing that could be said of it. But it was her beauty that sent Edward Phipps, languid and mannered Edward, into the most undignified state of primitive frenzy whenever she came near him. He kept gazing and glaring, hardly able to believe that anything so perfect to the eye could have existence; then she would make a little movement, touch him perhaps, and he would at once acquire the urgent rushing consciousness that she was flesh and blood, and that he needed her more than life.

She took very little notice of him. Her tilted fawn's eyes, set very far apart, looked up at him without shyness or guile. She liked him, and that was all. But Edward was aflame. She was actually the first human being he had ever wanted to have touch him. He wanted her every minute of the day, and first his pose, then his pride, went down before that hunger. Everyone at the studio knew of the affair; he, the secret Edward, was daily read like a book by the mocking eyes of extras and camera-men. He knew it, and cared exactly nothing. He was too far gone even to be pitiable; a madman is not pitiable. He was drunken and senseless with desire for her, drunken to the point of marriage, and letting his relatives and his future barony go hang.

But Leila Vane — odd, he thought, even in his delirium, that name cropping up — would not hear of marrying him. She gave no reason; she just jibbed at it. He did not interest her.

The other women, who found Edward attractive, and his little title more attractive still, told her plainly that she was out of her senses. Who did she think she was, the Virgin Mary? They gave her no peace; nor did Edward. His pride was in the dust; he took the silliest stratagems to speak to her, to see her for a moment. He wrote fantastic notes which she never answered. He plagued her. Everyone was sorry for Edward, and nagged Leila. At last, weeping so that amid his exaltation his heart nearly broke for her, she gave way. She was sorry for him, she said, terribly sorry; and if he liked — if he wanted her so much ——

" Dear! " said Edward. " Oh, God, Leila, don't cry; I can't bear you to cry. We'll have fun, my darling, truly we will. Get an Archbishop to tie us up, if you like, and then go somewhere heavenly — Sicily or Greece or somewhere."

She agreed, weeping, to Sicily or Greece if he wanted, but not to the Archbishop. Marry him she obstinately would not. So, after all, to the amazement of everybody, and amid much talk of having played cards badly and boasts from the other women of what they could have done in her place, it ended by being just an affair.

IV

Or rather, it did not end. Edward's passion should, according to the rules, have burned itself out in a couple of months, once he had what he wanted; but Edward was in love, and there he stayed, possibly because, although he possessed his Leila, he could not kindle her to any response at all. She was kind to him, but she just did not care, and told him so, pitifully. He repeated that it didn't matter, that he would make her care, and knew all the time in his heart that he could not. It was like making love to a polite person who is listening to someone else. Edward, who at Oxford had protested that companionship was the one thing, who had written flaming letters about sharing utterly all one's thoughts and longings, was in love with a woman before whom he was dumb, and who cared for him so little, while she yielded, that he could not even anger her.

It dragged on for months. They both went their way, worked, earned money, spent it. Everyone asked them about together. There were parties, at which both were conscientiously gay, and from which they went home together close-held and in silence — the wrong sort of silence. People came to their flat. People made love to Leila, who looked through and away from them. She did not give him cause for jealousy. There was no reason, it seemed, why they should not go on together all their lives long, desiring and thwarted, and making, as all their acquaintance said, such a lovely couple.

Edward suffered. He had always been accustomed to let go, at school, at Oxford, at home, and the silence was torment. He thought for a moment of Ella; but too much had happened, too long a time had elapsed; he could not have written now without self-consciousness. She, Ella, had become a shadow, and he knew that she had never been anything more, even while he had been blowing the froth off his soul, and clattering blasphemies on his typewriter. Leila was the reality; but she was as far away as though she viewed him incuriously with her fawn's eyes from a hilltop in Mars.

True, she deferred to him in small ways, even looked for his guidance; she imitated his voice and his writing, dressed where he told her, and reproduced the clipped yet lazy phrasing of his friends. She was eagerly adaptable, and Edward might have been flattered, happy, if he had not known that she did not care a halfpenny whether he was flattered and

happy or not. He tried to shrug; told himself that she was
getting experience, qualifying for better parts, and that the
whole affair, mysterious yielding and as strange withholding,
had some such aspiration for its motive. He could not trans-
late his film-self into real life, play the he-man, and shake her
secret out of her, poor gentle child. He could only make love,
unhappy one-sided love, and come out of his extravagances
to be polite again.

It was Edward's film company which, quite unknowing,
cleared the stage for a dénouement. This company — which
believed, among other oddities, that literature properly edited
for the screen could be made to pay — was in process of de-
livering to the public a winsome *Jane Eyre*. This involved a
shot or two of actual Yorkshire moors; and accordingly the
company was entrained, with its own sound-proof camera
rooms, and lights of a hundred thousand candle-power to
supplement the niggardly Yorkshire sun. Edward drove north
alone in his own swift stately car, and all the way was torn
by two thoughts; the longing to get back to Leila, and fear of
the silence that would greet him.

Only three shots of the actual moors were needed, and these
were secured with unheard-of expedition in five days. Edward
had left on the Monday; on Saturday he drove back to London
and Leila.

On the table in the hall of their flat as he entered were letters
waiting for him. He called Leila, but there was no answer,
and idly he began to tear the envelopes open; the usual rub-
bish, advertisements, begging letters, bills. One had no stamp.
As he was about to crumple it he saw incredulously that it was
addressed in Leila's version of his own fastidious scribble to
" the Hon. Edward Phipps." " What the hell —— " thought
Edward, dragging forth the folded sheet. It held very few
words.

"Edward, I'm very sorry, I just can't go on with it. I've tried, but what's the use? There's someone else, nobody you know, not your sort. I know just how you feel; I'm feeling just the same myself all the time. I'm really awfully sorry, Edward; I thought it might work, but it hasn't, so I'm just going to do a fade-out. Good-bye."

He threw this down after a moment, with the kind of laugh deluded lovers use before the microphone; but Edward was not acting. Staring down helplessly at the letter as it lay, he saw another envelope beneath it on the table. "Orlando Vane, Esq.," said the direction this time, "St. Mary's College, Oxford." So much was in Leila's writing; across it in red ink, in the hand of the porter, long-memoried as every college porter has to be, "Try Hon. Edward Phipps," and the address.

"I've just got to write," this letter began abruptly. "I'm in such trouble. You used to write me when you felt blue, so you won't mind my sending you this line.

"I have been living with a man, a real gentleman; he was at your college. I went to live with him because I thought I might get to like him. He's taught me a lot and he's ever so much in love with me, but it's no good. I just can't stand him, and so now I've left him. I've tried, but there it is: you can't make yourself be in love. He's got one of those thin, weak-looking kind of faces, just the opposite of you, and he's never unkind, and he'd give me the earth if I wanted, but always sort of polite and weak. Never goes up in a rage like you used to, and he's got a silly kind of laugh.

"He's on the films. It's all right, good money, but it's no sort of a life for a man. You said once you were going in for engineering in Mexico — well, that is the kind of thing I mean, more what a man ought to be like, instead of all this makeup and cocktails and all the rest of it.

"Well, as I said before, I've left him now and am at 104, Gladstone Street, Isleworth, where I was two years ago. I have plenty of money and don't want any help in that way, but I just thought I'd let you have a line to tell you how things are. I dare say you've forgotten my existence, but I've kept all your letters and photo; they mean a lot to me still.

" Hoping to have a line from you if you have not gone out to Mexico yet, I remain,

" Your sincere friend,
" ELLA."

After a moment Edward, taking the two letters with him, went to the dining-room, found some brandy, and drank off half a tumbler of it; then, in the cloudy but glowing after-math, sat down with his head in his hands to think.

It was hard thinking, that bruised his vanity at every turn. He had to face the fact that his own view of himself as a reck-less, rather splendid person, a brilliant yet tender person, suc-cessful, lovable, and good-looking, had not " got over." The Edward of the letters and the Edward of life stood confronted in Leila's mind, and were not the same; there was no faintest family likeness between them; unrecognisable, even to one who knew both.

He faced that, starting up from his chair and walking blindly to and fro while his vanity smarted. Leila's patience, Leila's silence, had contrived to set before him the cruellest picture of himself, such as no rage, striking to wound, could ever have made him see. With all the will in the world — " I've tried, but there it is " — she could not manage to love him. He was too far from the ideal, too dreadfully different from the Edward of the letters. And this other Edward, he of the polite weakness, was the true one.

He understood, and writhed, and tried to find a way of salv-ing his vanity by action. What could he do about it? Go to Gladstone Road, prove that he was the Edward of the letters? (Blast Josser and his photograph, the sweatered oaf!) Tell her the whole story; go up in one of those Edwardian rages she so much admired? Alas, the instrument of these cataclysms had been the typewriter; flesh and blood, topped with "one of those weak-looking kind of faces," could never equal the type-writer's fine frenzies. What were the other alternatives? To take another mistress, and let the whole thing slide with a laugh — a "silly kind of a laugh"? What use to pretend? Everybody knew he cared.

He-man stuff, then? Go round with a gun or something; smash in her mouth, and the fawn's eyes that saw him so clearly, too clearly? Ah, no, no! Her darling face — I couldn't bear it; I couldn't hurt her, thought Edward, rocking as he walked, and striking at the walls so that his knuckles bled. Besides, to be the Isleworth murderer; the sordid questioning, the newspaper gloatings — no, no, shrieked Edward's thoughts, never that! The glamour's gone from murder now, what with expert witnesses and finger-prints. God, no! I'd rather die myself.

"I'd rather die myself."

In this roundabout way Edward arrived at his solution, which, though really no solution at all, was what he needed even more; a gesture. He was of the generation that cries out when it is hurt, and even, sometimes, before. He wanted Leila and the world to know how much he cared, and he wanted to hide for ever the sickening secret, that their mutual hero had never existed. There was, it seemed to him, only this way out. He therefore made search in a drawer for the automatic which he had used in a Raffles part; and having burned the two tell-tale letters to ashes, put the barrel in his mouth and pulled something cold with his thumb.

Victim of misadventure, victim of a heartless little bitch, victim of the nerve-destroying whirl of modern life — every-one who saw the news was sorry for Edward, and found somebody or something to blame for his death. But it occurred to no one to blame the true and entirely unconscious culprit, that unknown undergraduate who started the low-brow fashion in Oxford with a bowl of goldfish and two pink silk garters bought at Woolworth's Stores.

VARIATION

By

L. P. HARTLEY

NOTE

Mr. Hartley has conceived the story as a one act play in three scenes. The first, which closes with the letter, is expository. The opening dialogue gives the impression of a household that is out-of-joint, and of a querulous, complaining and inefficient wife; by so doing it prepares the reader for the final scene of departure. The prominence given to the typewriter as a "property" in the theatrical sense is cleverly done. The letter, given in full, fills the function of the old stage confident. It will be remembered that early in the first act of the old fashioned plays the hero and his friends, advancing to the footlights, hold a conversation in which each tells the other facts that must be familiar but facts which it is essential for the audience to know. In the same way, the letter tells us how the correspondence started, and when, and why it stopped,—all facts that must have been equally well-known to the recipient of the letter. We are told that the typewriter is used to avoid recognition of the handwriting, because X uses the Greek e's. Thus by the introduction of the letter the reader is in possession of all the antecedent facts. We are now ready for the main scene, the recognition. This is accomplished by the somewhat improbable device of having one letter read aloud. He naturally recognizes his own letter. She understands that the letter is his because in it is repeated, word for word, a sentiment he has just expressed. The scene is carried almost entirely by dialogue, with an occasional analytical paragraph. Instead of the climax with the two natures emotionally in opposition, the scene ends uncertainly. And in a play, the last scene, one page only, would have been omitted. Mr. Hartley, then, is trying by suggestion to force the reader's imagination to fill in the gaps. Does he gain, or does he lose by this method?

VARIATION

By L. P. HARTLEY

WITH a sigh Myra Henning walked across the room and pressed the button of the bell. Nobody came. She waited. Save for the distant throb of a vacuum-cleaner, all was silent in the house. But the silence only increased her impatience; she went to the door and called:

" Gladys! "

The vacuum-cleaner stopped with a grunt in the middle of a respiration, and a moment later Gladys stood before her.

" Didn't you hear me ring? "

" No, ma'am, but I'm afraid . . ."

" I've told you there's no need for you to help with the vacuum-cleaner; they can do it perfectly well by themselves."

" I was only showing them how to be careful with the curtain where it's a bit worn, ma'am, and I'm afraid . . ."

" Well, what are you afraid of? "

" I'm afraid the bell's out of order again."

Myra made a gesture of despair. "And that on top of everything! However! When did you notice it was out of order? "

" This morning, ma'am, when Mr. Henning tried to ring."

" Oh, when did he try to ring? "

" Before you came down to breakfast; he wanted to know if there were any letters."

" And were there? I didn't have any."

" There was just one for him, ma'am. The postman had only that minute come."

" Oh," said Myra. " I really rang to ask you, where is Mr. Henning now? "

" He was in his room, ma'am, five minutes ago. I think he was writing a letter. He said he didn't want to be disturbed."

" Didn't want to be disturbed? "

"Well, he asked me not to put the things on his writing-table straight, ma'am."

"Oh, I see. And what made you think he was writing a letter? "

"He was fixing the notepaper in the typewriter, ma'am."

"In the typewriter? In my typewriter! He's always borrowing it now. He told me he'd forgotten how to use it."

"He didn't seem very comfortable with it, ma'am; he kept jiggling it about."

"As he does with the car. Will you ask him to put the typewriter back in the morning-room when he's finished with it? Thank you, Gladys; that's all for the moment."

Three times in the course of the next hour Myra visited the morning-room to see if the typewriter had been replaced. The third time she felt she could wait no longer; she sat down crossly in front of the empty space, took up her fountain pen, filled it at the cost of inking her fingers, and began to write.

" Dear Theodore,

"You will think I am always complaining to you, but this time I really have a grievance! And as you are partly responsible for it, I know you will sympathise with me. Though, indeed, you always sympathise. My grievance (you may have guessed) is not altogether unconnected with X. I usually forbear to mention him but he is really rather inconsiderate, growingly so, I think. He has taken to borrowing my typewriter! If I had the honour of receiving his letters, I should not mind so much — indeed, it would be a relief, for his handwriting is appalling. Or if he took the trouble to ask me first! But he just pinches it. I can't tell you, Theodore, how mutual civilities evaporate after a few years of married life! I can remember when X. used to stand up when I came into the room.

And now he doesn't even notice if I'm there or not. I mustn't go on in this strain or you will think I am disloyal. But do, when you next write, tell me about Y.'s shortcomings; it was so guarded of you only to say she was a little tiresome. There must be something more in it than that, or you wouldn't have suggested we should start writing to each other again.

" But to me belongs the credit of having begun it, of having answered the S.O.S. of the 'Demobilized Officer, depressed.' It was eleven years ago today — the eleventh anniversary! And *that's* why I feel so particularly furious with X. for stealing the typewriter this morning. He must have done it on purpose to spite me, for he got hold of it before I came down. Of course, it doesn't prevent my writing to you, but it does a little take the edge off the first fine, careless rapture when I remember this is only a rough draft, and I've got to copy it all out again! I wonder if it would matter, this once, if I didn't, and sent you a specimen of my handwriting? It's more legible than X.'s. He takes no trouble about that or about anything else — certainly not about me. I typed my first letter to you because, do you remember, I was working in that office; and you said it showed how prudent I was, and you would do it too, although you were a poor hand at it. You do occasionally make a mistake; but I think you must be good at anything you take up.

" It seems odd, doesn't it, that we 'entered into this correspondence' to relieve each other's loneliness; we dropped it when we married; and we took it up three months ago — why? To relieve our — well, whatever is the opposite of loneliness, I suppose. How paradoxical one's motive are! But perhaps we are lonely though married — unless X. has a private life of his own into which I am not admitted. But I don't believe it. He's grown so dull, poor old thing. The typewriter itself must yawn when he gets hold of it.

" I remember now that you gave another reason why we shouldn't write in our own handwriting. When you invented that system of forwarding that seemed so complicated but worked so well, you said we must do everything we could to preserve our anonymity. You had formed an image of me in your mind (you said) that was quite complete: you even knew the colour of my hair and eyes (you didn't tell me what they were). Ignorant people might call it an ideal image; but it wasn't: it emerged from the confluence of our thoughts, and I was as much responsible for it as you. I wasn't just the material of a statue you were carving. I was like a piece of music, that only needed rightly interpreting to be the most beautiful piece of music in the world. You said you aspired to be my interpreter. How well I remember that letter.

" Dear Theodore, you said we were never, never to fall in love with each other, or we should be exacting and jealous and perhaps get on each other's nerves. If you gave me a specimen of your handwriting (you said) I might get to hate the sight of your Greek e's. (How right you were! They always annoy me in X.'s brief notes: they are so much like his a's. I almost wish you hadn't told me that you make them.) We were to be as abstract as possible.

" I'll own to you now that that high ideal wasn't quite possible to me. I suppose, being a woman, my emotions are more concrete than yours. I have loved you once or twice — just a little. Do you mind?

" This letter transgresses all our rules, conventions, and traditions. You must forgive it! The next shall be much less declamatory. I was empty and nervous and irritable this morning; and when I began to write I suddenly felt so grateful to Fate (or whoever it was that arranged this outlet for my feelings) that I felt I must testify and make some sort of thank-offering — even on an anonymous and abstract altar! Consider it (if you can) not a tribute to you but to the kindness of Fortune! The anniversary seemed to require it, and then — my pen ran away with me! The typewriter would have compelled me to be more circumspect.

" It will certainly exercise a restraining influence, perhaps censor the letter altogether, if I copy it out. I wonder if I shall. It's so long and I'm so lazy. I think I hear J. outside, grunting under the typewriter's weight.

" Goodbye,

" Yours,

" Dorothea.

" I don't really *dislike* X."

It was nine o'clock in the morning, a few days later. A bell rang in the kitchen.

" Why," said the cook, " it must be the master ringing for his breakfast. He's been so early these last few weeks, I don't know what's come over him."

" Ah! " said Gladys, departing with the tray; " it's not breakfast he comes down early for, that I do know."

She found Mr. Henning standing by the breakfast table, staring down at an empty plate. He was facing her, and his head, slightly bowed, showed a bald patch on the top.

" Good-morning, Gladys," he said, straightening himself a little guiltily. " That is — er — good-morning again." He looked out of the window — though " out " was a euphemism, so opaque was the November weather.

" Not a very nice morning, I'm afraid," he amended.

" No, sir."

" Gladys! " He was elaborately casual. " Letters come? "

" Not yet, sir."

He glanced anxiously at the clock.

" Oh, the postman sometimes comes later than this, sir."

Mr. Henning hastily turned his head. " Oh, I know; I wasn't thinking about that. On these damp mornings I've known him to be as late as twenty-eight minutes past nine. No, I was just wondering why — why " (he seemed to search his mind for something to wonder at) " why you had brought in two cups."

" Because the mistress is coming down, sir."

" Oh, is she? " The disappointment in his voice was obvious. " But her place isn't laid," he added hopefully.

" We only just got the message, sir. I was to be sure to tell you not to go away before she came down; she wanted to see you specially, I think."

John Henning sighed. " That means a long wait, Gladys."

He was right. He had finished his breakfast and was longing to light the cigarette Myra had forbidden while she was eating, when in she came. Gladys was just behind her, with some letters on a tray. Involuntarily his glance slipped past his wife and rested on the maid. Myra stopped, turned her head, and stretched out her hand to the tray.

" Good-morning, Myra," her husband called to her from the fireplace.

" Good-morning, John; I thought you hadn't noticed me."

" On the contrary, I was waiting for you."

" You looked as though you were waiting for the letters."

" How subtle you are," said John Henning, ironically admiring. " You didn't notice if there were any for me? "

" You didn't give me time. Yes, there's one for you too, not very exciting. Typewritten."

She handed him his letter without looking at it, her eyes were so occupied with her own. She began to open it. Her husband noticed the action.

" Oh, I thought you wanted to speak to me specially about something, before I go about the business of breadwinning," he said lightly.

" I did, but do you mind if I —— "

" Certainly not, only I didn't imagine it could be very exciting, as it's typewritten."

With a simultaneous movement they both looked down at the letters they were holding.

"Very well," said Myra, put out but resigned, "I won't read it. I'll talk to you instead."

"Will that be a great sacrifice?"

"I can't tell yet."

"Well, go on."

"It's about the typewriter. You find you constantly need it now, don't you?"

"So many people complain of my handwriting, you amongst them."

"I know. I think it's an excellent idea," said Myra, "that you should learn to typewrite."

"I don't want to learn," said Henning, annoyed by the implication in his wife's words; "I want to use the confounded thing."

"That's just it — that's what I complain of. I want to use it too; and it is really mine, isn't it?"

"You certainly brought it with you from the office."

"Anyhow, when I was in the office no one else touched it. I sometimes wish I was there now."

"You can always go back," said her husband politely.

Myra recovered herself. "That would be one way out of the difficulty," she said more gently. "But before I do anything drastic, couldn't you buy a new typewriter? In any case, mine — ours — is getting worn. It blots all the eyes of the e's in a maddening fashion like — like these." She held out her envelope, half-torn across the flap, and indicated the smudged letters. "Now, give me your envelope for a moment, and you'll see the difference."

Disregarding her outstretched hand, he examined his envelope himself.

"But surely these e's are smudged too?"

"How can I tell if you don't let me look?"

"Ah, well, you must take my word for it," he said, putting

the letter in his pocket. " If I got a typewriter, I should choose one that made Greek e's."

" Oh, don't — you know how I hate them! "

He took his letter out of his pocket and studied the envelope. " They look very nice here."

" But you said a moment ago that the e's on your envelope were smudged too."

" Oh, did I? Well, these e's are all right: it was my eyes that deceived me."

" Oh, John, those loathsome puns! Can you ever be serious? Here, give me the letter."

" I can't; it's private."

" Surely you don't mind me looking at the envelope? "

" I think I'd rather you didn't."

" John, I can't make out whether you're just trying to tease me, or whether —— "

" Whether what? "

" Well, whether you are really keeping something back from me."

" Well, supposing I am? "

" Then I don't think you're very kind."

There was a pause. John Henning drummed with his fingers on the table. The sound irritated his wife as he knew it would. Her impatience showed in her face, accentuating a certain sharpness of feature that he had been increasingly aware of during the last few months. He said deliberately:

" All things considered, I think it would really be kinder not to let you see it."

" John, what do you mean? "

As Myra rose from the table she thought she was going to cry. But she did not want to give her husband an easy triumph, and, subduing the spasm in her throat, she said with all the indifference she could muster:

"From your unwillingness to tell me, I might suppose it was a letter from a woman."

"Your supposition would be correct."

While she stared at him disdainfully, Myra was mentally making an inventory of her husband's female friends. They were not of the stuff of which mistresses are made. In ordinary circumstances she would never have suspected him of an intrigue; but in wantonly setting his wits against hers, he had exasperated her beyond bearing, so that, in her present mood, she would gladly have believed him capable of any infidelity. When she spoke, it was really out of irritation with his defiance of her, not from conviction of his guilt; but the effect of her words was the same.

"I suppose that's why she uses a typewriter."

"I don't follow your reasoning."

"I mean that's why she doesn't use her own handwriting."

"Again your train of thought escapes me."

"You must be very stupid," said Myra. "I mean that your correspondent doesn't want anyone but yourself to know who she is."

"Whom does her identity concern except me?"

"Then why bother to conceal it?"

John Henning considered a moment.

"If you were writing a letter to someone —— "

"Well, go on."

"If you were writing to someone, and you didn't want anyone else to intercept your thoughts nor deflect them by a hair's-breadth, not even breathe upon them, as it were —— "

He hesitated.

"Well?"

"You didn't want them to collect, on the way from me to you — from you to him, I mean — any of the common dust of association, any contact that would make them, in however slight a degree, someone else's concern as well as yours and his — any little mark that helped identification or recognition —— "

" A Greek e, for instance," put in Myra.

" Anything that could connect them with one's everyday life, anything that could explain them by natural causes and make them less of a miracle — I'm afraid I express myself badly."

" No, you are most eloquent. I follow you far better than you followed me a moment ago."

" I mean, if you wanted to banish from the material form of that letter whatever tokens of its progress, through the hands of servants and postmen, through streets like Oxford Street, through trains like the 9.5 to the City, through post offices like the G.P.O. in Hill Street, through concealed approaches and gravel sweeps, through kitchens with serving hatches, to — to —— "

" A breakfast table like ours," said Myra, rather grimly.

" If you wanted it to come like a bolt from the blue, a welcome thunderbolt, a flying fragment of who knows what meteor — well, wouldn't you at least type the envelope? "

" Yes," said Myra slowly, " I suppose I should."

She looked down at the letter in her hand. She knew that it came from Theodore, and a moment ago she had been longing to read it. For four days she had been living on the expectation of it. But as she listened to her husband's impassioned plea for the privacy of his letter, her desire lost its orientation, and began to turn back upon itself. What did it amount to, after all, her secret correspondence? It was just an escape from reality, a playing at life: it could not relieve her inward suffering any more than beautiful music can charm away toothache. It was merely a substitute for experience and a laborious one at that. She heard the note of eagerness in her husband's voice; she saw the glow in his eyes; she was aware of the warmth of his whole being, alight and aflame with delicious exaltation. She was convinced, heart and mind, that he was in love with another woman, too deeply convinced to challenge him, to want to hear him deny or affirm it. Yet, though she accepted the fact, she did not realise its full significance.

Two streams, tributary to the main flow, contributed to her present wretchedness. One was the discrediting of her own secret romance, now shown up for the pitiful make-believe it was and must always have been — for the revelation of her husband's passion ran like a consuming fire through the fertile places of her memory, leaving them barren and comfortless. And the other, lesser source of grief, was the thought (that so often comes to one in disaster and for a moment seems to eclipse in painfulness the disaster itself) that she herself was responsible for her suffering — she and Fate combined. If she had had a cold, if she had not decided to come down to breakfast, if she had not provoked and wooed this horrible combination of circumstances, she need never have known how her life had been mutilated and the sources of its nourishment stopped up. She had come down meaning to make a slight scene. Well, Fate had called her bluff. She fumbled in her dress for her handkerchief.

"What's the matter, Myra?" asked her husband. "What have I been and said now?"

His words jarred on her and his stupid air of innocence, which seemed intended to insult her intelligence, infuriated and nauseated her.

"Do you expect me to feel happy," she gasped out between her sobs, "when you, when you——"

"When I do what?" His voice now sounded more concerned, but it was still brazen with pretended innocence.

" When you as good as tell me " — Myra hated the vulgarity of the words, but never having expected to make an accusation of this kind, she did not know how else to frame it — " that you have a mistress."

" Myra! "

They stared at each other, alarm and astonishment in their eyes, while Myra's charge seemed to take tangible form and lie between them like a gage of battle.

The words were no sooner out of her mouth than her anger melted, and her one wish was to recall them. They were much too violent; by overstating her grievance they put her in the wrong. And they gave the initiative in the quarrel to her husband, an initiative he was not slow to take. But, profiting by her error, he kept his temper.

" What makes you think I have a mistress? "

Myra longed to say that it was all a mistake; she didn't think so now. But his tone was so chilling that she had to make a show of defending herself.

" What you said just now about writing to somebody — and then you wouldn't let me even look at that letter."

" I'm afraid you don't distinguish very well between what is real and what is imaginary. I tried — feebly, I admit — to give you some idea of what an ideal correspondence might mean to someone who was . . . a little jaded by — oh, I don't know . . . the limitations imposed on life by actuality. And you mysteriously leap to the conclusion, because my imagination is capable of conceiving a happiness that I don't — er — happen to enjoy, that therefore I have a mistress."

" I'm sorry," said Myra, humbly and helplessly. " You seemed so carried away by what you said, I suppose I forgot that you were describing an ideal state of things."

" You are not the first to sneer at the ideal, and you won't be the last," said John, coldly and with scant justice, for Myra had not sneered. " It's that mental attitude of yours, so petty, so ignoble — if you'll forgive my frankness — that drives one into the arms of — the arms of —— "

" Into whose arms? " asked Myra in spite of herself.

" It's no good telling you," said her husband heavily. " You wouldn't understand."

" I can understand this," Myra countered, her resentment returning under the lash of his contempt, " that this morning you received a letter of which you won't let me see even the envelope."

" That letter! " said he with an air of weary indifference. " If you speak of it again I'll throw it into the fire. I don't ask to look at your letters," he went on moodily. " I don't suppose they would interest me, but if I wanted to make a nuisance of myself I might. The one you had this morning, for instance — what about that? You say mine is from a mistress; may I return the compliment, and inquire if yours is from a lover? "

It was the lovelessness rather than the hostility in his voice that appalled Myra. The flat, dead tones sounded the knell of the present, of the future; they did more, they tolled for the past, for the whole of their married life. It seemed to Myra, then, that John had rescued her from the office, made love to her, married her, given her everything she wanted except a child, simply in order that he might ask, after the ten years of their life together, whether she had a lover; not to ask it in anger or in pity, or in sorrow, but in indifference, as though he cared not which way she answered. Yes, and not only in indifference; for, if she could detect an emotion in his voice, it was incredulity; he did not believe that a woman so dull and charmless and lack-lustre as herself could have a lover. And at this her vanity rebelled. She would show him; he should know that in some man's heart she still sat enthroned.

"Let us make a bargain," she said, decision giving her voice a false air of briskness. "If I read my letter to you, will you read yours to me?"

Her husband was very much taken aback.

"What, out loud?" he said.

"Certainly; and afterwards, if you like, we will exchange them, to prove that we have suppressed nothing."

John Henning pondered a moment. "I suppose I owe it to you," he said.

Myra's thumb was already ripping open the envelope, but she checked the action midway.

"Don't flatter yourself," she flashed back at him in a sudden fury, "that the debt will be all on your side."

"If, as I suspect, the letter's a bill, the debt certainly won't be all on my side, even if I have to pay it," said her husband, walking towards the window and peering into the fog as if it held something that interested him. "Fire away," he added over his shoulder. With trembling fingers Myra smoothed out the thin broad sheet; and in a voice that also trembled she began to read:

"DEAREST DOROTHEA,

"After all, why not 'dearest'? It has been 'dear' all along, I know; 'dear' was our convention. But I have long wanted to change it; and what better moment than today, the eleventh anniversary of our correspondence? Something tells me it is a turning-point. Now I couldn't write 'dear' (with your name after it) even if I tried!"

Myra stopped reading and stole a glance at her husband's back. It was unresponsive. She continued:

"I appreciate your consideration in not asking me about Y. I think a letter ought to be in one key, don't you? and for that reason I haven't told you much about her. Not that it's exactly a sore subject, but it is so completely irrelevant to *our* relationship. It belongs to the world — I suppose it really constitutes the world — you help me to escape from. Her failings, poor thing, are not really serious; I am still fond of her in a way. I think if you met her you would see, probably better than I can now, the traces of the qualities that used to make her attractive, just as the perceptive can see the traces of beauty in an old, tired face. (I think you must be very perceptive.) For all I know, her charm may still be there, though I can't see it; and you know how not being able to admire something you once admired doubly aggravates the sense of loss. To me she seems over-emphatic, and strident, and resentful. We get on all right when I'm in good spirits, but if I'm depressed, she's like salt rubbed into a wound. I think she believes it is her mission to be a kind of moral antiseptic; but *you* know, dearest Dorothea, how much I prefer an anodyne! When we first met, Y. and I (*we* haven't met! — I'm coming to that), the circumstances were peculiar; I think they hastened on our marriage; and (I would only say this to you) she hastened it, too. She had a dull job, she was badly off; and her vivacity, which was what first attracted me, was really the result, I suspect, of the conflict between her vitality and her adversity. I hadn't yet found anyone to be kind to (one often doesn't, in life; in my correspondence with you the kindness is all on the other side), and I thought how delicious it would be to temper the wind to those pathetic high spirits and put them in a sheltered place where they could blossom undisturbed. *That's* where I made the mistake; they didn't bear transplanting; they grew rather rank. . . . And when I'm in a bad mood I tax Y. (in thought) with ingratitude and insensibility and many other things. I have even managed to persuade myself she married me for my money, little though there is of it.

" But *basta!* I couldn't have brought myself to tell you this any more than I can take nasty medicine without the promise of sweetness to follow. I know I oughtn't to ask it of you, but couldn't we meet just once — not on paper, but in the flesh?

We must, we must! One does well to be suspicious of life, even bringing gifts; I have proved that; but all the same, if year after year one goes on looking the gift horse in the mouth, how can it help getting old and long in the tooth, or whatever horses do become? One must have some confidence. Why, it's absurd even to talk about confidence. We have the best of guarantees; we have known each other so well and so long.

" When I began to write I had already decided on a meeting-place, but, oh, Dorothea, some unworthy little misgiving still holds me back! Ought we to take the risk? I think we ought; but let us remain anonymous and unidentified for two or three letters more; they will be marvellous letters written in the dawn of our great happiness. Only we will abide faithfully by our old rules; we don't let the letters collect, on the way from me to you and you to me, any of the common dust of associa-tion, any contact that could make them, in however slight a degree, someone else's concern as well as ours, any little mark that helped identification or recognition, anything that could connect them with our everyday life —— "

Something strange had happened to the cadences in Myra's voice; it went up and down in a sort of sing-song, punctuated by little gasps.

" Anything that could explain them by natural —— "

She broke off with a cry. " John, are you still there? I feel I can't go on reading. I'll try —— "

" Anything that would make them less of a miracle . . ."

" Oh, John, do come to me quickly — quickly! "

The letter fell from her hands, and as she clutched the table for support she saw a figure coming towards her from the window with great strides. Whose figure it was, the tumult in her senses hardly allowed her to dintinguish; it might have been John's, Theodore's, anyone's. . . .

When Gladys brought in the breakfast next morning she found John Henning already in the dining-room. He looked pale and agitated.

" The letters haven't come yet, sir," volunteered the maid.

" Oh, haven't they? Well, never mind about them. I've got something rather important to tell you — I'm going away."

" Very well, sir. Shall I put the usual things in the suit-case? "

" The suitcase won't be enough, Gladys. I shall want my trunk and — and all my luggage. I'm going abroad for some time — several months, perhaps. Your mistress will remain here."

" I see, sir. Then I'll tell George to get the trunks down from the boxroom and air them."

" There won't be time to do that, I'm afraid. I'm leaving this afternoon."

" This afternoon, sir? " gasped Gladys, who had hitherto concealed her astonishment. " And shall you be taking the typewriter as well, sir? Because that'll need packing separate."

John Henning smiled.

" No, I shan't take the typewriter. It's not much good really; an old model, out of date now."

" Yes, sir. Excuse me asking — only there's not much time and we are so short-handed, only five of us with George, sir —— " Henning smiled again, with conscious patience. " The mistress will know where to send the letters? "

" How kind you are, Gladys; you think of everything. But it doesn't matter about the letters; I'm not having them forwarded. And, oh, Gladys," he called to the maid, who had nearly reached the door, " will you ring up Dr. Hardman and ask him to come round some time today? In the evening would be best. Mrs. Henning isn't very well, but it's nothing serious."

IN XANADU

By

GERALD BULLETT

NOTE

In *In Xanadu* Mr. Bullett invites us frankly to play with him. There is no attempt here to suggest actuality. The scene is laid anywhere, nowhere, in Xanadu, or Bagdad; the characters may be Chinamen, or they may be Arabs, or what you will. By this means Mr. Bullett solves the problem of creating conviction, or rather, he gives up solving the problem. Smilingly he assures the reader that it is all too absurd to be taken seriously. He does not expect you to believe that a man, who has known a woman intimately for a year, would not recognize her in the dark, knowing her intimately for a week. So he works in little attacks upon the English customs, such as " a way of life, which . . . would have earned him respect in Oxford, or Ely, or even Muswell Hill," or " Anglican in nothing else, they at least shared, in advance, our detestation of the unusual," etc. For this reason, he envelops the story in the atmosphere of the Arabian Nights. There are, and there can be, no precise details, nothing to suggest concrete images to the reader. Instead, there are metaphorical phrases that vaguely suggest the Bible, particularly the *Song of Solomon*. To achieve this effect, he resorts to a marked rhythm in the sentences and recurrent vowel and consonant sounds. In the sentence, " Then is my dream dead, he cried, and I am desolate," watch the insistence upon the dentals *t* and *d,* and the repetition of the *e, ea,* and *a* sounds. Mr. Bullett's solution of the problem, then, requires a type of most elaborate writing, writing that might almost be analysed into a musical notation.

IN XANADU

By Gerald Bullett

IN the city of Xanadu and in the time of the great Kubla
Khan — unless my grandfather, from whom I had the
tale, was at fault in these particulars, which is very possible —
there lived a young man who, though of blood royal he had
the merest smatch, was by his neighbours accounted princely,
and so called. Prince Yafith — and my grandfather would
hear of no other name for him — was both valorous and wise.
Expert in military exercises, as befitted his station, he nevertheless spent as much time among his manuscripts as with his
horses. He had read the sacred writings, to say nothing of
others not so sacred; and he practised, with a certain indolent
skill, the arts of music and versification. Learned in many
lores, and master of many lives, he conducted himself with
modesty and wielded his power with discretion. He beat his
slaves but seldom; the pleasures of torture were repugnant to
him; and he had never been known to order the death of a
malefactor for any less crime than murder or treachery. This
eccentric behaviour, while it endeared him to his own depend-
ants, set the tongues of malice wagging in the world without,
and to such noisy purpose as only his wisdom in war could
silence. It added to the scandal that though he had been careful to furnish his household with all requisite amenities, including a variety of young women, he shewed himself somewhat indifferent to the delights of love, following a way of
life which, while it would have earned him respect in Oxford,
or Ely, or even Muswell Hill, was looked at askance by the
orthodox citizens of Xanadu. His heart being set, perhaps, on
a dream beyond mortal attaining, he was content to spend the
most of his time in retirement, browsing in his library, talk-

ing with his friends, or wandering lonely in his gardens. For
hours together, being of a contemplative habit, he would
slowly pace the broad lawns, pausing from time to time to
watch the dazzling play of a fountain, symbol of his own aspiration, or to stare entranced at the white dome of his house
that seemed to quiver in the sunlight, or, most frequent indul-
gence of all, to peer into the shadowy green dimness of the lake
and see as it were his own elusive thoughts in the vision of
lithe shapes, dissolving forms, softened colours, evoked by the
twinkle of a tail or the flash of a gold fin.

It was in precisely this daydreaming posture that he was
found, one day in the fourth month of his thirtieth year, by a
slave bringing rumours of war. A host was reported to be
marching upon Xanadu — or Baghdad, or what you will, for
my grandfather, as I have hinted, could never quite make
up his mind about it. Prince Yafith needed no second telling.
Saddle me Zarimba, he commanded, and let everything be
ordered for my going forth with the armies of our lord the
Sultan, whom heaven preserve. I hear, said the slave, and obey.
And he obeyed to such purpose that within half an hour of
the first alarm Prince Yafith was riding to war in the company
of other commanders and followed by a numerous soldiery,
little knowing that he was to be away from his home for a
year and a day; for the war was like a scattered forest-fire,
which, while you stamp upon it here, breaks out again yonder
where you were stamping but a minute since; it was an affair
of skirmishes and running to and fro, one thing leading to
another, and nothing, it seemed, leading back to Xanadu; and,
as is the way with war in all ages, there was more waiting than
fighting in it, though of fighting, too, there was plenty. Indeed
there was, my grandfather would say: how else would there
have been so many brave men slain? In the very first month of
the campaign the Prince's personal servant met his death

wound. Yusuf they called him; he was a goodhearted ugly fellow not yet bearded; and as he lay dying in his master's arms he asked forgiveness, saying: In my bosom, lord, you will find a letter. It was given me by a woman who had it from another, for this woman had as little art to write as I to read. But, answered Prince Yafith with a smile of compassion, she had perhaps other arts and was able to instruct you in them. It is true, lord, confessed the dying man, and for our love's sake I have cherished the letter that her hand gave me. With these words poor Yusuf fell silent and in a little while went beyond reach of questioning. The candle-flame fluttered at his going; the walls of the tent swayed gently; and tears stood in the eyes of the prince. So he has left me his letter, poor soul, he said musing; and when his vision cleared again, he turned, for distraction from his thoughts, to the thoughts of the unknown woman, who had written: *O companion of the brave, whatever your rank or state, a woman's heart beats for you. Because you have taken the burden of war upon yourself, I am to you as a conquered city yielding all her treasure. In victory you are my lord and I will praise you. In defeat, O lord, you are a cradled child whom I will nourish with the milk of my love. As a tree bending over a quiet water I will bend over you, and as the water holds unspoiled the tree's image I will hold you unspoiled. These eyes have not looked on you, nor these hands touched you; and the speech of your voice comes not to the ears of your adorer. But the eye of the heart can search you out, and the listening mind can know you. For your comfort and my glory let there be love between us, that division may not divide us, nor apartness keep us apart. If you will send me word to the house of Barsum the mercer of silks, in the Street of Saffron, I will requite you with another.* This was the letter that Yusuf had carried unanswered in his breast. It was signed with the name of Nurelhuda. A rare spirit, said Yafith, his eyes kindling; and sighing his deep delight he read the letter again. A rare spirit indeed, he cried; a very pearl among women; it is she of whom I have dreamed these many years. And at once his mind began turning over the phrases of his answer: an occupation the like of which, as weeks went by, and moons waxed and waned, beguiled many an hour of weariness and want. Of every rider who brought despatches from Xanadu he demanded, in another's name, a letter from Nurelhuda; and never went news from the front but included a message for her from her faithful Yusuf; for so, in memory of his fallen servant, and having the whim to disguise his greatness, he chose to subscribe himself.

Meanwhile the image of his beloved, whom he had never seen but with the inward eye, budded and blossomed in his desirous heart, so that his first care, when the war at last was ended and he home again, was to seek her out that he might fill his senses with the beauty his spirit had so long enjoyed. But this hope was frustrate. His question and his hunger paced the streets hotfoot. The inquiry was secret and subtle, but it brought no answer. His messengers first, then himself incognito, went into all the corners of the town. With many a strange woman he had speech. You are called Nurelhuda? Yes, master. You wrote letters to such a one and at such a place? Nay, master: I have no art to write. These failures having bent too far the supple bow of his patience, he at last went in person to the house of Barsum the silk mercer, in the Street of Saffron, where the quest had begun. An old man, this Barsum, with wisdom, the sum of many thoughts, scored on his face. But Yafith was in no mood to find him venerable. Fellow, you must tell me your secret. Who and where is the lady Nurelhuda? That I may not tell, sir. Dog, cried Yafith, I am a prince and powerful. The Sultan calls me friend. My word is given, answered Barsum, and I may not tell. I will have you flayed if you deny me, threatened Yafith: I am Prince Yafith. Honoured sir, said Barsum, I am your humble servant to command. But in this, being Prince Yafith, you will hold me excused. Nor, sir, will you flay me, added the old man with a smile. How so? demanded Yafith: who shall prevent it? — whom should I fear? None but Prince Yafith, answered Barsum with a deep salaam. In him is my protection.

In this plight the prince stayed rigid for many days. Prisoned in himself, he had no joy of the world, because Nurelhuda was denied to him. He sat silent and withdrawn at the feast; in the company of friends he was absent; sunlight was a weariness and the dark hours a desolation. At last he resolved: I will send word to her once more at the house of Barsum, and entreat her lest I die of this love. But scarcely were the words dry on the scroll when his glance fell by hazard upon one whom he took to be a new woman of the household, and his thought changed, and he called to her: What is your name, and why are you here? A pertinent question, for her look was strange to him, and he could not conceive how she had gained admittance to the house, or how, having gained it, she dared with such assurance to linger on the western veranda, so near his private apartment. Let not my lord be angry. His servant is called Mirramazoom. Mirramazoom, echoed Yafith: it is the voice of bees drowsy with sunlight. And why are you here, lady? That, she answered, is as my lord pleases. But though the words were meek there was a ripple of laughter in her tone, her speech running like clear cool water over the jewels left unspoken. Then, said Yafith, you will unveil to me? For it was part of his singularity that in all his commerce with women he preferred to entreat where he might have commanded; and already his senses were stirred by the sight and sound of this stranger, her form being slim and supple and softly curved, her hand white as a wild lily. With the fingers of this lily hand she raised her veil, and Yafith felt his heart stand still, his breath come short. You are the moon of desire, he said murmuring. You are the honey of the royal reason. But, he added in his heart, you are not Nurelhuda, whom I love. She, with no answer, let fall her veil again, and made as if to go; and this coquetry enchanted him anew, so that he seized her hand constraining her. Come, my panther. Come, my gazelle. Let there be rain in this desert of days. Let night be pleasant with our loves.

So for a year and a day the prince had great joy of Mirramazoom, and she of him. She was his friend and paramour whom he delighted to honour, admitting her not only to his bed but to the growing garden of his mind. She in her turn gave him all she had that might conduce to the perfecting of their union; and Yafith, being grateful that she had saved him from despair, contrived to think himself content with her and to refrain from providing her with rivals. So exemplary, by our western standards, was his behaviour towards her, except in the article of Christian marriage, that my grandfather professed to consider him an Anglican born before his time. The gossips of Xanadu, however, were loud in predicting disaster: Anglican in nothing else, they at least shared, in advance, our detestation of the unusual. Of this attitude to himself the prince, if he was aware of it, took no notice; and Mirramazoom, with no less equanimity, suffered the envy and hatred of her female companions of the household. But, while these lovers indolently drifted with the languid tide of their happiness, the Terminator of Delights was secretly spying out his chance, so that a day came when Mirramazoom, once too often for her lover's patience, began to question him. You are silent, my Yafith. Tell me your thoughts. It is nothing, he said: they are not worth the telling. She would not, however, let him rest with that answer. It is in my mind, she persisted, that you do not love me as you did, dear lord. Tell me in what I have fallen short. So Yafith, with a shadow in his eyes, rose up and left her and would not be stayed, going to the quiet verge of the lake that he might indulge undisturbed his new-quickened dream of Nurelhuda, the peerless, the unknown, whom written words, during the drought of his long exile, had been as a well of living water to him. And presently coming back to the house he shut himself alone in his room to compose a letter to this Nurelhuda, this Light of Day. Light of day she is indeed, he told himself; and balm of quiet hours. Thus musing, he began making verses of her:

She is a garden of spices, a land of pleasant herbs:
The joy of all seasons is in her breath.
Her valleys are for delight, her green hills for plenty:
And she is glad in her abundance.
She is the bending bow and the curving water:
She is the music of many instruments.
The secret of night is in her dark hair:
Her mouth is kind and subtle.
Her thighs are alabaster:
The stem of her body is a column marvellously wrought.
Her breasts are sleek as apples warmed of the sun:
In the cup of the hand they are warm as ripe nectarines.
The fragrance of dewfall is in her flesh:
And her eyes are dark with the shining of love.

These verses, after much sighing and hesitation, he embodied in his letter to their subject, and having despatched it by messenger to the house of Barsum he set himself to the cruel task of waiting. The day limped by on leaden feet; the night, in which he lay solitary, was as long as many moons; and morning came with a promise that evening found unfulfilled. There passed three days of weariness and fever, when he wandered disconsolate in his gardens, with Mirramazoom following dumbly at a little distance, grieving that he did not notice her. On the fourth day she approached him face to face. Has my lord no further need of me? He stared, unseeing; and she repeated her question. Whereat, as once before, he rose with a weary gesture and went out of her presence. So bitterness and grief made war in the heart of Mirramazoom, and she turned her thoughts towards the written words of a stranger, taking from her secret bosom a scroll in which love entreated her; and the next day there came a slave bearing a letter addressed to Yusuf in the service of Prince Yafith. The fingers of the prince trembled as he handled it, and his heart grew big with longing when he read the words of Nurelhuda and tasted the honey of her heart. But his appeasement was brief. For now nothing would content him but that he should see her in the flesh and find his imagination in all things fulfilled and surpassed. He resolved at last to make himself known for what he was. I whom you call your Yusuf am the Prince Yafith, he wrote, and my eyes ache for you. In my western garden there is an orchard enclosed. Tonight, when the rising moon reaches her second arc, may heaven give me sight of you there.

For what remained of the day he scowled at the sun, impatient for its setting; and when, evening at last being come, he sent his attendants away and hurried to the trysting-place, the very sky bending over him seemed to share his expectation. The orchard, girt by a high wall, grew on the slope of a hill; a little beyond it, in the valley, ran a broad stream whose voice, clear and continuous, was like the joyous babble of his own thoughts. With his private key he unlocked the door in the wall, and so entered a small fragrant world open only to the sky. The amber evening was now far advanced, the sky tinged at its edge with a pale luminous green; and against the background of this fading brightness the new moon slowly rose. The heart of the prince held but one thought, and to beguile the time of waiting he began trying to make music of it. In the season of plenty, he sang —

In the season of plenty I will forget the long famine,
The sky of my orchard being hung with mellow fruits —

But already, fevered with hope, he wearied of the endeavour, and his voice wavered into silence. She will not come, she is withheld from me, he said, picturing her as the wife or daughter of some powerful neighbour, perhaps a prince like himself; and, if she comes not, I will destroy the house of my life, for there is no joy in it. But the memory of the words she had written made him sheathe his dagger, for it seemed to him now that her coming was assured, and he wondered what madness had persuaded him to doubt of it. So swaying between the two extremes of folly he waited and watched for her, and across the half-open doorway a shadow fell. It is she, it is Nurelhuda, his heart said; but his voice could utter no sound, and they stood, he and she, with but a stride between them, in a stillness that seemed to gather all beauty and all desire into a bubble of time. That bubble vanishing, he recovered power of speech. O Nurelhuda, desire of the world, shew me your face. He trembled at the great joy in store for him; for, though she was darkly veiled, he knew her heart, he had read her mind, and he could now see, as formerly he had conjectured, that all womanly enticement was contained in the curves of her form. Unveil, he cried, and let me worship. She, making no answer, moved away from him, yet seemed by her gesture to invite his company. In an instant he was at her side, entreating her. Hush, she murmured; for the moon is with us. Let us find first a leafy covert where the grass will be kind and the shadow deep as our love. The sound of her voice, so rich in tenderness, so heavy with passion, enslaved him to her whim; and very soon, with no words said, they were lying side by side in a warm, fragrant darkness. And now she was unveiled and her mouth naked to him, but though he stammered praises of the loveliness his heart divined, calling her the lily of lilies and the moon of love, her face was a dim wonder not clearly to be discerned. Beauty, none the less, was in their bed, for he could see her pearly whiteness and the lyrical form of her, and his hands could worship. And, he said, with the first light of morning I shall see her face. But after many honeyed hours, in which they had great joy of each other, he fell into a blissful sleep, and morning found him lying alone. Yet he was not cast down. He felt that his life was now fulfilled, and in his heart he knew that Nurelhuda would come to him again.

So all that day he was at peace with the world, and coming by chance upon Mirramazoom he spoke kindly to her, seeing her in the light of his old affection, and perceiving that his new joy, the hunger for which had made division between them, now restored them to each other. But his thoughts were still in the orchard with Nurelhuda, and tonight, he said, she shall not deny me but I shall look on her face. But the second night was as the first, and morning found him lying alone; and for seven nights, and then seven again, Nurelhuda kept her face hidden. Often he entreated her, but she was loving and full of excuses. I have taken a vow, she said. I am pledged to heaven. Have patience a little longer and I will reveal myself. Yafith, because his joy in her was so great, suffered himself to be cheated many times; but at last, meeting her at the orchard door on a night when the moon was full, he fiercely seized her, and tore her veil away. And seeing that it was Mirramazoom who trembled in his arms, he cried angrily: What is this? Have you come to spy on me, Mirramazoom? I am Nurelhuda, she answered, with shining eyes. For seven nights, and seven nights again, you have had joy of me and I of you. The voice is the voice of Nurelhuda indeed, he said, dazed and dejected; but you are Mirramazoom. I am Nurelhuda, she answered. Ah now, he cried, it is the voice of Mirramazoom that speaks. So for the third time she said: I am Nurelhuda; adding expectantly, after a pause: And you, lord, are Yusuf, in quest of whom I came first to the house of Prince Yafith. And when the prince saw me —— But Yafith broke in upon her narrative. Can this be true, he asked, that you are Nurelhuda? As I live, she said, it is the truth. Then is my dream dead, he cried, and I am desolate. But seeing her sudden grief he was moved to take her hand and comfort her, whose heart's treasure, no less than his, had been spilled and squandered on a dream. So hand in hand, like our first parents, Yafith and Nurelhuda turned their backs on Eden and walked with sad steps towards the future, scarce daring as yet to wonder what it held for them.

THE END OF WISDOM

By

G. K. Chesterton

NOTE

A variant of the straight narrative type is that where the facts are given and the reader is expected to draw the conclusion. Here is what happened, the author tells us, now judge for yourself. The facts must be given with apparent fairness and fullness, but the skill consists in so distributing the emphasis that only one conclusion is possible, and that of the thirty-seven different morals the reader must automatically select the right one. Mr. Chesterton wishes us to realize the value of spiritual humility. Therefore John P. Crake experiences the futility of materialism, as shown in the Bisons, the futility of love, as shown in Mary Wendover, the futility of contact with the soil, and the futility of ideal friendship. The blue bird of happiness is not to be held in the cages of this world, and St. Luke's paradox still holds that " whosoever shall seek to save his life shall lose it." But this moral of spiritual humility contrasts comically with the intellectual arrogance of the manner. There is little sympathy shown in his treatment of the unfortunate Bisons, whom he sees through the eyes of Mr. Sinclair Lewis. But whereas Mr. Lewis knows his Babbitts, Mr. Chesterton does not. As presumably the story was written for the English public, the inaccuracy of detail may not matter; but the American reader can amuse himself in checking Mr. Chesterton's slips. The naïve assumption that any business man can run a farm is in itself delightful. This criticism is not so captious as it may seem, since in this type of story the truth of the facts must be well established for the reader; if the facts do not seem true, he will not make the desired deduction. Why Mr. Chesterton should have placed his story in a locality with which he is not well acquainted is another question, but the thirty-eighth moral to be drawn from his effort is that for this kind of work the author had better know intimately the character and environment of his story.

THE END OF WISDOM

By G. K. Chesterton

WE have all had dreams or memories about some gang of pirates, grim to the point of the grotesque, as they were in the story-books of childhood, who yet pointed with awe, and almost with horror, at some super-pirate in the background; a solitary and sinister figure, compared with whose unsearchable wickedness they were all as innocent as an infant school. Such was the attitude of the hard-headed and acquisitive business men of Bison City, Ill., U.S.A., towards a certain Mr. Crake, who had committed the Unpardonable Sin.

He committed it at a luncheon party of the B.B.B., supposed by some to stand for " Better and Brighter Bisons," but by the more moderate for " Better and Brighter Business." The room in the large hotel was already decorated with American flags and also with bright bunches of American ladies, the beauty and fashion of Bison City, who were allowed to lean over the stone balustrade of the gallery and look down on the Bisons feeding. But the Bisons themselves were rather late, as is the habit of the brisk business-like salesmen of those parts; and for some time there was only one lean, leathery, bilious-looking man, whose profound gloom was relieved by a large disc or label on his coat, inscribed, " Call me Johnny." After a time, however, similar revellers arrived with similar decorations; notably a light-haired withered little man, whose label bore the blazon of, " Please, I'm Tom," and a very hearty, heavy man, with dark sleek hair, whose disc was adorned with the words, " Oh, Boy, I'm Little Frankie." As the seats gradually filled up, it was seen that all the guests were decked with such gay proclamations, except two. One of these was evidently a guest of importance from outside: a compact, carefully dressed man, with yellow hair, which shone like yellow soap. The other sat further down the table, dark and angular, with a hatchet face, which was yet somehow handsome, and a rather sullen expression. This was John P. Crake; but there was no invitation, either in his dress or his demeanour, to call him Johnny.

He was far from being an outcast, however; his fellow-townsmen being only too delighted to recite the precise number of dollars which he made every week in the biggest business in that neighbourhood. For Americans, who are accused of loving money, have this most generous trait: that they can actually love each other's money. They were ready to put it down to his being " sick," in the American sense, if he really failed to rejoice in the eloquence round him. That anybody could be sick of it, in the English sense, never crossed their minds. He heard the big dark Bison still orating: " . . . A man like that's just God's own American citizen and won't stay down. He goes right out for the highest ideal in sight. He won't stay ' put ' with ten thousand dollars when there's twenty thousand dollars knocking around. Now we figure that about the highest ideal going is this Service. . . ." As in a dream, Crake heard the voice change, and knew that the yellow-haired politician was speaking: " . . . Here on false pretences, gentlemen. I am not a Bison. Nor was George Washington; but he would have been. (Cheers.) Wasn't it just this ideal of Service. . . ." There were more cheers, silence, a little commotion, and Crake heard his own name. Everybody was looking at him; the fat dark man was waving florid compliments at him; they wanted a speech; a speech from the first citizen of Bison City. He refused. They cheered and hammered the table as if he had accepted. He refused again. They called for him again. The man from Washington, shining all over with diplomacy and yellow soap, insinuated his persuasion; could not be expected to leave

Bison City without hearing its greatest American citizen. John P. Crake boiled with black indescribable rage and shot suddenly and rigidly to his feet. He began in a harsh jarring voice:

"Gentlemen. We're all here to tell lies, and I'll begin with that one. Gentlemen." He gazed round at the somewhat startled audience and went on: "We all tell lies in business, because we only want to make money; but I can't see why the hell we should tell lies for fun in the lunch hour. I don't care a blasted button for Service, and I don't intend to be anybody's servant; certainly not yours. Every business man here wants to make money for himself, including me; and though he may use other men, he doesn't care if they're dead and damned when he's used them. That's the reality, and I like doing business with realities. As for ideals, I've nothing to say of them except that they make me sick as a dog." He sat down more slowly and with a greater air of calm and relief.

It would be hard to say how the luncheon party broke up; but the first to come was the last to go. For, as Crake went out of the room, he found the lean bilious man looking more unpleasant than ever, because his face was deformed with a smile.

"Good for you," he said, showing his yellow teeth. "I daren't do it; I have to wear this fool thing. But that's the way to get on top. Treat 'em like dirt." After a pause, he added: "Say, can I see you about that consignment?"

"Come round to my office at four," said Crake abstractedly, and went out.

At four he was going through a pile of letters, not without a grim smile. Personal letters had already begun to arrive, sent round by hand as a sequel to his disgraceful outburst. Ladies especially, whom he had never seen in his life, remonstrated with him at enormous length over his unfamiliarity with Ideals. Some recommended particular books, especially their

own books; some particular ministers, at whose feet a taste for
ideals might be imbibed. As he turned them over, the bilious
man was shown in, a certain J. Jackson Drill, a broker, and,
incidentally, a bootlegger. Crake pushed the papers across to
him with a gesture of contempt; a contempt, it is to be feared,
which included Mr. Drill as well as the papers. For Crake was
inconsistent, like many such men; and did not really like the
dirty pessimism of Jackson Drill any more than the greasy
optimism of Little Frankie. Perhaps the cynic does not respect
somebody else's cynicism.

Drill picked up the letters with his unpleasing grin, and
began reading fragments aloud: ". . . If your ideals do not
satisfy you, I am sure you have not heard the real message of
the Broad Daylight Church, which promises spiritual progress
and business success for all. The Church is now in serious need
of funds. . . ." Drill dropped the letter and took up another:
". . . May a sister in the sight of God express her grief at
the dreadful avowal revealing your spiritual state touching
dollars. Wealth is worthless in itself (seem to be a lot of· Bible
references here; handwriting very illiterate); it is a means to
an end, and some of our wealthiest citizens set a noble example. . . ." Drill picked up a third letter, remarking, "Not
so illiterate; nice handwriting," but continued in the same de-
risive sing-song, "I have been thinking about what you said
today, and I cannot decide whether it was the Only Way. Of
course, I see your point. If these people go on being idealists,
there won't be a decent ideal, or a decent idea left in the world.
Somebody must do something to stop their befouling everything. Courage has come to mean readiness to risk other
people's money. Service has come to mean servility to any
rich man who waddles along."

Crake had lifted his head and was listening, suddenly alert
with curiosity, but the other went droning on:

"Somebody must do something; and you did do something. You broke the back of it with sheer brutality; but I can't help wondering whether there isn't another way. I expect you've wondered yourself; because you are not a brute. You're supposed to be sulky because you are always longing for a little time to yourself, to think these things out. So am I."

"Here," said Crake sharply, "give me that letter."

"Rather a scream, isn't it?" said Drill; "it goes on, 'If we can't shut off this deafening nonsense, we shall have no inner life at all. . . .'"

Crake snatched the letter out of his companion's hand with a violence that tore it across at the corner. Then he spread it out before him and looked at Drill; and Drill knew that he was not wanted in that room any more.

The letter was an extraordinary letter. The extracts he had heard gave no real idea of it. There were moments when he thought he was reading his own diary. In some cases it was rather as if he were looking into his own subconsciousness. It was signed with an evasive female pen-name, and had an address that was no clue to identity. Yet he was not primarily impressed with how much, or rather how little, he knew about the writer. He was impressed with how much the writer knew about him. She knew one thing at least, which he hardly knew himself till he had done reading. That he hated ideals and idealism because he was himself very much too bitter and fastidious an idealist. That he hated his wealth and his work and his fellow-workmen because of an unnamed comparison and because his kingdom was not of this world. He sat down and wrote a long and even laborious letter in reply; the beginning of a prolonged private correspondence that spread over years. And through all those years he never made an effort (so strong was something in him making for refinement and renunciation) to find out the name or dwelling of the woman who was his best friend.

For some little time Bison City did regard Mr. Crake as something between a leper, a lunatic, a wicked wizard commanding the elements and the blasphemer whose duty it is to be struck by lightning in the religious tracts of that region. Americans do not worship riches in the sense of forgiving anything to the rich; and they do not easily fogive a blasphemy against the gods whom they do worship. Mr. Crake had defied the gods of the tribe that were of stone and brass — especially brass. He had violated the highest morality of Bison City, which is well named, because its morality consists of going at anything with your head down. Yet, strangely enough, Mr. Crake grew happier as time went on, and even more good humoured with his fellows; so that his unpopularity began to fade away. In fact, his loneliness was ended. He no longer boiled with an incommunicable disgust. He poured out his feelings every night in long letters to his unknown friend; and received letters which had a slow but steady effect of restoring him to sanity and even to sociability. In this respect his invisible companion both puzzled and pleased him. She had read much more than he, though he was not an uncultivated man; but she seemed to have reached a balance from the study of opposite extremes. Left alone, with one book at a time, he might have been tempted to go mad like Nietzsche or turn peasant like Tolstoy. But she seemed to have accepted all the abnormalities and then returned to the normal. She was sufficiently cultured to know even the case against culture; and he could not shock her by cursing books as he shocked Bison City by cursing business. The result was that, unknown to himself and by minute gradations, he was turning from a mono-maniac into a man. And then, one fine day, something happened to him, that suddenly revealed to him his manhood; which came on him with a rush like a return of boyhood.

And the strangest thing about it was this: That when he sat down, on the evening of that fine day, to write the letter that had become like a diary, to be read only by a second self, he found for the first time that he could not write. At least it seemed in a new unnatural way impossible ... almost indecent. Nothing might seem more remote than that relation; yet his friend had always remained a woman; the mere fact, the slope of the feminine handwriting, a hundred delicate details, had left hanging over the affair that distant and disembodied sentiment that can never be conjured away; something like the smell of old gardens or that dust of dead roses that was preserved in old bowls and cabinets. He knew now that he had been living through a long convalescence in the large rooms of some such ancient and quiet house; under the large tact of an invisible hostess. And what had just happened to him, in the street outside, was so vivid and violent, so concrete, so incongruous. After poising his pen for a moment of doubt, he dismissed the matter, and only answered her remarks about the poetry of Claudel. And then a strange thing happened; giving him a rather terrifying sense of being watched in that house of healing by an all-seeing eye. For she wrote, in her next letter, quite casually and even humorously: "Something has happened to you. I was very much interested in what you did not tell me."

Then he told her; but it was an effort, and he felt for the first time that he was living in two worlds. As he walked where the town opened into a country road, he had suddenly realised that he was happy. His cure was complete. The disease of disdain for common things no longer devoured his brain, and yet his appreciation of the common was no nearer to the vulgar. Indeed, the common things around him, the stones

in the road, the weeds in the ditch, stood out with a distinct-
ness that was the reverse of flat. It was as if he had felt the
third dimension for the first time. It reminded him of something his friend had said about religion, as compared with
the mere herding both of Capitalism and Communism. " There
is a delicacy about the Day of Judgment." It was at least supposed to deal with individuals. " Yes, that is it," he said to
himself. " They used to say in the sight of God we are all
equal. But if you only say that, it sounds flat; like all those
flat-faced Bisons. No, in the sight of God we are all distinguished. We may be damned; but, damn it all, we're
distinguished."

He was wandering away into the nondescript landscape outside the wooden town, dotted with frame-houses and the thin
trees of those plains, now lit up with the delicate clarity of
the Indian summer. A born critic, born in a world where
criticism is rare, he had often felt something frail and col-
lapsible about the frame-houses of his country; as if they
would fold up flat like a portable stage; something of the
nomadism of a travelling show. But in his new normal mood
it pleased him — not so much that they should shut as that
they could open — as a child is pleased when a hinged toy
opens like a telescope. Then something happened which
showed sharply how very new was the mood, and even how
very abnormal was the normality. He caught sight of a string
stretched across a backyard, with some coloured clothes hanging on it; some of them seemed to be blouses or pinafores
such as artists wear; some pyjamas of a garish cut and pattern.
Before he had begun to browse in that great library of his
literary correspondence, he would have felt the sight as the
most unsightly sort of commonplace. A woman hanging out
the washing would have been something on a level with the
Comic Strip in the loathsome local paper. But at this queer

moment of his life he actually liked it. The headless figures of the shirts, the dancing legs of the pantaloons looked like giant marionettes acting a pantomime in the sunlight of Italy; the stripes and patches of crude colour had the note of carnival. He thought inconsequently of the double fate of the word "Pantaloon." A very strenuous young woman was struggling with the line; and her copper hair in the sun gave a touch that brought to life the colours of a blue and green frock fluttering behind her. The garments on the line were puffed out by the wind into preposterous shapes of hollow solidity; and just at that moment a very big one, looking like a complete suit of yellow, broke from its peg and went careering across the bushes towards him, like some fat yellow buffoon dancing across the countryside. He made one wild leap and caught the runaway, which collapsed like a balloon and then hung like a rag; and, bounding across the grass plots and pathways, solemnly handed it to the young woman, who was already laughing.

"Oh, thank you very much," she said, "that's Uncle Bill. He's supposed to be an artist and like yellow. Used to have to do with something called the Yellow Book."

"The Yellow Peril, I should think," said Crake, "but artists are proverbially liable to abscond."

"So all my business uncles tell me," she said. "I'm afraid I don't understand either sort. They would never condescend to run after the washing."

"I wish they ran after anything so clean," replied Crake. "In the business and politics I've seen —— Well, there isn't any washing, only whitewashing."

She was looking at him in an unembarrassed manner, slightly amused; she had a square, open face which would have been even conventionally handsome if her wide, blue eyes had not been a shade too far apart; everything else about her expressed only the strength and strenuous bodily vigour of her first attitude; and she had one trick that is only found in people who are physically almost perfect. When she was not darting and dashing about she stood absolutely still.

His eyes strayed towards the little wooden house to which the yard was attached; and she answered his unspoken question without losing her steady smile.

"No, I'm not the Hired Help; I rather doubt if I'm a Help at all. But the rest of the family's out."

"Ah, of course," he said, "the yellow gentleman is your uncle."

"The Scarlet Woman is my aunt," she said, indicating another garment. "She has gone to hear a Hindoo who lectures on Health-Spirals and the Super-Gland."

"I know him," said Crake gloomily, "he deepens your inner life and gives you tips about Wall Street."

"The peacock blue and green contraption is my sister," she went on. "She's gone to the Purple Possum, the celebrated playground of the New Youth. All very brilliant, I believe, and prides itself especially on being Frank. What did you say?"

"Oh, nothing," said Crake, who had involuntarily murmured, "Oh, boy, I'm Little Frankie."

"Uncle goes to a speakeasy; but it's supposed to be one for artists. It's all too intellectual for me. Will you come inside?"

"Intellectuals haven't intellect enough to boil an egg," he said as he went inside. "I'm all for the eggs."

And as he went in through the sheds and sculleries and kitchen, bowing his head a little, something was whispering in his ear: "You will not return; you will not come back free; you are going into a new world; a little, real world. You are going to live in a dolls' house; and you will come out a doll."

And the change that was already in his heart made him answer with a challenge: " What a fool Ibsen was," he muttered. " What could be jollier than living in a dolls' house? "

And when he went through the dark interior and saw at last the light from the front windows, it was not the dead daylight he had left behind; for those windows looked on to the strange streets of some other star; he was in love.

A few days afterwards, with his head full of these new things, that capered in many colours like the headless puppets in the sun, he came back suddenly into the cool shadow of that older friendship in which he had lived so long. He opened the letter, which went straight to the point, silently and from within, as was her strange habit.

" You understood my first letter at once; when most men would have thought I was mad. You will understand that this is my last letter quite as easily. You will not think any of the vulgar things: jealousy or the fear that somebody else will be jealous. You could not be vulgar; at first you had almost nothing except not being vulgar. You began with nothing but a hatred; but I knew your hatred was noble, and I know your love would be noble. No; it is not that sort of obvious difficulty at all. We must end here because we have gone round the whole world and thought as far as thinking will go. That is not conceit; it is not a question of knowing everything now, but of being ready to understand anybody at any time. You would not melt into a Regular Guy; you did not dry up into a Superman; and after that you will become a man and understand all men. We must end now, because of all those who have thus understood all things, from the cedar to the hyssop, hardly any (not even Solomon himself) have resisted the temptation to say a last word, to sum it all up, and to say, Vanity of Vanities. Let us, let me at least, resist the temptation, and say, not *Vanitas,* but only *Vale* . . . Farewell."

John Crake sat down and wrote a long and earnest and delicate letter of thanks, surveying all the thousand things that he had gained in that voyage round the world with that invisible companion. Then he sprang up like a spring released and rushed down the road like a boy freed from school; all the noises of nature seemed to be shouting and cheering him on, for he felt for the first time that he had a body, and it was racing to outstrip his soul.

Before that autumn had turned to winter he was married to Mary Wendover, the lady of the clothes-line; and it is typical of the tail foremost or back-door fashion of his intro-duction that he never knew her name was **Wendover until** about a month after he knew it was Mary. She was apparently a guest in the house of her relative; but the guest seemed to do all the work while the hosts pursued self-development. " Very self-development," said Crake, " but I think, as usual, the Cinderella was the favourite of the fairies." And indeed she seemed to show a more artistic ardour for pots and pans than they did for arts; as if the teapot were indeed a familiar goblin or the broom a benevolent witch's broomstick. After their marriage her creative concentration increased; and Crake, remembering his own chance words of encouragement, felt it natural to be infected with the same fury of efficiency. He wanted to deal with things directly, with his own hands, as she did; and he announced one day that he had sold out his business and was going to work a farm he had about ten miles from the city. She only laughed, and said: " I thought you were already doing business with realities."

" Why," he cried, " that is out of my celebrated disgraceful speech. I didn't know. . . ."

" You must have known ladies are allowed to overhear Bisons eating," she said.

" Well, it shows how little I knew in those days. Business

men do business with unrealities. Only with unrealities. With rubber forests nobody has seen or ivory from elephants who might be fabulous like unicorns. I want to cut down a real tree and ride a real horse and be real."

Indeed, there was a reality in their very romance; and their common passion went back to its romantic origin. Slight as had been the gesture of their introduction, it had been active and abrupt. What he had seen had been a woman wrestling with a rope; and what she had seen had been a man bounding over a bush; and all their love and life went with that gallop of bodily vigour and the high gestures of the mastery of man.

It was about three years later, and, save for the noise of two children in the old farmhouse, a man would have said that their whole life was unchanged. He still rode his horses round the farm, and his body was still young enough to find automatic exultation in the exercise; she still practised a hundred arts and crafts under the name of housekeeping, and would have let loose a violent scorn against anyone who called it drudgery. They both enjoyed to the full the pleasure of doing things well, and there are few pleasures more enduring; and yet a more subtle critic might have said that things were changed. But John Crake could only think of one critic who would have been subtle enough to say it.

Perhaps it was a proof that things were changed that he had thought of that subtle critic at all. But he did now recall that cooler background of friendship, and told himself that she would have understood. Above all, she would not have misunderstood. She would not have been cheap, and supposed that he was merely tired of his wife. In reality, he was not tired in the least. He felt that he wanted her and he had missed her, in spite of having married her. Moreover, there grew upon him a dull pain in the feeling that his wife herself had become sad and estranged. He had seen her staring out of the window on bright summer days; and her face was sadder for the sunlight. Her plunging practicality was often interrupted by her sudden stillness. She liked more and more to be alone. John Crake was no fool, and would have thought nothing of these moods if they had occurred in a moody person. If she had been of the sentimental sort it would not have distressed him much even if he had thought (as he was sometimes inclined to think) that they were somehow connected with personal memories, and even with personal memories of another person. He was shrewd enough to know that romances do very little harm to the romantic. The sort of person for whom lost loves or faded fancies can be stirred by music or turned into minor poetry is generally the sort of person who can indulge them without much danger to the solid loyalties of life. But Mary Crake was not particularly romantic; and certainly the very reverse of sentimental. She had a passion for the practical, for translating thoughts into things. She would no more desire to have a romance without turning it into a reality than to have a recipe without turning it into a dish. She could no more have lived on dreams than she could have dined on a cookery book. Ever since he had seen her wrestling with a clothes-line like an Amazon lassoing a wild horse, he had been affected by her powerful impatience and directness of design. People of that sort do not brood for pleasure. If she was brooding, she was suffering.

He, in his turn, brooded long upon that brooding; pacing up and down the long verandah into which was extended the wide porch of the American farmhouse. All round him was that dreary plain that is the incongruous background of that cheery people, and one straight American road ran up to the very steps of his own porch, a road lined with lean, spidery trees. The road ended with the farm, and it seemed to his sullen eye like the road of destiny, that leads so straight to achievement and disappointment. With an abrupt movement, he turned his back upon it, went into his study, and sat down at his desk. Before he had risen from it he had broken the silence of four years, and written to that long-lost friend and counsellor who had never had a name.

He came out again upon the porch, with his sealed and stamped letter in his hand, and saw that the long road between the thin trees had a black object upon it, the dark angular figure of a man, with a hat tilted over his eyes, so as to show nothing but a sour grin. It was Jackson Drill, the bootlegger; and Crake had an instant overwhelming sense of repugnance. There had been a time when they were the two cynics of Bison City, and seemed to be in a sort of sympathy in their lack of sympathy. It measured the distance that Crake had really travelled along that road of destiny, that the distant sight of Drill was like the sight of a black scorpion. He had long felt that that sort of pessimism was mere poison. The hand that held the letter made an involuntary movement, as if not wishing even the externals of such an understanding to be exposed to such a misunderstanding. The movement, of course, produced the very effect it was meant to avoid.

"Very confidential correspondence, I suppose," said Drill. "Three years after marriage is about the time they start. In fact, old man, I fear it isn't the only confidential correspondence in the house."

Crake said in a very low and restrained voice: "What the devil in hell do you mean?"

Drill laughed with disagreeable agreeableness; for Americans are not afraid to be familiar with their wealthier employers, so far as language is concerned. "Well," he said, "if you have your private correspondence, why shouldn't she? By all accounts, she used to have letters, even in the old days, that you didn't see. That you weren't meant to see."

" Oh, indeed! " said Crake, thoughtfully, and hit the man a crack on his crooked mouth that sent him from the top of the steps to the bottom, and left him spread-eagled on the flat road below. Then Crake turned and entered his own house in so towering a passion that it might have shaken the topmost chimneys and brought them down.

His wife was sitting with her back to him at a writing-desk, reading an old faded letter, and, though he could not see her face, he knew when he first heard her voice that she had been in tears; a terrible and portentous thing in her case.

" Who is that letter from? " he asked, with his voice on a dead level.

She rose and faced him, and her low voice rang out:

" Who are you to talk about letters? " she said. " Who is that letter for? "

Then, after a deadly silence, she added, almost grimly:

" Give me that letter."

" Why should I? " he answered, frowning at her.

" Oh," she replied, almost lightly, " only because it is addressed to me."

And with that he looked across at the old letter she was reading, and saw that it was one of those that he had sent to the same address.

There are thirty-seven morals to this story; but one of them is that it is he who has really gone round the whole world who is anxious to come home; that the end of wisdom is the beginning of life; and that God Himself bowed down to enter a narrow door, in the hour when the Word was made flesh.

PERCY AND PANSY

By

FRANK SWINNERTON

NOTE

If Mr. Bullett solves his problem by placing the events in a far-away country and at an indefinite time, the same result may be obtained in a known locality and at the present time by having the characters in a social class quite removed from that presumably of the reader. And here also is the obvious advantage that, as the reader does not know the characters, he has no standard of judgment of the plausibility of their actions. In *Percy and Pansy* Mr. Swinnerton leaves us in no doubt as to the caste of his characters. That of the hero is given in the first sentence; Percy is a cockney clerk. To make quite certain that the reader understands this, the whole account is written in Percy's dialect. On the first page in quick succession are found *guv-nor, blighter, hopped, miking, kids, Cord,* and *watch 'em work.* Still more, Percy is the conventional cockney clerk, with his head full of romantic tomfoolery, which he expresses without punctuation. And Pansy is the feminine analogue. Both characters are drawn broadly; the reader is supposed to laugh at them, not to sympathize with them. So, although Percy is the nominal hero, actually it is Pansy that in every case takes the initiative; Percy merely falls into the traps set for him. And this is done to make him appear unheroic. Neither the author, nor the reader expects much of so ridiculous a little man, and the final note of exultation rings pathetically true. This story, consequently, well represents the value of the type.

PERCY AND PANSY

By FRANK SWINNERTON

I

YOUNG Percy Mears was alone in the warehouse. It was
after five o'clock — seven past, as a matter of fact. The
guv'nor had gone. Adolph had gone — little blighter. Siskin
was supposed to be there, but Percy knew full well that Siskin
also, taking a risk, had hopped it. Full well.

Percy shuddered at that risk. What he meant to say, supposing Adolph . . . Quite likely. He gnawed at the end of his
pen. Nothing to do, and another hour to wait. A summer
afternoon, mind you. Furthermore, you could tell it was bright
by the way the echoes came down the open shaft.

The warehouse was like a dungeon, always chill. Except for
the wan light of his own worn-out electric light bulb, everything was black. Silence in the building above, where all the
others were miking; just an occasional whisper — probably a
rat — along the dark aisles between the racks of shelves, and
the warm roar of traffic out of doors. If he hadn't got to stick
here, he could get out and stroll in Battersea Park. Watch the
kids at cricket.

Cord! Only eight and a half past!

Although he was no player, Percy knew all about cricket.
Sometimes he felt he knew all about everything. He was quick
to see the mistakes of selection committees; he dreamed of
centuries made by himself against the Australians; but he
ducked if the ball came towards him through the air. He was
not strong. He never had been strong. His father and mother
were both dead. He was always pale and very thin. But brains!
Watch 'em work! Nine past.

Sighing, Percy picked up his much-folded and soiled copy

of *The Spokesman,* and began to do the children's cross-word puzzle. Then his eye was caught by something in the next column. It was a set of verses.

> " Sometimes " (read Percy) " I dream a king will come
>   And say ' I love you.'
> He'll tell me tales of derring-do,
>   And say ' I love you.'
> And I shall listen open-eyed
> To stories of the world so wide,
> And courage, honour, noble pride;
> And if he says ' Wilt be my bride? '
>   I'll say ' I love you.' "

The words had a curious effect upon Percy. He felt he had never read anything so beautiful in his life. " Courage, honour, noble pride! " His heart swelled. This was poetry. " I'll say ' I love you.' " Could anything be sweeter? Eagerly, he sought for more. As he did so his cheek mantled. Apparently he had stumbled upon the column of " Advice to Our Readers." He read:

" Louise de la Valliere (The Gables, Whittlecombe, S. Devon) sends me some of the verses she has written. She asks if they are poetry. Here are some of them. [The lines followed.] I am afraid not. You will have to work hard to be a poet, Louise. Read Tennyson, Browning, and some of the moderns — Sitwell, Noyes, Bridges, etc."

Percy swore. He said " Hell! " For a moment he was blinded with anger, so that he could not read the lines a second time. When he could do so his previous opinion was reinforced. " Fool! " he ejaculated. " *He* don't know much."

The hour was forgotten. He seized a sheet of blank paper from Siskin's rack. Without knowing what he did, he began to write.

" DEAR MISS DE LA VALLIERE " (he said),

" Do not take any notice of what the editor says. Your poem is beautiful. I know it is. He does not know. You say so truly courage, honour, noble pride — what could be greater than these? It is a fine idea. I should like to tell you some of my adventures but modesty forbids. I expect you have noticed how really brave men never say anything about what they have done — they pass it off with a laugh, saying Oh, it was nothing at all did I tell you the story of the old man who walked in his sleep, etc. When a man boasts they generally tell lies so as to make an impression but you can see through them, it is the way of the world. But I must not run on, I only wanted to tell you I think your poem is the greatest poem I have read and miles better than Tennyson, Browning and the Moderns. I hope you will go on and fill a museum with poems. With best wishes I beg to remain yours —— "

For the first time Percy hesitated. Several thoughts flashed through his mind. Then, with his chin up, he deliberately concluded:

" truly GUY DE MONTMORENCY."

Using one of the firm's envelopes, he addressed it to Miss Louise de la Valliere, The Gables, Whittlecombe, S. Devon. This done, he awoke as if from a dream. Coo lumme, it was twenty to six!

A strange accident befell Percy that evening. It was his habit — in order to save a short walk — to make a rather spectacular leap from the number nineteen omnibus just as it reached the end of the road in which he had a single room. He scorned to stop the bus, but, as it slowed down in response to the conductor's ring, jumped. The act, performed by an expert, is successful ninety-nine times out of a hundred. Tonight, perhaps because Percy was thinking more of the poem than of his step, it failed. True, he leapt; but as his foot touched the pavement he stumbled. His legs lagged behind him. They felt innumerable, but too short for effective service. He was falling. His hands were wildly thrown out.

He was almost lost, when his arm was strongly clasped. He was supported. Feeling sickish, he took another involuntary step, turned, and clung to the giver of support.

"Oops a daisy!" cried a cheerful voice, which Percy instantly resented and disliked. He looked into a face that smiled. The face of a young woman. Smiling! All her teeth showing! A pretty young woman of about middle size. A girl. She was dark, neatly dressed in blue, with a hat that shaded her eyes and gave them a dark, amused air of knowing all a young man's hesitation. The bitterness of wounded pride rose in Percy's heart. "All right?" asked that calm, unimpressed, motherly voice.

"Yes, thanks," retorted Percy briefly. "Quite."

"Sure?" His arm was released.

That hideously kind smile! He saw it again, ducked, frowned. He was thankful, recovering equilibrium, to get away from the woman. She seemed to be laughing at him, carelessly, kindly, interestedly, as if he were about ten years old, and no hero at all.

"Cord love a duck!" said Siskin. Percy looked disapprovingly up from the morning paper, in which he was still finding matter for condemnation of selection committees.

"Whasser row!" he demanded.

Siskin, who was short and plump, with a discoloured fair moustache and a red face, held a letter between his finger and thumb. His red face was redder. Sniggering. If he had had any teeth, he would have shown them between his richly parted lips.

Percy clambered off his stool.

"Here! That's mine!" he cried, snatching the letter. It was addressed: "Sir Guy de Montmorency, Goods Department, Jones and Carruthers, 8 Totters Court, London." And it read:

"Dear Sir Guy,

"How am I to thank you enough for your splendid encouraging letter about my verses? It is so kind of you. Do tell me some of your brave deeds. I should like to know them, so that I can make verses about them. Alas I am not brave myself, far from it, but I love heroism in others. Perhaps that is because I am a woman. Alas I am bed-ridden — had an accident when a child — has made me such a wreck. But shall be so grateful if you will write again, should appreciate it very much, as a quiet life in the country is not at all my idea of things. Well, good-bye, and thank you so much for writing, I really feel flattered from yours sincerely,

"Louise de la Valliere."

"My father was French. Was yours? Should love to see your photo."

Percy's eyes goggled out of his head. His breath was drawn and expelled as if he had been running swiftly. He devoured the written words. They were easy to read, for Miss de la Valliere had a small, flowing hand. A poet! She wanted him to write again. She asked for his photo. Asked if he was French. Percy laughed, then frowned. French! As to her being bed-ridden, it was a shock; but an impressive shock. It appealed to him. Poor little girl, poor little thing. Somehow that made it sort of finer . . . "courage, honour, noble pride." He was inspired.

Siskin sniggered again. He kept on sniggering. He — he — he! Fool! Percy put the letter away.

"It's a competition," he explained loftily. "That's my —— "

"Oh yeah?" mocked Siskin. "Well, now; this requisition.
. . ."

For three hours they dawdled through their work. Then
Siskin went to his dinner. He would eat it in the Embank-
ment Gardens, and stroll about for a time before returning.
Take his time, too, and wink at the girls. They wouldn't look
back, but would shrug their shoulders in contempt. Percy was
free.

"Dear Miss de Valliere" (he wrote),

"I beg to acknowledge your letter. I think you are a very
brave little woman. There is other kinds of bravery than running risks. What I should do if I had to lay in bed I cant imagine. A man like me has to have an outdoor life to keep fit.
No my father was not French but pure English with a dash
of Scotch and Irish. I am like him. I am sorry I have no photo,
but although the camera cannot lie they say I do not think
much of men who are always prinking themselves before the
glass in an unmanly manner. They say I am rather like
Ronald Coleman but I cannot say as to that, as the truth is I
never look in the glass. Never have time, for when it is not
one thing it is another — hunting, riding hard, playing polo
and cricket and what not. But I must not speak to you of
these things, as I am passionately fond of poetry and literature.
I hope you will send me some of your poems as I should appreciate this very much, being keenly appreciative. You ask me
to tell you some of my deeds, well really Miss Valliere I fear
I cannot do this just yet it would not be the thing. I should
like to tell you of some of my experiences in the African
jungle, I think they would interest you but shall have to do
this in my next as it would take too long at present. What do
you think of these men who are flying round the world in a
week? Fine, are they not. I have not done much flying as yet,
only week-ends, but mean to do more, as I am passionately
fond of it. One gets about so much quicker, not like buses
which crawl along till you are going to get off when they

put on a spurt but that never troubles me. Now dont forget to send me some of your poems I look forward to these, and am inquisitive as to what you are like I expect you are lovely like your poems.

"With kindest regards from your sincere friend,

"Guy de M."

The rest of the day passed in a dream.

In the evening Percy was strolling in Battersea Park, thinking deeply, when he saw the young woman who had saved him from falling. She had a short fit of coughing as they drew near each other, possibly having swallowed a fly; but Percy politely raised his hat and passed on without attempting to render first aid. He had no thought to spare for the world of flesh and blood; he was living in fairyland.

A day came, however, about a month afterwards, when a letter was delayed; and Percy, distraught, made a muddle of his work, was severely rated by young Adolph, who was a sort of unofficial manager, and in the evening left the warehouse very much cast down. He hardly cared what happened to him, caught his bus mechanically, leapt off it without spirit, and turned the corner of his road, blind to everything. In this way he did, without premeditation upon either side, collide with Pansy Spale, with whom, since she had helped him, he had in mysterious ways formed a tenuous acquaintance.

"I say, I'm fearfully sorry!" cried Percy. "I am, really."

Pansy was biting her lip. She was pale.

"Heavyweight!" she retorted, with a little venom. "Rhinoceros! Look what you *done!*"

Both concentrated attention upon her very small shoe, which was split. From the shoe rose a slender ankle.

"I say!" ejaculated Percy.

"I bet you do!" said Pansy. "But nothing to what I do!

My best shoes! What you want to barge round corners like that for? "

" Well, I wasn't thinking," stammered Percy. " I mean to say . . ."

" Make me look a sight! Oh, well, I'll have to go back, that's all."

" Does it hurt? "

" Bit. Not much. But what you want to —— "

" I was worried."

" What's the matter? Got the sack? "

Percy shook his head.

" That wouldn't worry me," he boasted.

" I don't think," replied Pansy, with a quick glance. " Well, then, it ought to."

She limped along by his side. Percy began thinking. His heart felt very cold in his breast. It seemed to be falling lower and lower. His throat was dry.

" I say," he stammered. " I mean, what do they cost? Shoes, I mean."

Pansy put her head round in a droll way and stared in his face.

" Don't be silly," she said. " Boy like *you!* "

" No, I mean it." He was flushed.

" You buy yourself a new cap," suggested Pansy. " Look a bit smarter. Never thought of it? Do it now. Then I'll let you come to the pictures with me."

Smart? Smarter? Percy's breath caught. Fumbling movements occurred in his brain. The pictures? Let? *Let?* No letter; he was miserable; she was pretty. Damn his heart, — like water!

" All right," he said, slowly. " Tonight? "

A nod. They walked a little way. Past his home, onward, to hers.

" Quite a bit of luck, you not looking where you're going,"

observed Pansy, drily. She placed her hand for an instant, un-expectedly, upon his arm.

" Who for? " asked Percy, stumbling after the lightness of repartee.

" Oh, me," she answered. " Who did you think? "

No letter. No letter. Then, four days late, it came. Though as cordial as ever, it was very brief.

" DEAR SIR GUY,

" You will have wondered at not hearing from me, and I am sorry if you have thought me unkind or neglectful, but the truth is I am going to be married. This will surprise you, I know, but I am sure you will understand. Getting letters from you has been lovely. I expect my husband will want to take me abroad. Perhaps I'll write to you again later on, but perhaps I shan't be able to. Thank you very much for your kind letters — they have been so nice. I hope you will be happy.

" From your sincere friend,
" LOUISE D. L. V."

Married! It was a blow. Married? But it was impossible!

" She said she was a cripple," thought Percy, rather dully. He sat at his desk, neglecting his work, his head buried in his hands. Yes, it was a blow. He had always thought — well, he did not know *what* he had thought, but ——

" Mears! " cried a sudden voice at his elbow.

Startled, Percy sprang to his feet. Young Adolph! He had a stupefied glimpse of a small, dark, sneering face; of eyes peep-ing from under creamy lids; of a thin nose wrinkled in dis-taste. Then his stool crashed to the concrete floor. His knees trembled. He felt sick.

" You muddle. You idle. You're no good," hissed Young Adolph. " What good *are* you? "

"I'm sorry, sir," stammered Percy.

"No good!" repeated Adolph. "You're a fool! D'you hear?"

Percy stood there at attention, saying nothing.

"You'd better look out for something else," snarled that bitter voice. "I'm tired of you."

Still Percy said nothing. It was not fear of Adolph that checked him, for he surprisingly felt no fear. It was something else. What was it? Disdain? Paralysis? Neither. It was stupefaction at the sudden appalling loss of a secret image of romance, the collapse of his dream of fairyland.

For three nights he did not see Pansy. On the fourth she was waiting at the end of the road when he left the omnibus. Percy caught sight of her as he leapt; and he nearly fell. Not quite. Yet, if he had judged by his sensations, he might have imagined that he had fallen through hell, and that only two hands were stretched out to save him from an eternity of torture.

Pansy did not say anything as he came up to her. She merely looked straight into his eyes. Her expression was not one of laughter. Her lips were slightly parted, but she did not smile.

They walked along together in unhappy silence, past Percy's home, past Pansy's home, into Battersea Park, and along the paths until they were alone. Every now and then Percy swallowed quickly, but he did not speak. At last Pansy said:

"What's the matter, Perce?"

He struggled to speak.

"I'm fed up," he said.

"With me?" She caught quickly at that.

"You? No."

"Somebody else?" Pansy could hardly breathe. "Some other girl?"

It would not have been true.

"No. Everything," answered Percy.

"I wish you'd tell me." There was a very long pause. Somebody passed them. "I've been thinking it was me."

"Rot."

"Well, you've been funny. And then not seeing you."

Good God! She was crying.

"I tell you —— "

She was pressing closer to him, not deliberately, but because she could not help doing so. With her handkerchief she wiped the tears from her eyes, and began smiling again. But it was a different smile from the one with which in earlier days she had offended. It was coaxing, as if she wanted Percy also to smile.

He looked at her. Such bright eyes, so near to his own! Percy had never noticed before how funnily her face twisted when she smiled. Her lips looked irresistibly soft. Suddenly his heart rose. It was thumping in his throat. He was deafened by the roar. He raised his arms. The eyes were so close that he could not longer see them. Her breast was against his own. The old dream was obliterated in a new one.

Next day, still in the warehouse, Percy replied to Louise de la Valliere.

"DEAR MISS VALLIERE (he wrote),

"I beg to acknowledge yours, and am very glad to hear that you are going to be married. By a curious coincidence, so am I, to the sweetest little woman in the world. It is like fate. I hope you will be happy, and hope I shall be happy. My wife and I intend to fly round the world for our honeymoon. I shall always think of you and remember your poetry with true appreciation, and am as always your sincere friend,

"GUY DE M.

"P.S. — My address in the near future will be uncertain, but I shall send you some p.p.-cs later on."

II

It was a murky day in March. From the front windows of the flat in which he and Pansy lived, Percy could hardly see across the street to the houses opposite. Not fog, but a gloomy darkness enveloped the town. Moisture hung from a bare tree just outside. Everything seemed miserable — as miserable as Percy himself.

He had been married for six months. He had been out of a job, in a job, and again out of a job. Now he had something that seemed more promising, but he was feeling unwell. He thought he had eaten something which had disagreed with him. But Pansy had dismissed that notion. She had been quite unsympathetic. "You've imagined it," she had said. "Well," Percy had retorted, very sarcastically, "of course, *you would* know better than I do."

And with that he had stumped out of the kitchen, which was at the back of the flat, into this melancholy, half-furnished room at the front. In five minutes it would be time for him to leave for his work, and in his present state of mind he took pleasure in being as cold and uncomfortable as possible. He had half expected that Pansy would follow him and apologise; but she had not done so. She seemed to have no notion of apologising. He had noticed it before. It was one of his complaints about her. Not to apologise, he meant, *when she was in the wrong.*

It was all very well for her, at home, with nothing to do but wash the dishes and make the bed and get his dinner, to sneer at his illness; but how would she like it if he died? He meant to say, she'd be sorry enough then, he supposed. Would she? His heart gave a jerk. *Would* she?

The doubt made him walk smartly about the room. Good God! Six months married! What a tragedy! Percy went to the door. He listened. Firmly he took his hat and coat from their hooks, and put them on. Then he hesitated. Should he?

Some instinct made him go back to the kitchen. There sat Pansy with a curious enigmatic smile upon her lips. She was rather red in the face. She looked up, but no higher than the middle of his waistcoat. Percy, for his part, though conscious of this, did no more than sweep his glance about the room, as if Pansy had been a plate, or a teacup glimpsed *en route*.

" I'm off," said Percy.

" All right," answered Pansy.

No more than that. No kiss, No " good-bye." No promise or inquiry as to the time of his return. He strode out, shutting the door very deliberately. He really felt most awfully ill. But *she* didn't care. It was a joke to her. See her smile? She made a joke of everything.

His new job was in a street near Piccadilly Circus. He was his own master. He was called " stockkeeper," and had no troubles except loneliness. He even had a fair amount of work; and, as he was now twenty-four, he was beginning to take an interest in efficiency for its own sake. Since his marriage, also, he had grown ambitious.

Yes, by jove, he'd married a girl with no poetry in her. No sympathy. She could laugh all right; but she couldn't understand how you felt. No sympathy. No poetry.

Into Percy's mind stole the memory of an old poem, read long ago. He began to feel better as he recalled it. How many months it seemed since he had first read those lines! And the letters ——

He had never destroyed them. He had kept them in an envelope. When he had come to his new job he had brought the envelope with him. No good leaving it at home. Better run no risks. Pansy might one day be inquisitive — they *were*, you know.

He was in his warehouse; and he felt better already. It was a light warehouse, with lofty ceilings. Everything arranged as he wanted it. He knew where everything was, could find it at once. Here he was his own master.

It would be interesting to turn up those old letters. He did so. First the poem, then the first letter, the second, the third, fourth, fifth, and so to the one in which Louise announced her marriage. He wondered what *her* marriage had been like. A failure? Percy expected she would be happy. With that lovely spirit. Probably she'd be writing more poetry than ever, now. Or perhaps not. Who could tell?

She would have forgotten him. Would she? He wondered if she had ever suspected that he wasn't a baronet. What did *that* matter? It made no difference. He had a good mind to write to her again. Not lies, but something — he didn't know. The craving for sympathy, understanding — she'd know how he felt. She'd appreciate it.

Not like Pansy. Little devil!

Hardly realising what he did, Percy took a sheet of paper — ordinary plain notepaper — from the drawer of his desk. He wrote the address of his warehouse, knowing that he would be the only one to see any reply; and he began the letter with a remarkable recovery of old fluency.

" Dear Miss de la Valliere (he said),

" I expect you have forgotten all about me by now, but *I* have not by any means forgotten *you*. I remember our correspondence with great pleasure, and I take this opportunity, during a visit of uncertain duration to the old country, of writing to hope that you are quite well. The story of my experiences since I last wrote you would fill a volume, and I sometimes toy with the idea of writing them. But I must not give way to temptation, and, seriously, I am only joking, when I speak of taking up the pen. I wonder if your marriage has yet taken place, and if you are happy. I sincerely hope so, and yet there is so much unhappiness in the world that I am sometimes inclined to ask what is happiness and where does it hide. In my own case I am as happy as can be expected. I have an excellent little wife who studies to please me and has a blithe merry spirit, always laughing and turning things to jokes, so that I have no cause for complaint. I hope you are equally happy and that your husband, if you are married, sees the funny side of things. Sometimes this is a little hard for those who have *serious interests,* but you will agree that it is better than being always mopy and too sympathetic. Hoping to hear from you I remain your sincere friend,

" G. DE M."

As he wrote, something of the old oblivion of common things returned to Percy. He forgot his feeling of sickness, he forgot the cloud under which he had left home in the morning. A curious lightness took possession of his heart. He whistled as he worked. The parcels of stock did not seem heavy; the time did not hang. Even the winter weather, which blistered his hands with chilblains, did not seem as severe as it had been. He was happy.

He was still happy when he reached home in the evening, to find Pansy with the same strained smile upon her face, satirical and unresponsive. He had not been home an hour when his happiness was gone, lost in twenty exasperations. But the exasperations were hidden. Always, as if to console himself, Percy was able to count the days between the sending of his letter and the receipt of a reply. Devonshire was a long way away. How he wished that he could fly there with his letter and bear away the answer to it!

A day passed, two days passed. There was a change in the domestic atmosphere. It was now Pansy who bubbled with cheerfulness, while Percy, slightly more anxious as his time of recognised waiting began to expire, grew quiet, nervous, troubled. Not until he found his letter waiting at the warehouse did he allow exultation to carry him high. Then, indeed, with a shout of impatience, he tore open the envelope. His hands trembled.

" Dear Sir Guy,

" First of all thank you so much for your welcome letter — a treat all the greater because I did not expect it. I did not know where you were or anything, it is such ages since you wrote. I am so glad you are happy, it is a treat to hear of someone perfectly happy, for though you say you are a serious person I am sure you must like your wife to have a cheerful spirit. It is far better to have this than a face as long as a fiddle like some people I know. Yes, I am married, and am happy in a way, but oh, Sir Guy I wish my husband had a cheerful spirit. He is full of fancies as to his health, not at all a brave man in that respect I fear and, though I try to keep him from losing heart it is sometimes a heavy task and I have a job to keep from losing heart myself in these dark days — that would never do, would it ? However, there are worse troubles at sea, and when the brighter weather comes he will be himself again. I hope so, as I must tell you Sir Guy (you will excuse me I know because of our old friendship, because although I have never seen you I feel you are so sympathetic) that I am expecting to become a mother in the autumn. I have not dared to tell my husband, in case he is not pleased — have nobody else I can tell — am alone in the world. I never do any writing now — my husband is not at all literary but cares only for sport and politics, which he reads in his newspaper. I hope you will write to me again. Though I am not living here any longer, the letters will be sent on and it will not matter to you waiting two days longer, besides which I can still sign myself by the old name your sincere friend

" L. DE LA V."

Percy spent the day as if upon wings. He did not notice its passing. But as he went home through the dark streets he saw a girl selling violets, and bought a bunch for Pansy. That evening both were happy.

They were sitting beside the fire, both dreaming, she with a book in her hand, and he pretending to read a paper, when Pansy gave a little exclamation. It was a whisper only.

" Eh? " demanded Percy. He saw that she was flushed.

" I was thinking," said Pansy. " Where you work. Is it flats? "

" Wodjer mean, flats? "

" Where people live. Like this."

" Offices," he rejoined, briefly. " Our people's. All of it."

She had grown paler again and was thinking absorbedly. Percy, after eyeing her in disquiet, returned to his paper. But he did not read it. His mind was repeating the letter from Louise. He was troubled by a wish to tell Pansy something about it — something disguised, not the facts, but *something*. . . . The truth was that his head was full of Louise and what she had told him. About her husband, about the coming baby. . . .

" . . . read between the lines. . . . " he was thinking to himself, in a manly way. " that . . . what I mean, a little woman . . . all alone . . . afraid of her husband, and *that* . . . afraid to tell him what ought to make him feel like a king. It's pathetic." He had a flying notion that Pansy might go down and nurse her. Then he shook his head violently at the thought of anything so outrageous.

Pansy saw the shaken head.

" D'you know the people in the office? " she asked.

" No. See, it's different."

" How? "

" Well, they're in one street, and I'm in another."

" Thought you said —— "

" They're front entrance. I'm back. I'm ' goods.' "

" Goods! " Pansy gasped. " Goods department? " Percy nodded. " Anybody else there? " He shook his head. " Nobody? Nobody but you? " She was crimson. She became very thoughtful again. Her mouth drooped. Her head drooped.

Percy saw all that. He was staring at her.

" It's *you*, then," murmured Pansy. " I know it's you. But I never guessed. I really never guessed."

" You're talking in monosyllables," protested Percy. " I don't know what you mean."

" Sir Guy de Montmorency! " cried Pansy. " Oh! " She shouted the exclamation. " Fancy me being taken in like that! "

" Wha-at! " Percy felt hot all over. " What d'you mean? "

She jumped up, ran out of the room, returned, and threw a packet of letters into his hands. They were his own.

" Where's mine? " demanded Pansy. " You shown them to anybody? "

Percy staggered to his feet. He was trembling violently.

" You little liar! " he exclaimed. " You cripple! You poet! You —— " He had been going to add something when he checked himself.

" Well, I *did* write verses," protested Pansy. " They were all mine."

The astonishing fact passed almost unappreciated.

" And bed-ridden? " he stormed.

" That was to show I wasn't looking for a boy."

He chewed it. He glowered. Then, accusingly, he pointed a finger.

" And getting married! "

" That was when I began to go with you."

" But . . . but . . ." He spluttered. " Your husband always

fancying . . ." The truth dawned upon him. He uttered a long-drawn-out " Go-o-o-ord! "

For a few minutes they stared at each other. At last Percy remembered his final charge.

" What a liar! " he muttered. " And I suppose you put that in about the baby, and being afraid to tell your husband —— "

" It's true," said Pansy.

She was inspired. She sank faintly to a chair.

" It's not! " shouted Percy. " It's not! You don't mean it! Pansy! " His face had changed. As she lay back in the chair, as one dead, he bounded to her side. " I . . . say! " he breathed. He was aflame with excitement.

" It's all spoilt, now," moaned Pansy. " Everything. Everything."

Percy clouded. Then he threw his hands forward. He had glimpsed a new heaven rising from the ruins of the old one.

" 'Tisn't! " he cried. " It's A.1. I feel like a king! "

FANNY BAINES

By

MARGARET KENNEDY

NOTE

Like Scott with *Waverley* Miss Kennedy might almost have used the sub-title *'Tis Sixty Years Since,* for *Fanny Baines* is a "costume piece," although the setting is unobtrusively mid-Victorian. The Sunday bonnet, lined with *gros-de-Naples* and made of white *chip,* strikes the keynote, followed by *chignon, tarlatan flounces, gauze bonnet, plaid trousers, crinoline,* etc. Slight deft touches build the picture in the garments of the middle of the nineteenth century. These external properties are easy to work up, but what is vastly more difficult is the mental attitude of the period, expressed in the appropriate phrasing. The poems they contribute bear the keepsake titles, *Thoughts from the Tomb* and *The Muted Minstrel.* Beverly is " some curled and scented darling of a lady's boudoir." The raffish countesses and the moustachioed adventurers, the Italian count, the cold, vain, shallow and heartless beauties, all suggest the dissipation, if not debauchery of 1850. Selina's exclamation " If our verses have given consolation and guidance to any human creature, however misguided, however sinful, however far removed from ourselves in station " would seem appropriate in any Godey's Lady's Book. And Fanny's novel might be the opening of a number of the cheap writings of the time. But this stage setting, physical and mental, is by no means put in for its own sake; it is used to explain the motivation of Tom and Fanny. Tom is the mid-Victorian husband, insistent upon his marital rights, on the obedience promised him in the marriage ceremony, while interpreting his own vows with great latitude. Fanny's revolt, then, takes on epic significance; like Nora, in the *Doll's House,* her protest symbolizes the new age. But greater than Nora, she does not leave, closing the door behind her; the pathetic futility of Tom's sleeping face brings comprehension, and she remains to be the modern wife.

FANNY BAINES

By Margaret Kennedy

I

FANNY took off her Sunday bonnet and gazed at it
fondly for a moment before she put it away in its band-
box. It was more satisfactory, however, upon her head than
in her hand, for it did not look quite as fine as it felt. The
lining of *gros-de-Naples* and the broad blue ribbons were very
well, but the brim was too large and white chip was, as she
had complained to her sisters, a governessy sort of contriv-
ance. Once perched out of sight, she could imagine away the
white chip. It would sit far back on her chignon, showing her
beautiful smooth forehead, a bright thing of purple gauze,
filled with lilac at either side, and half concealed, perhaps, by
a fall of finest Brussels lace.

"But you are quite wrong," Emmeline had said, when they
discussed this point; "a fall doesn't go down over the back.
It hangs forwards and conceals the face."

"Oh! don't be tiresome. I mean a veil."

"But only married women wear veils like that, Fan."

"I know. But I'm just as likely to be a married woman as I
am to have a Brussels fall, so why spoil the ship for a ha'p'orth
of tar?"

Emmeline and Selina sympathised. If one had to be content
with pretending things instead of having them, one might as
well do it thoroughly. They did not care as much for clothes
as Fanny did, but they were tolerant to all the pleasures of the
imagination. Selina, indeed, went further, for she would have
thought it a weakness to take any pride in the bonnet as it
actually was. Its inadequacy, had she been interested in bon-
nets, would have prevented her from making any compro-

mise. She would never have smoothed the ribbons and pinched the bows as Fanny now did, or laid it so carefully away in layers of silver paper. And she looked on at these operations with a cynical eye.

" You lead a double life, Fanny," she declared.

Fanny started guiltily, blushed, and asked what she meant.

" I mean that you talk about Brussels falls and a lilac filling, but for all that you quite enjoy wearing white chip."

" But it's a very pretty bonnet," protested Fanny.

" Pretty! " said Selina with a snort. She added: " And what's more, you enjoy sharing a hymn-book with Tom Baines."

" Well, if one can't do what one wants, one had better do what one can."

Selina assumed the air of a granite cliff repelling an Atlantic wave, and said shortly:

" I don't see the necessity."

" Oh, Selina! "

Fanny looked with despairing admiration at her sister. It was quite true. Selina never did see the necessity for lowering any of her demands upon life. She would take all or nothing, but she would never be content with half. Not everybody can hope to attain such a sublime strength of mind. But if she was unsparing to herself, she was humane where the problems of other people were concerned. She would probably be sympathetic when she heard all that Fanny had to tell. She would be a kinder confidante than Emmeline, for, in spite of her lofty temper, she never turned aside from truth and she recognised hard facts for what they were. Besides, she did not know all about Fanny's double life, and Emmeline did.

They went down to the kitchen, their refuge on Sunday evenings, and Fanny knew that the moment had come. Her heart almost failed her. She looked from one sister to the other. Selina, tall and ghostlike, paced thoughtfully backwards and forwards through the dusky caverns of the room, lost in the reverie that filled up three-quarters of her life. Emmeline crouched on the floor by the fire, trying to read a book by its uncertain light, her long curls falling forward on the page. The clock, hidden in the corner, ticked like a slow pulse, and Emmeline coughed, flinging back her curls impatiently as she turned a page. Fanny thought:

" This is their life; not mine any more." She said:

" Tom Baines proposed to me this evening."

Selina stopped her prowling and stood still. Emmeline looked up from her book. Their bright, childish eyes were fixed on Fanny. After a few seconds they both said together:

" Well? "

" I've accepted him," said Fanny.

There was a little note of assurance in her voice which surprised them all. They grasped its meaning immediately. For they were creatures of infinite imagination, and the first swallow always meant summer to them. Their minds leapt forward into time, framing a new Fanny, placid, alien, jingling household keys. They had lived through the parting before they spoke again. Selina, facing it squarely, broke the silence.

" I expect you are in the right," she said gravely. " You always hated being a governess and you are not likely to get a better offer."

" But no," broke in Emmeline. " How can you, Fanny? You don't love him."

" I knew you'd say that," said Fanny coldly.

Selina came into the ring of light on the hearth and stood over Emmeline, looking down at her.

" Don't be an idiot, Emmie," she protested. " Fanny must marry somebody, or earn her living as a governess. When you talk about love you mean something that will never happen to any of us. How could it? What likelihood? There's nobody here that we can love. What choice have we? One of Papa's curates, the new clerk at the bank, young Mr. Postlethwaite, and Tom Baines."

Fanny looked at her helplessly. Between Emmeline's romantic fastidiousness and Selina's implacable common sense, she hardly knew how to defend herself.

" Tom Baines! " repeated Emmeline, almost shuddering.

Such a figure of fun, she was thinking. They had laughed at Tom Baines all their lives. Any girl in her senses must have laughed at him. He had a perfect genius for making himself ridiculous; even his salutation in the street was liable to set them off into a secret paroxysm of hilarity, for he always removed his hat as if it had suddenly become too hot for his head. He could do nothing simply. A consequential awkwardness ruined all his attempts to make himself agreeable, and no girl danced with him if she could help it.

" He is not handsome," said Selina judicially, " but I would not call him plain. There is a certain want of openness in his countenance which I do not like. A fearless frankness is essential to manly beauty. But on the whole there is not very much amiss. I think that he should grow a beard. It would give more consequence to his chin."

Emmeline said nothing. To her mind there was everything amiss, and she did not think that a beard would improve matters. To begin with, he was too short. Fanny, though slender, could give him a couple of inches. His chest was narrow, his nose in cold weather was inclined to be red, and he never looked at the person to whom he was speaking. Half fox, half rabbit, she thought contemptuously, remembering with what an air of cunning foolishness he had slunk up to her on the occasion of their last meeting, and how the cup of tea which he offered had been spilt over her tarlatan flounces.

" I'd rather be a governess," she murmured.

"You've never tried it," pointed out Selina. "Tom Baines is a very good match. His uncle has taken him into partnership, and will make him his heir. He is very sensible and steady. . . ."

"Oh, pray stop!" broke in Fanny.

Selina looked surprised.

"But I entirely support you, Fanny."

"Yes, I know," said Fanny miserably. "But you don't give me the support I want. I am not as mercenary as you seem to think. I would not marry Tom Baines, though he were twice as rich, if I did not like him. I . . ."

"Oh, Fanny!" said Emmeline with a meaning smile.

But Selina rose to the defence once more.

"I dare say she does like him. Just as she likes her Sunday bonnet. Fanny is not like you, Emmeline, or me either. She has a strong vein of practicality. I have often wondered which side of her would win. She could never be entirely comfortable sitting on the fence. She must jump one way or the other, and, for my part, I think she has jumped the right way. It would not do at all if Fanny were to grow into a sour old maid."

"And shall we grow into sour old maids?" asked Emmeline.

Selina shook her head.

"But unless we marry . . ."

"We shall never marry anyone."

"Then . . ."

"Oh, I don't know. But I am not afraid of turning into an old maid."

Selina could not have told why this was. But the future never frightened her.

Fanny, who had been reconnoitring her position, now said:

"Tom says that I shall be a very good influence in his life."

Selina gave one of her abrupt laughs.

"Is that why he proposed to you?"

"Not altogether."

Again there was that new-born note of confidence. She looked into the fire and smiled to herself. Her sisters watched her. They could each of them have written an imaginary love scene which would have knocked the daylight out of any halting efforts on the part of Tom Baines. But the fact remained that Fanny, alone of the three, had tasted actual experience. They wondered what it was like, and whether she now knew something that they did not.

A door opened at the end of the long flagged passage and a loud halloing was heard. It was their father calling for his evening grog. Fanny got up and hurried to answer him. When the parlour door was shut behind her Emmeline leapt up from the floor.

"Sallie," she declared, with flashing eyes, "we can't let Fanny marry Tom Baines. She must not do it. She cannot. She loves another."

"Ha!" exclaimed Selina in astonishment.

"Indeed she does. She has loved him for two years."

"But who . . ."

"Nobody here. But they write to one another. I wonder you should not have guessed. I'm sure I always know what she is about when she slips off to post a letter. And when one comes for her it is the same. If she had not told me, I should have known it from her face."

"But she never does get any letters, except from Harriet Simpson."

"Just so. He writes to her, under cover to Harriet Simpson, at Clapham, and Harriet sends the letters on. They contrived it in that way so that Papa should not find out."

Selina began to look very grave.

"Emmie, who is he? Somebody she met at Mrs. Longman's?"

"Mrs. Longman indeed!" cried Emmeline, laughing heartily. "Imagine Mrs. Longman introducing anybody to her governess. Oh no! Mrs. Longman may keep a carriage and be a very good sort of woman, but I fancy that she has not many men of title on her visiting list."

"Men of title!"

Emmeline laughed so much that she began to cough, and had to drink a glass of water before she could continue.

"No. She did not meet him anywhere, as a matter of fact. They have never met. But she loves him. She admitted as much to me, once, when I pressed her. But you will never guess. It is all too strange and odd and delightful. You remember those verses we published anonymously in the *Cumberland Courier?*"

"*Thoughts from the Tomb?*"

"No, no. Before that. The first verses that they took. *The Muted Minstrel*. Well, you must know that we got a letter, complimenting us on these lines, from an unknown but titled admirer. It was when you were from home: when you were staying at Litchfield with my Aunt Crabshaw. So Fanny answered the letter. It was very shabby of us not to tell you, but we thought you would not approve. They have continued to write to one another ever since."

"A titled admirer? Did he say he was titled?"

"Not then. That came out later. But we could see, in the very first letter, that it was written by a man of fashion."

"A man of fashion," said Selina, in tones of deep disgust.

"You need not speak so, Selina, for you have never met any."

"But I know what they are like," said Selina with conviction. "Some curled and scented darling of a lady's boudoir! Upon my word, honest Tom Baines is a better choice."

"I am not at all sure that Tom Baines is honest. He looks uncommonly sly to me. And indeed you are mistaken, Selina. Fanny's lover is not in the least what you think."

"You have never seen him."

"No. Of course not. But I have seen all his letters."

"Where does he live?"

"In Europe," said Emmeline largely.

Selina could not help looking impressed. She would have liked to live in Europe so much herself that she was inclined to be respectful to anyone who did.

"He travels," explained Emmeline. "There is a reason why he can never return to England. Oh! Selina, if you knew all you would pity him. Misfortune claimed him from his earliest childhood. He had the most unnatural of parents. And his first love was blighted. She was false. His sufferings have been unspeakable, and he has admitted that they drove him to the edge of despair. It seemed as if every human being had turned against him, except such worthless creatures as always fawn upon a title and whose regard will be secured by wealth and position. In such company, unsolaced, unguided, can you wonder that a man so driven should have attempted to drown his sorrows in dissipation, if not debauchery?"

"Debauchery?" said Selina.

No. She did not wonder. She knew as much about debauchery as she did about men of fashion.

"It might be possible," she mused, "to save him from himself."

"That is what Fanny thought," said Emmeline eagerly. "That is why, at first, she allowed the correspondence to continue. She is the one good influence in his life. He says so.

She has convinced him of many things which he doubted before. The superiority of her intelligence and the purity of her mind . . ."

Emmeline dropped her voice as Fanny's step was heard in the passage. But Selina was never a safe recipient of confidence.

She turned on Fanny at once.

" Fanny," she said in tones of deep reproach. " What is this that Emmie tells me? Can it be true? Have you indeed been drawn into a clandestine correspondence with a man of title? "

Fanny shot a black look at Emmeline and said that it was quite true.

" But Emmie had no right to tell. It is all nonsense, and I have been thinking so this great while. Now that I have accepted Tom Baines there must be an end of it."

" But why did you not tell me, Fanny? Am I so untrustworthy? "

" I thought you would not approve."

" Oh, Fanny! " cried Selina earnestly. " How little you know me! Why should I not approve? If our verses have given consolation and guidance to any human creature, however misguided, however sinful, however far removed from ourselves in station . . ."

" Yes, but it's all nonsense to imagine (as Emmie has probably told you everything, I can be frank), to fancy that I had fallen in love with him. I should never have given way to such folly, if I had not been beside myself at the Longmans', so melancholy and in such low spirits. Those long winter evenings in the schoolroom . . . and the tedium of never seeing anybody but the children . . . the want of any rational company. . . . I had read all the books in the only bookcase that Mrs. Longman left unlocked. And you know I have always detested needlework. And then it was so delightful to get his letters, describing all the places that I would like to see, the

Alps and the Bay of Naples and Seville, just as I'd always pictured them. But to call it love was very foolish, and if I were to refuse Tom Baines for the sake of Beverly, as Emmie would have me do, I should deserve to go on teaching spoilt children for the rest of my life."

"Beverly?" repeated Selina. "His name is Beverly? Lord Beverly?"

"I don't know his real name," said Fanny. "He is obliged to conceal it, for the sake of others as well as himself."

"But how do you write to him?"

"I write to an address that he has given me in Doncaster. And the letters are forwarded to him."

"I wish his name had really been Beverly. There is something noble about such a name. He cannot be all bad, worldling though he may be, or he would not have deigned to correspond with a poor governess."

But Emmeline broke in here.

"He does not know that Fanny is a governess. He believes her to be a fashionable woman and that her name is Eleonora."

Selina frowned and Fanny hung her head.

"I knew that you would not like it, Sallie. That we should correspond, you would have allowed that, but you would have obliged me to tell the truth about my humble circumstances. But if he had known all he would have despised me."

"He did not despise the hand that wrote our verses," Selina pointed out. "Did you tell him that *The Muted Minstrel* was not all your own work?"

"No, Selina. I did not. And if Emmie can forgive me I think you might. It would have looked so foolish."

"Nay, it is not for myself that I care," said Selina in some distress. "But you should not have told him what was not true."

"I said nothing that was absolutely false. I told him that I too had my reasons for concealing my name and true station, which was perfectly true. And I said that I lived in the country in retired simplicity and that luxury and idleness had long since been strangers to me."

" They were never anything else, my dear Fanny. I must say that I cannot think it right."

" But think of the good that she has done," broke in Emmeline. " If it were not for her influence he would now be lounging on some Italian couch in the arms of his mistresses. . . ."

"Good heavens! " exclaimed Selina. "Does he say so? "

" Indeed he does. You should see his letters."

Selina looked as though she should very much like to see his letters. But Fanny said firmly that she must burn them now that she had accepted Tom.

" I'll do it tonight, while the fire is still good, and there will be an end of it."

She marched out of the room in a decided way, and while she was gone the other two heard a knock at the door.

" Don't do," said Selina, as Emmeline got to her feet. " The cold air in the passage will make you cough."

Lighting a candle, she went out and came back in a few minutes smiling grimly.

" Tom Baines to see Papa," she told Emmeline.

They shivered sympathetically. Poor as their opinion of Tom Baines might be, they could not help being sorry for anyone who had to see Papa.

" Did he seem very nervous? "

" It is impossible to tell. He is always so odd. He ate his hat and fell over the door-scraper and said ' Good-morning.' When I said ' Good-evening ' he said: ' Ha! ha! Very good.' "

Emmeline sighed. One of the sweetest chapters in her secret dream had been a gorgeous interview between Papa and Beverly.

When Fanny came back they told her that her lover was in the parlour. She heard it with composure, being very sure that her father would make no real objections. And she produced a little casket that she had brought with her from upstairs. It was tied with blue ribbons, which she burnt first of all, being a methodical creature. Then, opening the box, she took out a packet of letters.

Her sisters, silent and embarrassed, drew away from her, wondering if she would rather be left alone. But, as the blue ribbons caught fire and the flames danced on the ceiling, she beckoned.

" Come, Sally! I know you are dying to see these letters, and it is only fair that you should, before they are burnt, since one-third of the poem was yours. Read them, but pray spare me any more reproaches."

Emmeline and Selina approached the fire, and three heads drew together as Fanny took out the first letter.

" What extraordinary writing! " exclaimed Selina.

Fanny explained that Beverly was obliged to write with his left hand, since the other had been injured.

" We think in a duel," added Emmeline.

Selina looked at the strange, stiff, upright strokes in great disappointment. They conveyed nothing of the man.

" You think too much of handwriting," said Fanny. " You are always complaining that mine has no character."

" Nor has it. Every young lady who ever left boarding school writes just like you, Fanny. Even I can scarcely tell your hand apart from Harriet Simpson's or Ellen's or Charlotte West-hope's."

Selina broke off as Beverly's warm and respectful praise of *The Muted Minstrel* caught her eye. She had to allow that he was a good critic.

" But how did he come to be reading the *Cumberland Courier* in Baden Baden? "

" You will see. He says it lit into his hands."

Selina devoured the description of the gaming tables, the raffish countesses and the moustachioed adventurers. She reached out an eager hand for the next letter, which she read more easily by the light that blazed up from the first. Beverly was amazed that such strong lines should have been penned by a woman.

" By women," murmured Selina.

He begged that the correspondence might continue. For the next two or three letters there was no mention of Baden Baden, only a few passing references to the higher Alps and a short description of the Hospice of St. Bernard. Books were the main topic. Fanny and Beverly were agreeing upon their favourite authors. But later on there were hints of something more dramatic. Beverly had left the Alps. He was in Venice. He begged her not to ask him how he spent his time. There were some pages in the book of life which should not, could not be turned before the eyes of one who . . . But in the course of time they were turned. Fanny's exhortations began to work upon him. The confessions of despair grew blacker, the acknowledgment of dissipation more open. The scene changed to Rome. Beverly rode on the Campagna, which rolled, mused in the Forum, which was ruined, and reflected cynically upon the morals of the Principessa — in whose boudoir he had just spent the evening. She was typical of all the ladies who succeeded her, cold, vain, shallow and heartless. Fanny, Emmeline and Selina were not surprised. They would have expected as much. But they wondered a little if all the ladies in Europe were married. Beverly never spoke of any who were not.

" Did he never meet any young ladies? " wondered Selina.

" Oh yes. But he found out that they were all as bad as the rest. They were set on by their mothers to try for his fortune," said Fanny. " Besides, he is afraid of young girls. There is one

letter . . . Stay . . . I will read it to you. . . . He was in
Vienna. . . ."

She found a letter some way down the pile and read:

". . . Here I come from an unusual entertainment. I have
been drinking beer with a very honest coachbuilder, under the
lilacs in his garden, and feasting my eyes not a little upon the
charms of Fraulein Gretchen, his daughter, all white muslin,
cornflowers and innocence.

" And what have I, you will say, to do with innocence? I
will tell you. I looked at her for twenty minutes by the clock,
and I spoke to her not at all. When I took my leave, she smiled
upon me very sweetly and I had the privilege of seeing a very
fine complexion suffused by a most charming blush. Poor
child! She little knew that she was smiling on the devil and
all his works!

" So now good-bye to Fraulein Gretchen. May she make
some Viennese tradesman a happier man than I can ever hope
to be. And so to the Opera, and afterwards to supper not a
hundred miles from the Ball Platz, *und so weiter*. . . . And
you, dear friend? How are you spending this summer afternoon? Do I not see those clear eyes, that calm front of yours,
bent over this letter in reproof. . . ? "

Fanny broke off and there was a little silence. All three were
thinking of that girl in white muslin, a little enviously because
she spoke a foreign language and drank beer under lilac trees
in a town that they had never seen. At last Selina said:

" I think he imagines a good deal more than he has any
warrant for. She may not have been thinking of him at all. He
seems to suppose that he has made another conquest. I should
have told him that only coxcombs take these things for
granted."

Fanny and Emmeline exchanged glances. They had often
felt it to be a little unkind that they had kept the thrill of these

letters to themselves, and allowed Selina no hand in the replies. But now they knew how right they had been. Selina would never have remembered that she was writing to a lord.

" He shows very different feelings toward the end," said Fanny. " You will change your mind when he goes to stay with the monks."

" Monks? "

Selina frowned and Emmeline hastened to say that they were Greek monks, not Roman Catholics.

" I'll go back and read them all in order," said Selina, " while Fanny puts them into the fire."

But Fanny got up.

" You can put them into the fire yourself," she said. " I don't care. I've thought a great deal too much about him, and about a life that I shall never see. Half of me always thought it foolish. As Sallie says, I've been sitting on the fence. Now, and for the rest of my life, that half must be all of me. Never again . . ."

Her voice failed her. She drew away, out of the circle of fire-light, where her sisters sat reading and burning. And presently the door at the end of the passage was opened and her father's voice called:

" Frances! "

She went slowly away, her Sunday gown whispering over the stone flags of the passage. But her sisters, sitting in the charmed ring of light, were so intent that they did not know she was gone.

II

Fanny got a gauze bonnet for her wedding, but not a Brussels fall, and she went with Tom to Paris for a honeymoon. At the end of three days she was so tired that she could scarcely breathe. For Tom was an earnest sightseer. He had never been abroad before and he was never likely to go again, so he determined to make the most of it.

They rose at seven o'clock, and soon after eight they would set forth from their hotel with guide books in their hands. Fanny felt that she might have enjoyed it more if her new cloth-topped boots did not hurt her so much, and if the naked statues in the galleries had not embarrassed her so terribly, and if being married had not made her so inordinately sleepy. She yawned and blushed and sometimes felt very much inclined to cry.

Tom yawned a good deal too, but they kept up an appearance of creditable, if sober, enjoyment until the ninth day, when they went to Fontainebleau and got lost in the forest. Having walked, as it seemed, a great many miles, Fanny sat down suddenly on the grass beneath a tree and said " Oh dear! " so dolefully that Tom was quite startled.

" My love, what is it? Don't you feel well? "

" No, no, no! " cried Fanny, petulantly pushing him away. " Do leave me alone. I am perfectly well. I'm tired. Leave me alone."

" I beg your pardon," said Tom stiffly.

He was offended. For it was she who had insisted upon walking so far.

Fanny fought against her tears. She had been fighting them for nine days. They had been rising all the time and now the floodgates broke. She burst into a passion of sobbing, but all that she could say, in answer to Tom's enquiries, was that Paris was no better than an exhibition.

" Oh no. I'm perfectly happy. I'm not sorry that I married you. But I don't like Paris. I don't like it at all. I don't like exhibitions. They always give me a headache. If I have to look at any more famous sights I shall scream. We have famous sights at home and we can see them a great deal more comfortably. I'm sure that hotel is not healthy. It is enough to give anybody the fever."

Tom grew more offended than ever, though he secretly agreed with her. He, too, was disappointed. He had expected much more from the trip. But he had been more successful in disguising this fact to himself, especially since he, being a man, had to do all the parlez-vooing. That, and making sure that he was not being cheated, had kept him fairly busy. It was pleasant, he found, to be the most normal, rational and honest person on the stage. At home he was seldom called upon to play such a rôle. There everybody was larger and more sure of themselves than he was. But here, in this world of outlandish foreigners, he was able to enjoy the sense of being a true Briton. He would strut along beside Fanny on the Boulevards, carefully protecting her from any possible jostlings, proud of her slender height and the magnificent amplitude of her bridal array, and satisfied with the cut of his new plaid trousers. It was very ungrateful of her not to be enjoying herself when he had spent so much money, and so he gave her to understand.

"I thought you liked Paris," he said coldly.

"So did I," said Fanny.

Her tears had stopped and she was dabbing at her eyes with a ridiculous handkerchief upon which Emmeline had embroidered an F. B. monogram. But there was something a little crushed and pitiful about her; she looked fragile, like some flower that has bloomed too early in the spring. Tom saw for the first time how black were the shadows beneath her eyes.

"By Jove!" he exclaimed. "You *are* tired."

He sat down on the grass beside her and took her hand. He was tired himself, and unable to pretend any longer that Paris and Fanny were all that he had expected. But of this second disappointment he was determined to say nothing. It was his own fault. He had desired he knew not what: some tremendous bliss, some fusion of mind and soul that should change the whole of life for him. He had imagined that he would be able to tell Fanny everything. But it was not so, and he had only himself to blame.

He knew now how extravagant had been his hopes when he proposed to her. It was so astonishing to be accepted and not laughed at that he had begun to expect a miracle. He had always thought her quite different from other girls. There was a mystery about her, a secret. He did not know how it was, but he thought that the expression in her eyes had something to do with it. She would look past you and through you as if she was seeing something that nobody else could see, and her smile was slow and beautiful, like the sun breaking through a cloud. Those eyes, that smile, did not frighten him; they had no malice or mockery, and in the sharp-eyed simper of the belles of Drummondale he was used to discerning both.

For a little time it had not seemed impossible that she might one day come to his aid and help him to bridge the gulf between the man that he was and the man that he would have liked to be. She might share his longing for travel and adventure, new scenes, and company far different from any that could be attained by a provincial attorney. She might hear, without disapproval, of the boredom which had almost suffocated him sometimes, of the despair which seized him when he knew that he had nothing better to hope for. He had thought that he would never be able to speak of these things to anyone in the world, and this thought had been a torment to him even in childhood, for he was an orphan, and his uncle and aunt, though they had brought him up as their own son, had never been able to help laughing at him. From his earliest years he had suffered from a twofold shame, fully conscious, on the one hand, of the poor figure that he cut in the eyes of the world, and weighed down, on the other, by the humiliations of the dreaming egotist, the incipient Malvolio, who feeds upon imaginary success and knows it to be futile.

But if, to Fanny, his outer self did not appear entirely ridiculous, then he had thought that possibly, with the growth of intimacy, his inner life might be shared with her too. He might even bring himself to confess to her the extent of folly to which his loneliness had brought him. And he was sure that the greater part of his trouble would disappear if ever he could speak of it. He would never be happy in Drummondale, but he might become, with Fanny's help, a self-respecting man. He would settle down with her, and perhaps they would have children, and Fanny would teach them to be good children, looking up to and admiring their father.

But now, after nine days, he knew that this could never be. She was not what he had thought. She would never love him as he had hoped. She was sweet-tempered, obliging and prosaic. Those hints of wild, strange sweetness which had reached him during their courtship were all illusions. She was sweet enough, and in her beauty he found considerable consolation, but wild or strange . . . never! With marriage she seemed to have vowed herself to the commonplace with the zeal of a St. Teresa. Duty and sound sense governed everything that she said or did. She kept a wise check on their expenditure, disapproved of any work of art that did not teach a moral lesson, and spoke soberly of novel-reading as a dangerous occupation. It seemed that he had married a first-class prig.

She was cold. She accepted his caresses, but she never invited them. But he supposed that all good women were cold. He had been mad to expect anything else. He had helped himself to an excellent and prudent wife, and he must learn to put up with her, to have her always about him, to listen to her prim little remarks about waste of time or money. If the prospect sometimes made him want to go out and drown himself in the Seine, he must resist the impulse. He wondered what other men did about it. For he was certainly not the first fool to be taken in by a pretty face. And he came to the conclusion that even his sensuality was inadequate, a thing which, before marriage, he could never have believed. He could not really enjoy so one-sided a passion, as a grosser man might have done. And that, too, was probably his fault.

This sudden tearful outburst, therefore, shocked and shook him. He knew that ladies are unreasonable and liable to hysterics. But he had at least expected to be spared that sort of thing with Fanny. It seemed that she had suddenly forgotten the rôle that they had both cast for her. And he was sorry for her too, because she was really tired and her physical inferiority to himself was going to be important in their relationship. He sat on the grass and sympathised with the unfortunate creature because she was a woman.

"Take care of my bonnet," said Fanny immediately.

Tom swore. He had been taking care of that damned bonnet ever since they left Drummondale.

"I'm sorry, love. But I often feel as if I'd married a bonnet instead of a wife. Supposing you take it off? It must be confoundedly hot, down over your ears like that."

"Take it off? Out of doors?" said Fanny.

"Why not?"

"Oh, it would look *so*."

Tom eyed her thoughtfully, and then said, with a little hesitation:

"I saw you running on the moors last summer, you and your sisters, and you hadn't a bonnet between you."

But Paris was different, as Fanny explained. An example

should be set to the foreigners. Besides, last summer she had not been a married woman.

"A married woman does what her husband tells her," said Tom, boldly untying the strings.

She gave in, for the lilac filling was scratching her neck uncomfortably. And without it she looked quite different. Tom could not take his eyes off her. She was flushed. The tears still hung on her eyelashes, and the soft wind blew in her hair. Tom thought: "I should like to write some verses about a pretty woman sitting on the grass without her bonnet. If I were a poet, I should write some verses about it."

In secret he had written a great many verses, but they were not about Fanny; they were full of arms and charms, snowy bosoms, rolling eyes and raven tresses, for his muse was a kind of tenth cousin to *Lallah Rookh*. He did not remember them now, when he wished that he were a poet.

He felt happier, more at ease with her, than he had ever felt since they married. And there was no bonnet to be considered.

"Now don't be foolish, Tom. That's quite enough."

"Fanny! Fanny! This isn't foolish. You don't love me."

"You mustn't say such an unkind thing."

"But you don't. If you did, you wouldn't keep on saying that's quite enough."

"Would I not?"

"No, indeed. You'd say: 'Dear Tom, please go on.'"

"Oh, Tom!"

They both knew that no lady would ever dream of such a thing. But Fanny, without her bonnet, was only half a lady.

"Do you like being married?" whispered Tom.

"I'm not very . . . used to it yet."

"But do you think you will, some day?"

"Perhaps."

"Just now do you like it?"

" Yes."

" Really? "

" Really."

" Oh, Fanny. . . ."

" Listen! Oh, quick! Give me my bonnet. I hear somebody coming."

" Nonsense! "

" Oh yes! There is! Somebody is coming up the path. Please, please, give me my bonnet! "

There were voices and footsteps behind the trees. Tom relinquished the bonnet. Fanny scrambled to her feet, gave her creased skirts a shake, twitched her mantle. The bright hair disappeared under the bonnet, and her flounces settled into full, discreet folds over her crinoline.

" Get up, Tom," she whispered.

He still sat on the grass, looking at her hopelessly, knowing that the moment of approach was gone. She had escaped him. Then he too got up. But as they strolled away he made one more effort.

" I say, Fanny. I've got a plan."

" Yes, Tom? "

" How would it be if we left Paris? "

" Left Paris? "

" You don't care for it. And I must admit that I've seen quite enough of it. Shouldn't we go somewhere else? We might enjoy it more. We might make a little trip down the Rhine. We might even go to Italy. . . ."

" But, Tom, we only have five days more."

" I don't think my Uncle would mind very much if we stayed a little longer. He might look blue, but after all it's only once in our lives."

" It would be so expensive," said Fanny. " Besides, our rooms here are paid for."

" What's the use of that, if we don't enjoy it? We shall never have such another chance to see the world. Why not take it, Fanny? "

" Such a waste of money. And we shall have had a fortnight."

" But Italy! Don't you want to see Italy? "

Fanny did want to see Italy, but not with Tom.

" Life is not all pleasure," she reminded him.

" No, dammit! But we've had no pleasure at all so far. Fanny, do let's. It would be such a lark. Fanny, do be a brick."

" Of course, you are the person to decide," said Fanny dutifully. " But . . ."

" We might go to Baden Baden. I've always wanted to see the life there and the gaming tables and all that."

" Oh *no*! " cried Fanny.

She began to walk so fast in her agitation that Tom had to stride to keep up with her. He could not have mentioned a worse place than Baden Baden. She was reminded of all the follies upon which she had so resolutely turned her back. She had pledged herself to decorum, common sense, and wifely duty, and if she had not forgotten herself, sitting bareheaded on the grass like any village wench, Tom would never have suggested such a thing.

" No, Tom. It's absurd. What should we do at Baden Baden? It's quite out of scale with our state of life."

" I think our state of life is a great bore," muttered Tom.

" God put us into it," said Fanny.

III

God had put her into it, she said, but she really meant that she had put herself into it. Pride rather than a sense of Divine Justice upheld her. Of her own will and with a collected mind she had married Tom Baines, thereby renouncing all that Tom

Baines could never give her. And, since she must have a vocation of some sort, she threw herself into the business with the single-minded energy of a fanatic. She gave up novel-reading. She learnt to make fringe. She jingled her keys, hemstitched all the sheets, and drank tea with the ladies of Drummondale. Not a moment in her day was ever relinquished to idleness or reverie. She even began to cure herself of the habit of running about, and as the summer ripened into autumn a demure and thin-lipped stateliness seemed to settle round her like an enveloping shawl.

Sometimes she would climb the fells to visit her sisters, but since she had come to regard these visits as a holiday, they were but sparsely made. After a time she only went if some errand justified the outing. Nobody in Drummondale could deny that she was a pattern wife, and nobody was surprised when Tom, after the manner of men so happily mated, began quite openly to neglect her. His shortcomings were the talk of the provincial tea-tables. He was moody and boorish, pleased at nothing that she did, and, moreover, taking to bad company, which was an agreeable surprise, for though he had never been popular, he had always been accounted a very steady, good sort of young man. More evenings than not he was to be found in the billiard-room of the Drummondale Arms, he was not always perfectly sober, and there were rumours about a barmaid in Keswick. The jury of matrons began by pitying Fanny and ended by blaming her. For she did not seem to be taking it to heart as she ought. She gave no confidences, asked no advice, and pursued her course of excellence serenely.

" Poor fellow! " said the ladies at last. " He must be disappointed that she has no children."

They had always thought it a mistake for a young man to marry into that delicate rectory family. A wife, however perfect, has not done her full duty until there are little feet running to greet the breadwinner on his return. Tom Baines ought to be ashamed of himself, but really Fanny was very foolish not to seek the advice which older and more experienced women might be able to give her. Veiled hints were dropped, but Fanny did not seem to understand them. For it was the turn of the year, and she was fighting an inward battle that had nothing to do with Tom or babies.

The spring had always been a dangerous time for Fanny. It was then that all those inclinations, which she had come to regard as dangerous, beset her most sorely. The sap rising in the trees, the new, tender colour of the fields, the soft rainy skies would fill her with a languid melancholy. The temptation to dawdle and to dream became almost irresistible. She would drop her work and stand at the window for minutes together, wondering what it was that she had once known that was so urgently worth remembering. In the spring it was impossible to find it important that the butcher's book should balance.

Every year she had been obliged to fight off the insidious mood, and before April turned to May she would always succumb. A lost look would come into her eyes and Emmeline would say:

"Fanny is writing poetry again."

But this year she would be strong-minded. She had disowned her muse. Married women did not have muses. Her pen must be allowed no licence. It must be kept for account books and ladylike notes. There must be no scribbling.

The daffodils came out in the fields above the lake. The larch woods turned pink. Fanny did a great deal of tatting. And if she looked out of the window it was merely to watch Keziah and Janet beating carpets on the lawn. And one afternoon, while penning an elegant billet to the doctor's wife, the sight of her own writing, that careful, stereotyped, sloping hand at which Selina had mocked, set her off. It was too much for her altogether. She sat staring at a half-sheet on which was written:

" My dear Mrs. Harding,
    " It would give me so much pleasure if
            The vestal flame is burning low dim. . . .
        Remember him. . . .
            tore
        I forced thine image
        the vestal flame
        No knew that under   skies
        My tears would flow again."

                    To B——
        " I bade thy suppliant ghost depart,
        I tore thine image from my brain,
        Nor knew that 'twas my living heart
        That I had rent in twain.

        I've watched the earth in barren guise
        Lie all the winter void of pain,
        Nor recked that under milder skies
        Green leaves must spring again.

        The altar flame   ashes cold,
        The vestal lamp is burning dim,
        When every flower that breaks the mould
        Bids me remember him.

        Of what avail? "

A footstep in the hall brought her to herself with a guilty start. She thrust the paper out of sight and took another sheet. Her letter to Mrs. Harding was half written when Tom came in.

" I beg your pardon," she said vaguely.

Tom was mumbling something, in a shamefaced way, about having to go into Keswick. She heard him with mild acquiescence, but her eyes were abstracted.

" Yes, dear," she agreed.

He felt that she would have said the same thing if he had announced an intention of going to Cape Horn.

" By heaven! " he exclaimed suddenly. " I believe you like it."

" Like what? " asked Fanny bewildered.

Like being badly treated was what Tom meant. He was ashamed of himself, ashamed of the company into which he was going, at the coarse opiates to which his disappointment had driven him. It seemed as if there was no escape for him but that of degradation. Those daydreams in which he had figured as a carefree romantic, an elegant leader of fashion, a travelled man of the world, a sinister and fated hero, would no longer suffice him; company of some sort he must have, if he was not to go quite mad, and he must seek it amid the grog and tobacco of the bar parlour. He had found that he could talk when he was drunk, and among his new friends, since he would always stand treat, he was accounted a wit. There, at least he was a person of consequence.

And Fanny seemed to like it. That was his excuse. She was glad to get him out of the house so that she could go on being a good wife without his loutish interruptions. Yet when she looked at him like this, with bright vague eyes that always seemed to be gazing at something through and beyond him, he had moments of intolerable doubt. The belief that she was cold, narrow-minded, a bore, the concentrated essence of complacent virtue, would crumble. He would find himself wondering again, uneasily, what she was really up to. There was something behind it all. He had not been deceived when he saw her in the spring last year, and thought she was different from other girls. There was a mystery, a secret. But she would never share it with him. She did not think him good enough for her. She had married him, as all girls marry, because she could do no better for herself. And she had put up a barricade of model behaviour behind which she might hide herself for ever. If she had given him her confidence, if she had ever come out from behind the barricade, he could have loved her madly. She might have done what she pleased. A slut or a slattern who loves you, thought Tom, remembering the barmaid in Keswick, puts more heart into you than ten thousand paragons who do not. Sometimes he almost hoped that if he baited her sufficiently, put her completely out of patience, she might be driven from her stronghold. But nothing put her out of patience. She seemed, as he had said, to like it.

"Don't wait up for me," he mumbled. "I may be kept late, and if I am I shall not come back till tomorrow."

Any other wife in Drummondale would have pricked up her ears at that. But Fanny merely asked which boots he was going to wear, as she would ring for Janet to fetch them.

"Oh, the devil take the boots!" cried Tom, and flung out of the room.

Fanny sat waiting to hear him go. Presently the house door slammed and there was a clatter of hoofs as he led his horse out of the stable. He mounted and the sounding clatter died away down the lane. It echoed, died away, echoed again as he turned into the high-road, and drew further and further away until it was no louder than the ticking of a watch in the still, rainy air. Fanny listened until she was really sure that the ticking had stopped, and then she pulled out of its concealment that scribbled half-sheet that she had pushed away, together with a letter that had arrived two days before under cover from her old school friend Harriet Simpson. It was a very illegible letter, scrawled over a signature that she had not seen since the night when she accepted Tom and sat with her sisters beside the kitchen fire, reading and burning.

" For God's sake write to me. I must hear from you. Do not reproach me for this long silence. I have an excuse to offer. Dearest of friends, you will pardon me when you know what it is. Some eighteen months ago I discovered how much you had become to me. I love you. Dare I say it? I love you with all my soul. We can never meet. Fate forbids it. And yet existence without you was insupportable.

" I did what I could. Bear with my folly when I tell you that I married. I took to my somewhat thorny bosom a young creature . . . but I will not speak of her. She has not deserved, poor soul, that I should reproach her. Need I say that she is beautiful, pure, amiable . . . that I am accounted on all sides a most happy man? We live in a state of connubial bliss (they call it that, don't they?), which is the envy of all my acquaint-ances. Oh, we are a pair of turtle-doves, I can assure you.

" You are revolted? Already, perhaps, you have dashed this letter, this last cry of a soul in despair, to the ground. I cannot think it. 'All my faults perchance thou knowest, all my mad-ness none can know.' What will you say when you learn that I have been unfaithful to her? what scorn . . . what contempt. . . . But believe me, nothing that you can feel will be half so bitter as the reproaches which I level against myself. Faithless to you, faithless to her! Better a millstone . . . but enough!

" I will be brief. . . .

He was far from brief. But the upshot of it was that he loved her, and Fanny would not have welcomed briefness on this theme. He had married in the hope of smothering his passion by a new attachment. But his wife, of whom he was continually saying that he must not speak, did nothing to help him in the matter. She was an angel, but she did not understand him. How could any good woman, save one, do that? Convinced

that his marriage was a failure, he had yielded, in a despairing
frenzy, to the charms of Giulia, his new flame, but of her, for
obvious reasons, he must not speak either. Parted from one who
had been the lodestar of his life, what else could he do? If
Fanny would not write to him, if she withheld her sympathy,
her counsel, he should not answer for the consequences. But if
she would relent, if she would resume that spiritual commun-
ion which was more than life to him, he thought there might
still be some possibility of repentance and reform.

Fanny looked from the letter to her own half-written poem
and frowned unhappily. She had not answered, because she
thought it would be wrong. But it now came into her mind
that these lines to *B* —— were inexcusable. They were everything that was bad. They were false. She would purge her mind
of them. She would write to him once, avowing the truth,
and finish it for ever. There should be no more schoolgirl
verses.

Tearing the half-sheet into a dozen little pieces, she took up
her pen and began to write rapidly the words that came to her.

" You must not write to me any more. It would be very
wrong. I am married too. I married, I think, for the same
reason that you did. Your letters meant too much to me, and
yet not enough. Your image had become too dear to me. Yet
it could never be anything more. Had I preserved a firmer
temper I could perhaps have resigned myself. But I could not
live so. Women are not like men. They cannot exist for an
ideal.

" Now my duty and faith are to my husband. I must never
think of you. But if we are to meet, in another, more blessed
existence, we must be worthy. May Heaven bless you and preserve you, my dearest Beverly, and remember, when you think
of me, that though happiness on earth is not possible to us, yet
we may still achieve, by right conduct and good principles, a

bliss which will surpass all that we can imagine here. For this reason, do not forget me.

> " ' All my hopes, where'er thou goest,
>   Whither, yet with thee they go.'

" Do not write to me again.

" ELEONORA."

A blackbird whistled in the briar at the garden gate. It had rained all day, but now it was clearing and a yellow, watery sunset lit the slopes of Callow Fell. Fanny was devoured by an impulse to do something violent and energetic. She must go out-of-doors, and walk quickly. Scarcely waiting to seal her letter, she hurried out of the house, towards the town. Her neighbours, peeping out between their curtains, wondered where she could be going in such haste, for she had unthinkingly put on her Sunday mantle and was skipping over the puddles with very little care. When she had put her letter into the hands of the old postmistress she could think of nothing better to do than race up the hill to find her sisters. The air was so sweet and fresh that she could never breathe enough of it. She felt as if she had been shut up for many months. She pined for the wind on the hillside. Emmie and Selina must come out with her, and they would go racing over the fells until dusk had fallen like a curtain over Barton Water.

But, though they were very glad to see her, they could not come because they both had coughs. She found them sitting in the kitchen, trying to warm themselves, for all the sour cold of the winter seemed to have lingered on in that great stone room. Selina, looking up, smiled her rare, lovely smile and cried:

" Here is dear Fanny come at last."

" Oh! " cried Fanny. " It's been so long . . ."

She broke off, choked by an emotion which she did not

understand. They hung about her fondly, untying her bonnet and exclaiming over the handsome folds of her mantle. But she, returning to that half-forgotten world, was filled with thoughts which had never come to her before. They had changed. Or had she changed? She looked anxiously at Selina's thin cheek, her sunken eye, the transparent frailness of her body. Had Selina always looked like this?

"Oh, Sallie!" she cried. "How ill you look!"

A quick glance passed between Selina and Emmeline. Selina said:

"I am perfectly well, thank you."

And Emmeline added:

"Oh, Fanny! How well you look!"

Fanny did look well. There was a healthy bloom on her cheek, and she had grown fatter living in the valley. She ate better food than they did and she lived in warmer rooms. Standing there, in her handsome merino, conscious of beauty, health and a secure future, she felt once more that she was a stranger. They had secrets now of which she knew nothing. It was she who had changed, not they.

"And they will be the same for ever," she thought. "There is something in them that time can never touch."

She tried to think of the future and could see herself there, but not Selina or Emmeline. She would grow old. She would learn many things which were now, perhaps, hidden from her. Time would touch her, but they were already beyond it. Her reason told her that they could not remain unchanged for ever, but in her heart she believed that they would, and when she tried to imagine them grown old she could only see an empty room, a deserted hearth.

Thrusting that vision aside, she roused herself to listen to them. They had a great deal to tell. The new curate was more ridiculous than ever. A girl at an upland farm had drowned herself for love. During the winter they had begun to teach themselves Greek, and Selina was writing a novel.

"Do you know what I should like to do?" said Fanny. "I should like to make some toffee, as we used to do."

"But, dearest, can you stay as long as that?"

"Oh, as long as I like," she told them gleefully. "Tom is gone into Keswick."

So they made toffee and she stayed to supper, and afterwards she brushed out Emmeline's hair, while Selina read the opening chapters of her novel.

The flickering firelight, the soft rhythm of the brush in Emmie's curls, worked like a spell on Fanny. She listened dreamily, uncritically, drawn into that peculiar world which Selina would evoke, which was so much more exciting than the world of Drummondale and yet not entirely unlike it. Only when she was bounding down the hill again did it occur to her how little Selina knew about life compared with herself.

"People are not like that," she thought. "Love is not like that. Only she is like that, so she makes everything else seem so. I know more than she does. I have a husband and a lover and I have been to Paris."

She could not imagine what Selina's book would have been like if Selina had had a husband and a lover and had been to Paris. Something of Selina's overflowing vision seemed to have lingered with her, and she went on, for some time, seeing everything with Selina's eyes till she was obliged to begin writing a novel herself. She began it a week later, not expecting to do better than Selina, but feeling that a husband and a lover and Paris ought not to be wasted. The opening chapters were quickly planned. Adelaide, the illegitimate daughter of a duke, having been put out to nurse at a farm, spent a carefully recorded childhood at school in Bristol and later went to Paris with a disagreeable old lady not unlike Mrs. Longman, was turned out by her into the streets and lit into the arms of a Mysterious Protector. Fanny had meant to introduce him earlier, but there was so much to say that it was June before she got to him. And in June Tom discovered what she was up to.

IV

She had no place in which to hide her manuscript, and she often looked with an envious eye at the desk where Tom kept his private papers. The key of it was never out of his pocket. If only she had a desk of her own like that! But she managed to conceal the growing pile of foolscap in the wardrobe, under her chemises, where nobody would ever think of looking for it. And Tom had no inkling of the matter until he came home unexpectedly one afternoon, in search of a paper that he had left behind.

" What's that confounded smell? " he asked, as he came into the parlour.

Fanny leapt to her feet aghast.

" Good heavens! The milk! . . . "

She had put a saucepan on to boil and forgotten it. She rushed into the kitchen. When she came back her secret had been discovered. Tom's eye had been caught by the sheets of foolscap lying about on the parlour table. He picked one of them up.

" What's this? " he asked.

"Nothing," said Fanny hastily.

His eye travelled down the page and he gave a gasp of amazement.

" What's this? " he asked again. " Have you turned authoress? "

She could not say that he was wrong. He stared at her in contemptuous amusement.

"I didn't know that I had married a blue-stocking."

With a curling lip he took up the next page. But Fanny snatched it from him.

"Oh, pray don't read it."

Gone was the placid acquiescence, the measured precision of the pattern wife. She glared at him like some savage woman guarding her young. He broke into loud laughter.

"So this is what you've been up to!"

"Oh, Tom, please give it back to me."

"I don't know that I will," he said coolly.

So this was what lay behind all that puritanical parade! This was her secret! She was a fraud and he had known it all along. As soon as his back was turned, this was how she spent her time. At the sight of her agitation his resentment burst into flame.

"I won't have it," he blustered.

He held her back while he gathered up the rest of the sheets from the table.

"I won't allow it. No man in his senses would allow it. You have the house to look after. I come in and find the pudding burnt while you sit scribbling nonsense. . . ."

"It's not nonsense. . . ."

"I'll form my own opinion about that when I've read it."

"You've no right to read it."

"No right? What do you mean? No right? Are you mad? You're talking to your husband, remember. It's not merely my right. It's my duty."

To have her, at last, at his mercy was a bitter but intoxicating draught. He felt dimly that he was coming into his own. No longer was she the injured wife and he the peccant husband. He was being master in his own house. He was putting his foot down.

"Women," he pointed out, "had better not meddle with

such things. To begin with, it's unfeminine. And, besides, everyone knows that women can only write the most nonsensical stuff imaginable."

"That is not true."

"Then why are you so ashamed at having it read?"

"Tom, I shall never forgive you if you read it. I shall hate you. Give it back to me."

She made one more effort to snatch it from him, but he held her off and flung the whole bundle into his desk, which he locked. The key went back into his pocket.

"On Sunday," he said, "I'll glance through it if I have time. And then I'll let you know if I think it's worth a burnt pudding."

Fanny, livid and dishevelled, said nothing. Her words choked in her throat. He was almost out of the door before breath returned to her and she called out hoarsely:

"I'm not your slave!"

"What's that?"

He turned round in the doorway.

"I don't belong to you. I'm not a dog to feed out of your hand. I hate you! If you want me to stay in your house after this you will have to live with a person who hates you. I shall wish you ill in everything that you do: I shall hope that harm will come to you. I shall rejoice if I can find means to make you suffer. . . . I . . ."

She fell suddenly down upon the floor.

Tom laughed again and all consciousness dissolved into the sound of his laughter.

He did not see that she had fainted, and went, still laughing, out of the house.

The little scene had raised his spirits. For now that Fanny had come down off her high horse he would see to it that she did not mount again in a hurry. As the afternoon wore on he began to feel more kindly towards her than he had done for a long time. His indignation over her scribbling craze had been but momentary. He should not really mind if she wrote books on the sly. But she must not, in future, give herself such confounded airs. He would keep the manuscript for a little while, tease her, and then give it back to her. But he would read it first, for he was very curious to know what she had written. In a softened mood he returned to supper, three hours later, and met Dr. Harding in the lane.

"Ah, Baines! I was just coming down to see you. They called me in this afternoon, you know, to see to your wife."

"What?" cried Tom. "Good God! Is Fanny ill?"

"Nothing to signify. A fainting fit. But your little maid very sensibly sent round to my surgery. Pray don't be alarmed, my dear fellow. There is nothing to be alarmed about, I do assure you. The pulse is excellent. There is no fever. She was a little hysterical when we brought her round, but . . . ah . . . that was what I was coming to ask you. . . . Has she had a shock of any kind?"

"Not that I know of," muttered Tom, looking sideways down the lane.

"Ah! I thought that perhaps . . . Ladies, you know . . . liable to these . . . highly nervous . . . but this little attack is nothing. You must keep her quiet. I've given her a soothing draught and sent her to bed. You mustn't excite her on any account. I'll look in tomorrow. Possibly . . . ladies . . . it's not unusual . . . young wives . . . but I'll look in tomorrow."

Tom scarcely heard what he said. He ducked his head and squinted sideways, looking so guilty and miserable that Dr. Harding was sure that Fanny must at last have heard something about the barmaid in Keswick. They parted and Tom stumbled into the house. He went into the parlour and stared at the place on the floor where he had last seen Fanny lying.

Janet had put his supper on the table. He sat down when she brought in his beer, but when, half an hour later, she came to clear away, both food and drink were untouched. Reports of this, carried to the kitchen, softened the judgment of the household a little towards him, for it was known that he had left the Missis lying in a swoon.

Once he got up and went to his desk. There was something that he had meant to do. But when he saw the tumbled sheets of Fanny's manuscript he shut the desk again, very quickly. He would have taken it up, there and then, and given it back to her, but the doctor had said that she ought not to be excited. She might be sleeping. He must wait.

At ten o'clock he crept cautiously upstairs, the light of his candle bobbing on the ceiling in front of him. No answer was given to his timid tap. She lay at the extreme edge of her side of the bed, and the frills of her nightcap hid her face so that he could not be sure if she slept. He whispered her name once or twice, but got no answer. Very softly he took off his clothes, blew out the candle, and clambered in beside her. He had meant to lie awake all night, in case she should wake and ask for anything, but trouble had made him drowsy and in half an hour he was fast asleep.

Twelve o'clock struck and one, and two. Silence and darkness pressed down upon the room, on the bed. It pressed on Fanny's eyeballs as she lay staring about her, until it was full of dancing coloured spots. One or twice, after Tom had fallen asleep, a shuddering sob escaped her. But he never moved. And when the clock struck two there was a faint rustling in the room. Fanny had slipped out of bed on to the floor. There were other tiny movements, and a metallic jingle. Tom's keys were being pulled out of the pocket of the coat which he had hung over its accustomed chair. The door creaked.

A ghostly figure stood by the staircase window in the wan light of a setting moon. Step by step she stole down the stairs.

The parlour smelt of cheese and beer, the supper that Tom had not eaten. Closing the door, she struck a light. A candle flame spluttered. Her giant shadow on the wall stooped over the desk as she fitted the key.

Her book lay in a tumbled confusion among Tom's private papers, where he had flung it that afternoon. Shivering and sobbing, she took a little time to sort it out, for the tears kept blinding her and splashing down upon the close-written pages. She counted them. Had she got them all? But no, peeping out from a pigeon-hole, another scrap of writing caught her eye. It looked like hers. Yet it could not be part of the book. It was only a half-sheet. What letters had she ever written to Tom? She pulled it out a little way and held the candle closer. *All my hopes, where'er thou goest, Whither, yet with thee they go.*

"Oh, God!" she whispered. "Oh, God!"

Her tears fell no longer. The shock had put an end to them. She stared at the letter as if she had been an idiot, and the idea that she was betrayed so appalled her that she did not immediately try to identify her betrayer. It was only after many minutes that she began, dimly, to search among possible names. Who had done it? Who had sent the letter to Tom? Harriet Simpson? Emmeline? Beverly himself? Some hidden enemy? And what did Tom know? How long had he known?

She had no scruples. Tom was her enemy and she hated him. She wished him ill. Eagerly she began to search through the desk for any clue that might help her. An inner partition baffled her. No key on Tom's chain would fit it. She fetched from the kitchen a little file and cut through the thin lock. A dusty packet lay within. It was securely sealed, but at the top there was pinned a letter addressed to herself in Tom's clerkly, copper-plated hand, and dated some months earlier. *To my wife, in case of my death.* Caution stayed her hand. Before she broke the seal of the packet, she read the letter:

" DEAR FANNY,

" It is my last request that you should burn this package un-opened. You are too fair, you have too just a mind, not to do as I ask. You will not refuse the last kindness that you can do for me. Be assured that these are not proofs of any disloy-alty to you. I would to God that I had nothing more serious on my conscience than this.

" You must know that before my marriage I corresponded for some years with a lady, unknown to me and in a station of life far above my own. We never met, but the sympathy of our minds drew us together. Some verses which she wrote at-tracted my attention. I wrote to her. She replied. We had much in common. On my marriage the correspondence ended. That is all. But as these letters were written for my eye alone, it is only fair that they should be burnt, unread, when I die.

" Fanny, I wish that I could be certain that you would do this for me. I wish that I could be sure that you would not read these letters. I am a fool not to burn them, but, however that may be, I cannot. They are too dear to me. I will confess all: It is better so, for if, in spite of all that I have said, you do read the letters, there is something that will puzzle you.

" The correspondence was continued, on my side, under false pretences. I assumed a character and a position to which I have no claim. I did this, partly because I feared she would despise me if she knew the truth, and partly because it pleased me to fancy myself as really being the person of whom I wrote. It was folly and I was always ashamed of it, as indeed, I am ashamed of everything else that I do and am. But *she* is blame-less. Her motives, through it all, have been noble and lofty. Despise me if you must; if it is possible that you could despise me more than you do already. But have charity and do what I ask you.

" Your husband,
" T. F. B."

At first Fanny did not believe it. Beverly remained solid. He could not be destroyed like this. She did not weigh the case. She simply rejected it, until confirming circumstances began to assemble themselves and she grew frightened. At the back of the secret partition there was a torn scrap of paper, the rough draft of a letter, and it was in Beverly's crabbed hand. She remembered getting the letter, and the description of the Coliseum by moonlight of which these were the notes. Tom had evidently taken great pains over it. There were notes at the side, in his own hand. And she remembered that he could use his left hand with unusual skill. Very slowly conviction was forced upon her. Astonishment gave place to terror and despair. She saw that Beverly was being taken from her. All faith and hope must go with him. Tom had destroyed everything: he had made her love and her sacrifice alike ridiculous.

When she had lain beside him in the dark she had thought that no human creature could hate so violently as she did. But his cruelty over the novel was nothing. She had forgotten it. This final betrayal made it seem a childish, petty thing. She stood by the desk and prayed that he should suffer. And she came at last to see that her revenge was in her own hands now. She could pay him out. She could make him feel all that she had felt: the ridicule, the humiliating exposure, the loss. She would go upstairs and wake him, where he lay there so securely asleep, and she would spare him nothing. The ghost of Beverly should pursue him to the grave, and after. If he died first she would put those lines on his tombstone! *All my hopes where'er thou goest.* He should remember Beverly whenever he looked into the eyes of his wife. And if the knowledge was a torment to her, it would be death to him. She knew that. A man cannot survive exposure as a woman does, because to the male truth is a more absolute thing. She might get over it in time. But it would be the end of Tom.

Her mouth set in implacable lines, she replaced the package and the letter, shut up the partition and locked the desk. She need not take the letters up with her; she would plan some subtler way of routing him. She would trap him.

On the stairs her candle guttered suddenly and went out. She had been sitting at the desk in the parlour for several hours. But there was a grey light on the staircase. The moon had set and dawn was creeping into the sky. She stole hastily past it, realising the passage of time, frightened at the ghostly premonitions of tomorrow. In the bedroom it was pitchy black. No light got through the heavy curtains over the window. She felt her way across the room that seemed to have grown strangely large. There was no sound from the bed. She listened. She could not even hear his breathing. Tom might be dead for all that she could hear.

She could not speak to him in the dark. She must see his face. And she stumbled across to the window, pulling the curtains wide apart. The luminous greyness of the dawn stole in. It fell on the chairs, the wardrobe, the bed, and on Tom's face where he lay sleeping. In the immobile deadness of the room that face seemed to float like a vision by itself. She drew nearer and looked down at him.

There is upon some sleeping faces a sadness which transcends any grief that the guarded soul can know. Tom's face had that sadness now. The cautious, sidelong gaze was hidden under calm eyelids. The uneasy mouth was still. The whole face was calm, resigned, defenceless. He looked as though he were waiting for the pain which she meant to give him, as if in his heart he had already accepted it.

She thought of his story again, saw it for the first time apart from the injury done to herself. Nothing in his life was now concealed from her. She knew it all — the solitude, the wounded egoism, the thousand small humiliations. (*All my faults perchance thou knowest, all my madness none can know. All my hopes . . .*) She looked into the mind of this man whom she had hated and found that hatred was falling away from her. There was nothing there to hate, and much to pity. A deep sigh escaped her.

She had nobody to love and nobody to hate any more. But love and hatred are the enemies of understanding. They are born and die in an hour, and when one human being is fully revealed to another they disappear. Compassion, terror, these are the only emotions which survive that test.

Fanny sighed again. She got into bed and lay down quietly beside Tom, watching the light grow stronger in the room. Her eyes were vacant and intent, like the eyes of a new-born child looking for the first time at a world where everything is strange.

VARIATION

By

Edward Shanks

NOTE

Mr. Shanks's technique is interesting in his stress upon the essentials only. Notice first what he omits. The reader is not told why Eileen put an advertisement in the paper, nor in what paper she put it; he is not told why Bill answered it, nor how long the correspondence continued, nor why it ceased, etc., etc. He properly calls it *Variation,* in that it has only a general likeness to the plot suggested. Bill has a case of hysterical paralysis. During the first attack he has been helped by an unknown. The story opens with the beginning of the second attack. The horror of the disease is so strong that he attempts suicide. Failing that, he turns to the one that previously cured him, and finds that it is his beloved wife. The credibility of the story, then, turns upon the character of Bill. To have such an attack possible, Bill must be an emotionally repressed individual. His courage, his " nerve," and his self-sacrifice are brought out. The fact that he is happily married and is pleasantly situated with John, who is naturally warmly attached to him, is definitely indicated. But the medical theory back of Doctor Harrison's diagnosis might well escape the casual reader. Since Bill has never told Eileen, both he, and the reader, assume that she does not know. Actually, since she is the unknown correspondent, she has known the truth the entire time. She must have been a superb actress if she could go " gaily in and out of the sick-room " while she was waiting for him to call for her. And her temporizing had nearly fatal results when Bill tried to kill himself for her sake. Common sense would have suggested her telling him that she knew before waiting for so dangerous an extremity. Such criticism as this suggests the liability of this compressed treatment; the asset is that, free from the restraints of the dull exposition, the author has the space to create a pleasant atmosphere.

VARIATION

By EDWARD SHANKS

I

BILL'S cousin, John, had fixed him up very pleasantly in the little gatekeeper's lodge which was now the estate office. The trouble had been to prevent him from doing too much. The walls were gaily coloured and the furniture was new but good. On Bill's desk there stood the bowl of flowers which Eileen never failed to keep replenished from their own garden. Nor were there any signs that Bill had too much or too troublesome work in front of him. There were but few papers on his desk, and those few were neatly sorted and docketed. In the outer room the cheerful clicking of a typewriter suggested sustained but not excessive industry.

Yet a casual stranger who entered the office might well have suspected that Bill was sick of his job and his surroundings. For Bill was sitting back in his swivel-chair with his hands clasped in his lap, and he was frowning savagely at the blotting-pad.

"This young man," the stranger would have said, "is plainly, from his build and his appearance, no lover of an indoor life. Today, with the sun outside, it is getting on his nerves more than he knows how to bear."

And if, after that, someone had told him a little of Bill's past history, he would have been more certain than ever that his diagnosis was correct. Can you expect the great airman, Captain Castle, who did fly the Atlantic and who, in a failure more glorious than any of his successes, almost flew across the Himalayas — can you expect such a man to settle down at his cousin's park gates, as his cousin's estate agent, when he is barely turned thirty?

Tactless people sometimes asked Bill questions like this. But it never occurred to him that they were tactless. He had no difficulty in answering them, and they produced not the slightest ache of regret in his heart. He had a hundred times assured his questioners that being estate agent at Wethering Court was a jolly interesting job. If he had been expansive about his emotions he would have said that it was more like heaven than anything he had ever known.

Even now, with that frown on his brow and the deepening expression of pain in his eyes, he would not have given it any other name. The trouble was that his heaven was horribly threatened, and he did not know whether to tell someone else about the threat would make it harder or easier.

Once or twice he half rose as though to make for the door. Once he put out his hand to the telephone and let it fall again. That way, he told himself, the danger lay. It was two days before, while he was telephoning, that the threat had first made itself apparent. He dared not risk now an action which would make it apparent to the wrong people.

At last he picked up a paper from the table and thrust it into his pocket. He had decided that it would serve as a pretext to fall back on. He might change his mind about confessing before he had reached his cousin's house. Even so much action served at once to relieve his pain, and it was in an almost cheerful voice that he told the clerk in the outer office that he was going up to the house to see Mr. Everard about that matter of the churchyard.

"Very good, Mr. Bill," said the clerk, and then added: "If you're in a hurry, sir, my motor-bike's outside. I shan't want it; I'm not going home for a bit yet."

Bill shook his head hurriedly and murmured something about a fine morning and a bit of exercise. As he went out he shook his head again in answer to his own thoughts. " No, dear me, no! A motor-bike would never do."

The walk along the drive to the great house seemed at one moment interminable, at the next horribly short. Bill wanted to tell his secret to John and to see what John could do about it. He also dreaded that putting it into words would make it nearer and more real.

He had in his pocket the letter which, if his courage failed him, would provide a reason for the visit. Not that, if he had been in a normal condition of nerves, either he or John would have considered any reason, save a desire for companionship and possibly a drink, at all necessary. And John, who was prac- tising in a desultory manner on the little putting green below the terrace, shouted with joy at the appearance of an opponent and relief from solitary boredom.

" They're going in too easy," he cried. " I was getting sick of it. Come and play me all the way round the clock, and if you beat me we'll get out a bottle of fizz."

" And supposing you beat me? " Bill asked.

" Then we'll get out the same bottle," John answered.

At that moment Bill felt that his mind had been made up for him. He could not evade the challenge, and he had no desire to do so. He would do his best, and, if nothing hap- pened — why, then perhaps he had been frightening himself unnecessarily. He would at any rate have postponed the evil day. If, on the other hand, that which he dreaded did happen, the confession would come naturally — or, rather, there would be no need to make it in words.

" Infirm of purpose," he cried with exaggerated boisterous- ness, " give me the putters." And he stretched out his hand.

" It's my honour," John objected, and, when Bill asked why, explained that it was because he was playing so well that morning.

The boast was justified by his first shot, which left him in such a position that only a duffer could fail to get down with the next. "There, my young friend," he declaimed triumphantly, "if you can get a half on that, you'll be putting better than you've ever done before or ever will again."

Bill, much on his mettle, put his ball within three inches of the hole. "I don't mind," John asserted. "You'll only get a half. Nobody but the completest fool in Christendom could possibly miss this — and that, I suppose, is what I am," he added reflectively as he missed with something to spare.

"You'll have to do better than that if you're going to beat me," Bill told him, and addressed himself to the ball. And then, suddenly, without warning, the club slipped from his hands. "That's that," he said firmly, but with drawn mouth. "Putting is just one of the things I shan't ever do as well again."

John's grin was stricken in an instant from his face. "You don't mean . . ." he whispered.

"Yes, I do," Bill nodded. "It has come again."

When he had said that, he felt that John needed help far more sorely than he did and that it was his business to supply it. "Don't take on so, old thing," he said gently. "What about getting out that bottle?"

John's grin returned like a horrible spectre of itself. He turned away and began to yell for Hawkes, the butler, and Bill yelled even more lustily. Presently Hawkes had had his instructions and was returning towards them with the tray.

"By the way, John," Bill suggested, "you'd better send him away quickly. You'll probably have to feed this stuff to me."

But when Hawkes had gone, Bill made the attempt and found that his fingers closed quite naturally around the stem of the glass and that he could raise it to his mouth without difficulty.

" There, you see," John cried unsteadily. " It was only an accident; it hasn't really come back again."

" Not a hope, John, I'm afraid. That's the fifth time since Tuesday — once on Tuesday, twice yesterday, and that makes the second time today. You remember how it came on before . . . a little at a time. . . . Oh, God! Williams wanted me to come up here on his motor-bike. . . . I told him I wanted exercise. . . ." He shuddered.

" Well, what are we going to do? " John asked miserably. " What does Eileen think about it? "

" Eileen? You don't suppose I've told Eileen? She never knew anything about this trouble. I never asked her until I was certain — until I thought I was cured."

" But, my dear old boy," John protested, " you aren't going to tell me this will make any difference to Eileen. If anybody else suggested such a thing, I'd knock his block off."

" You can knock mine off, and welcome." Bill shrugged his shoulders and went on speaking with an effort. " Difference? Make no difference to a girl of nineteen to have a husband of thirty paralysed in both arms, and no particular reason why he should ever get better? I tell you, John, I lay awake all night trying to think up a way of staging a gun accident that would look natural. Best I can do for Eileen, seems to me, is to make a widow of her. But I don't somehow fancy having my hands fail half-way through and just tearing holes in myself. I got to wondering whether you'd do something of the sort for me."

" Good God, Bill," John exploded. " I'll see you damned first."

" That's just about what you will see. If everything else fails, you'll have to help me, and I won't take ' no.' "

John peered at his wonderful, beloved cousin with earnest, short-sighted eyes and could see dreadful signs of strain. The set jaw dragged all the lines of the face, the cheeks had grown thin and paper-white. It was the countenance of a desperate man.

"The only thing I can think of," said John after a long pause, "is to have Harrison up. These little local men sometimes think of things when the specialists can't."

"Get him up if you like," Bill assented. "He's a good little man and he'll keep his mouth shut. Better ring Eileen and tell her I've had to go off somewhere for lunch."

II

It really was not a bad idea to send for Dr. Harrison. He was that best sort of doctor for stubborn patients: he not only confessed the limitations of his skill; he emphasised them. John stared at him with anxious disappointment. Bill, who had reluctantly and wearily given an account of his symptoms, was more appreciative.

"Yes . . . yes, I see." The little doctor nodded gravely. "It came on gradually and it was pretty well established and continuous before you came home?"

"It began just like this," John broke in. "It began in India, before I was out of hospital. You know, that was the damnable thing about it. Bill wasn't hurt when we crashed in those filthy mountains; I was. He was fit enough to get me twenty miles to the nearest village. He carried me in his arms some of the way. When we got to Peshawar, I was put in bed and nearly croaked, and Bill was asked out to lunch-parties. And then——"

"Go on, Mr. Travers," said the little doctor.

"Then it began—just after he was first allowed to see me. As a matter of fact, he was getting me a drink that they said I wasn't to have, and the glass slipped out of his hand just as he was giving it me. He looked frightened, and I told him it was all right; he could sweep up the bits without anyone knowing. Then I got it out of him that the same thing had happened before."

The doctor nodded again and looked at Bill.

" It had happened enough," Bill said, " to scare me a bit. But I didn't tell anyone about it. I didn't know quite what there was to tell. But while we were coming home I got worse and worse, and before we landed both my arms were useless."

" I see. It does happen like that, sometimes. And now it's beginning again in the same way? "

" Do you think it's really coming on again? "

To John's terror-stricken question the doctor gave no better answer than a shrug of the shoulders. " We must just hope it isn't," he said. " Listen, Captain Castle. This is a thing in which no doctor can help you. The springs of it are inside yourself. If you can find them, you can cure yourself. If not —— But I won't tell you that there's anything I can do for you."

" Oh, but there is," said Bill, without expression, as he rose and went out. He was absent for three or four minutes, during which John and the doctor looked at one another.

" He's not ——? " John cried, jumping up.

" Not yet," said the little doctor grimly.

When Bill came back from the gun-room, what they both noticed first was that he was staggering and that his face was much whiter than before. Then they saw that his hands were dripping blood.

" Sorry about your rugs, John," he muttered. " Had an accident —— " He took a step this way and that, and collapsed at Harrison's feet.

" Get him to bed," said the doctor after a period of feverish activity. " He mustn't use his hands for several days. Razor-blade, I suppose. But still . . . you know. That doesn't get rid of the trouble. It's inside him. Can you help him to get it out?"

"I don't know," John said helplessly. "I'm just a fool, you see, Harrison, no good at all. It's really my fault, all this. I was no good on that flight, except buying the machine. And when I think how he carried me in his arms through all that damnable country . . ."

"Don't be sentimental," Dr. Harrison advised. "Ring for your man and we'll get him to bed."

Bill opened his eyes as they were carrying him upstairs and said: "Fell off a wall on a heap of flints. . . . Tell Eileen." Then he seemed to faint again.

III

Eileen, accommodated with a room in John's house but unwilling to use it this night, had just been sent off to her bed by her husband. John fussed with her to her door and then sneaked cautiously back to her cousin.

"Like a bottle, Bill?" he asked in a timid voice.

"No. Is she all right?"

"Right as rain," John answered well-meaningly. "Doesn't give a damn."

"I want those letters, John."

"What letters?" But John knew well enough.

"*Her* letters. You've got them, haven't you? You haven't lost them?" There was a rising anxiety in Bill's voice.

"You don't want *them*. *They* won't do you any good."

"Go and get 'em." Bill was really commanding, and John obeyed. He left the room and returned after a few minutes with a packet of thin typewritten sheets which he threw on the bed.

"Open 'em," Bill ordered. "I want to look at the last one."

John slipped off the rubber band and smoothed out one sheet on the bed under Bill's eyes.

"She said to come to her again if I needed her," Bill remarked absently when he had read a few lines. "It must be on the other side." John turned the paper over. "Yes, there it is. 'You understand why I must stop, but I couldn't if I thought you still needed me. If you do, you'll write again, won't you? But you mustn't unless you do need me.' I suppose she meant that, John?"

"I expect she did," said John sagely. "But a lot's happened since then. She's married and she knows you are. She's grown up a bit by now, I expect."

"She'd want to help, all the same."

"She thought she would then. But she must have been only a kid. Had an elder sister, I suppose, who did the lonely soldier business in the war. That's why she put that advertisement in. She'll have grown out of it now, Bill."

"She told me to write again to the same address if I needed her," Bill persisted. "And you'll have to write for me, just as you used to. Get your typewriter, John."

"It's all foolishness," said John. "I never could make out why you wanted to go into such a mysterious business. Girl gives a false name and makes you give one. Won't know anything about you. And now you're married, and she's married, and that's that."

"Get your typewriter," Bill repeated. And John got his typewriter.

"Here, I say . . ." said John, quite early in the proceedings. Bill was pressing him too hard. Besides, he was, John thought, saying too much. "You're going into details."

"It's my last chance."

John looked once at his cousin, then went on pounding at the typewriter with two fingers of his right hand and one of his left. He said no more except, "That's right," or, "I've got that," until Bill had signalled rather than uttered that it was finished. Then he murmured timidly: "You know, you've told her who you are."

"I don't care," Bill said. "Post that and be damned to you! And give this address for the reply."

John tucked him up and went into the dressing-room till he was sure that he was asleep. Then he crept back and settled himself for the night in the armchair.

IV

During the next three days a stranger might have supposed that it was John whom Fate was threatening. Eileen went gaily in and out of the sick-room and was full of news of baby Cecily. Bill reposed absolute confidence in the magical powers of his unknown correspondent. Only John shook his head sadly from time to time. His view was that Bill had committed a grave disloyalty to his wife, and he didn't know what would come of it. And Bill, able to move his arms quite freely though his hands were still bandaged, merely laughed at him.

It was on the fourth day that Bill began to show some signs of strain.

"It always used to take four days, didn't it?" he asked rather wistfully in the morning.

"I hope she won't write," said John bluntly. "I believe you're all right again. Hold your arms up."

"I tried just now," Bill said, briefly and sombrely. "I say, old man, you'll recognise the envelope, won't you? Take care I get it when — when I'm alone."

"Eileen shan't see it, if that's what you mean." There was bitterness in John's voice, and a long pause followed.

"John, when does the second post come?"

"Some time around eleven, I think."

" Of course, it might have to be sent on to her from the old address."

To this John made no reply.

Bill hesitated a little, then said: " John, old thing, would you mind seeing if the post has come? "

But there was no letter.

And yet the letter came at last as mysteriously as Bill expected it to work on him. He went to sleep in the afternoon, thinking of that once familiar envelope with the name of the newspaper on the flap in which the desired envelope would be enclosed. Once he had looked to that boon once or twice a week, but never with this ache of anticipation.

Suddenly he woke with a feeling that someone had been in the room, someone who had come to help him. He lay for a moment with a sense of benediction about him. Then he saw dimly an envelope lying on the bed. Something odd happened for a moment in his heart. He tried to take it in his swaddled hands, but his arms would not obey him.

" John! " he screamed. " John! John! " He was amazed at his own voice. But there was no reply. He screamed again and then lay back, panting as though he had run a mile. After a little while he scrambled out of bed with difficulty, his arms hanging limply at his sides, and shoved desperately at the bell-push with his shoulder. At last a maid came and he endeavoured to control himself, but the effort was so great that he could only stare at her helplessly.

" Mrs. Castle has gone sir," she said, when he still failed to speak. " She came up, but she said that you were sleeping so nicely she wouldn't disturb you. She told me to tell you she would be here again after tea."

" I don't want Mrs. Castle," he uttered hoarsely. " I want Mr. Travers. Go and find him quickly — please."

" Very good, sir."

When she had gone he rolled over on his side amid the tumbled bedclothes to look at the outside of the letter. Instantly that something odd happened in his heart again, and he began to laugh at himself, loudly, hysterically. He was still laughing when John entered with a troubled expression.

" Look at the damned thing! " Bill chuckled terribly. " God knows where it came from. I thought it was a miracle, and it must be a bill or something. It hasn't even been through the post."

John was bewildered, and not unnaturally, for Bill in his tossings had hidden the letter from sight. But presently he caught sight of a corner of it and inspected it with increased bewilderment.

" Here, where has this come from? " he cried. " I gave orders that all letters for you were to be brought to me first." As he spoke he ripped open the envelope, pulled out a type-written sheet, glanced at it with amazed eyes, and muttered: " But it *must* be a miracle. Look at that, Bill." He spread the sheet before his cousin's eyes.

The letter began, as always, without form of address.

" You know (it said) that I couldn't ever refuse to help you. But did you never think of asking anyone else? And if you'd ever told me exactly what had happened to you, perhaps some-one else could have helped."

" What the devil does that mean? " Bill ejaculated.

" I'm being mysterious (the letter continued), and it serves you right. You've been making mysteries yourself. And didn't this come to you in a way you can't explain? You'll have to wait a moment or two before you understand."

Bill knitted his brows and stared hard at John. Then he went on reading:

" You'll never have any trouble with your arms again. Don't you see, you silly, Billy, that it all comes from the time when you carried John through those hills, and you thought your strength was giving out and that you'd have to put him down, and that he'd die before you could get help for him. That made you, without knowing it, hate your arms for useless things. But they aren't, Bill dear, and you must never again think that they are."

" The devil! " Bill muttered. " I didn't tell her your name or mine either. Turn it over, John."

" When you've read this, get John to telephone for me, and I'll come at once. And I'll bring baby Cecily with me, if you think you can face her after your faithlessness to her mother."

Bill gazed at John again, and for a moment did not speak. Then he waved his arms in circles in the air and peremptorily ordered: " Get Eileen here at once, you gaping old fool! "

BLAME ADAM AND EVE

By

J. C. Squire

NOTE

If the dramatic treatment aims to enable the reader to sympathize emotionally with the characters, another quite different aim would be that of so presenting the facts that the reader understands the motivation of the character. Such a type as this would obviously consist of analysis. In Mr. Squire's mind the interesting feature about the plot was why the characters should conceivably act as by hypothesis they are supposed to do. Granting the initial correspondence, why should two persons, persons such as we all know, ordinary, respectable, humdrum persons, yield to so outré a temptation to commit mental infidelity. The answer is curiosity concerning forbidden fruit. Then, why this cusiosity? To reply to this, there are first four pages of analysis of what is going on in the head of Charles; then a half page of Dorothy's mental processes. Later comes another page explaining her motivation. Consequently the story scarcely comes to the surface, and the climax is "Then they went to tea at Rumpelmayer's." Since this type of work consists in analyses of mental states, it demands high mentality on the part of the reader. Since there is no overt drama, no apparent story, there is no obvious appeal. If the reader is interested in the underlying causes of action, and then only, will he read to the end. In this sense it may be regarded as literary science, a problem carefully and thoughtfully worked out. And that is its appeal.

BLAME ADAM AND EVE

By J. C. SQUIRE

I

THEY sat on either side of the drawing-room fire glooming at it, Charles Cartwright in a dinner-jacket, Dorothy softly gleaming in a pale blue sheath covered with dull spangles. Charles sat bored and staring, with his knotted hands clasped between his knees, the hollow eyes in his strong dark furrowed face, staring straight at the flames; looking every inch of what he was, both an admirable novelist and a man. He was intent, desperate, bewildered but still determined. He did not see the Dorothy who sat there, for he was looking at the Dorothy of his dreams, who had often, though not so often recently, come to life: the Dorothy who had instantaneously impressed herself upon him the very first time he had met her, at a luncheon-party where nobody else seemed to be alive, much less to be living in the light of ideals. A luncheon-table, long ago. A dinner-table to-night. The last words that she had spoken at the dinner-table rang and rang through his head: " I simply can't understand how you can be so understanding as a novelist and so lacking in understanding as a man." " Rather hard-driving of one word," reflected the critic in him, with a twist of the mouth. And then the yearning, tortured mate resumed: " Oh, damn the wretched girl — no, no, I won't even in thought use such a derogatory phrase about the noblest and dearest — why *can't* she see that a man *must* have rules and principles to live up to though he may be ever so compassionate to those who don't recognise them, or break them. Why *can't* she see that one may have all the heart in the world, and still realise that it is one's duty to face the facts of the world, half of which are unpleasant, including most of the facts about men and women. Oh dear," he thought, with a sigh that he kept inaudible, " if only these goats of women would realise what we men are, and what the world is, and what the diversity of the world is, and how intractable are facts, and how we Englishmen have developed our hard faces simply through confronting them, but that we have confronted them from the most chivalrous motives in the world. What the hell," and his face twisted, and she watched it twisting, and she thought it was twisting out of dissatisfaction with her, her cooking, her management, her economy, her little efforts to have opinions of her own, which, after all, didn't matter, " what the hell did *she* know about India and the East."

He checked himself. For that matter, he had never been to India and the East himself, though Ostend, Switzerland and Seville he knew — at least the hotels, the casinos and the sights. But then he checked himself again.

Dorothy also looked into the fire. She did not look so intently as he, but more dreamily. She did not lean forward and stare fanatically; she reclined in her long arm-chair, with an elbow propped on the wooden rest, and her chin propped comfortably on her elbow — a chin as clean cut as the cheeks and brows, which framed the honest grey eyes and were framed themselves by the neat, straight, centrally-parted fair hair. " Why should he," she thought, " go on and on making a song about it? Why shouldn't she think, if she wanted to, that the Bolsheviks might be heralding a better world, that the Germans might be heralding a better world, that women should be allowed to do whatever they wanted to (and, after all, they only wanted to be faithful to a man who wedded them, however their thoughts might wander), and that Mr. Gandhi was a saint? It was on that point, after dinner, that the conflict had come. She had said that Mr. Gandhi was a saint.

And Charles had broken out. Charles had said, "Yes, I daresay he is a saint; but he is a crook as well."

And she had replied: "How *can* you say that he is both a saint and a crook?" And he had replied; but she didn't understand his reply; and he, Charles, reflected on it still, as he gazed into the fire.

Charles Cartwright, still not speaking, gazed into the fire. He could, with his own sex, discuss any subject in the world until late at night: and late at night, under the influence of liquor, both parties would agree that they both meant the same thing and that, at any rate, they were both good fellows. With women, even with the noblest women in the world, it was different. Whatever you said, they always thought you were having a slap at them. "Omne ignotum pro magnifico": a Latin proverb: "everything unknown, people suppose to be wonderful." True enough, but immeasurably truer of women than of men. For himself he preferred old Dizzy's remark: "If you have imagination you do not need experience." The old Jew had made it, being a poet, when young; and had confirmed it, only more so, when old. He hadn't been to the East; but, good God, couldn't one *see* the East? Couldn't one understand that one side of Gandhi was a saint and one side a sophist? Couldn't one *see,* wasn't it *obvious,* that one side was a Tolstoyan and one side a twister? Couldn't one *see,* that for all his charm (not entirely physical) that the ascetic prophet was a fact-dodger, who thought on "I'm sure they'll all love one another" lines, who would not face the untouchables, who would not face the appalling social conditions of Hindu India, who would not face the fact that there were seventy million Moslems who were at loggerheads with the Hindus and, physically, could wipe them out in three months, who would not *see* that things must be gradual, that we began by policing India, that we continued by giving it sanitation, that, in spite of the polo and the pig-sticking, we were involved in a process which might gradually give it Christian and European ideas of honesty, humanity and decent living?

Again Charles heard, though she never spoke, her voice coming in: " You and your silly Christianity! I bet you would have treated Christ just as you want to treat Gandhi! "

He had answered " The cases are not at all parallel. Quite apart from the fact that Christ was God, which I admit though you do not, I never saw a worse analogy. Pontius Pilate, and the washing of hands, and Pontius's wife! The Romans didn't mind Christ: in the end they made him. Do you really suppose that Lord Irwin would have executed Gandhi because the Brahmins had declared him blasphemous? My dear, you rather under-rate the British Empire! "

All that went on in Charles Cartwright's head as, with the muscles of his face growing tenser and tenser, he stared into the drawing-room fire.

But in Dorothy's head, all that went on was this: " Why on earth should Charles grow so angry, just because I said that Mr. Gandhi was a saint and a very nice man? Hang it all, just because one is a man's wife (and of course I admire him and think he's nearly always right) I don't see why one should always agree with everything he says. Besides, I *do* think that a great deal of what Mr. Gandhi says is *quite* right. I simply loathe those dull Anglo-Indian men with their rigid faces, and those hard Anglo-Indian women who (I don't mind betting) do a great deal more behind their husbands' backs than their husbands ever know — there *is* a certain excitement about fair-haired subalterns, although that silly darling old Charles could never, I'm sure, be brought to see it. Mr. Gandhi only says that India should be free. Why shouldn't India be free? Why shouldn't everybody be free? I simply *hate* all these restrictions which have come down to us from the past. I don't want to do anything outrageous, but I simply *don't* see why I shouldn't, if I don't do anybody else any harm."

And Charles thought: " If only she knew our sex." And Charles thought: " Oh, my darling, I must make one more attempt to get into contact with you. I simply can't *bear* that a love like ours — and we have such an awful lot in common — should break up simply because we differ about Gandhi or the Bolsheviks and all those ridiculous things beyond our horizon. And Charles said, impulsively and from the depths of his heart, " Darling."

And Dorothy replied: " Darling," with a certain frigid reservation that still did not quite close the road.

And Charles said: " Darling, it is simply loathsome that we should crash over a mere question of politics. But don't you see . . . ? "

And Dorothy said: " Oh, I'm simply sick of your saying ' Don't you see.' Don't *you* see that, although you may be right and you may be wrong, I want to think what *I* think, and not who *you* think."

And Charles said, looking up from the fire with such pathetic and appealing eyes, his face more finely cadaverous than ever in the firelight, " But, darling, it isn't a matter of what you think or what I think; can't you see that it is simply a matter of what *is*. For instance, what you said the other day about marriage."

" Well," said Dorothy, sheathed in the dress, and looking like virgin Diana in the glimmer of the fire, " what, I should like to know, *did* I say about marriage? "

" It was only this, darling," said Charles, with deliberate mildness, " that you said you didn't see why people shouldn't change their husbands and wives as they do their friends, if they want to."

Dorothy lowered her eyes, and her face looked sulky in the

firelight. "And that's what I *do* think," said she, "if they want to. I only said if they want to."

Charles became even more amicable, deferential even, than before. "But, don't you see, darling. . . ." he began.

"Oh, God," she spat, turning into a scaled snake, "I've had enough of your 'darling.' Why the hell can't you say what you mean instead of beating about the bush?"

He, at last exasperated into strength, at last responded. "Look here, Dorothy," he observed, "I don't very often play the still, strong man, but you've damned well got to listen now." He rose and walked about the room while she lay motionless in her long chair. "If you want to say anything, say it," said she, "I'm used to listening."

"Well," said Charles firmly, "it's just this. I've always loved you, and I love you still."

"Can't that be taken as read," replied Dorothy quietly, "I quite believe it, but it doesn't seem to make any difference. Of course, I know what it is really: you've been annoyed ever since I said I wanted to go out to dinner with the Fritzenheimers whom you can't stand, simply because they are Jews."

Charles raged on at her. "It's simply disgusting that you should say that," he protested, "you know damn well that half my friends are Jews. I know I've said that a lot of the Jews have more feeling for Jewry than for any of the artificial nations, as they think them, of Europe, but you jolly well know that I've never been prejudiced against any decent man because . . ."

"Yes," replied Dorothy, helping herself to a cigarette, "shouting as usual. Isn't it possible for you to discuss anything without shouting?"

Charles also sank, with a prodigious effort, into a chair, and himself produced from a case, and laboriously lit, a cigarette.

" Sorry, Dorothy, if I shouted," he said, " I was simply carried away. But it's a bit rough, isn't it, when a man is trying to talk about things in an impersonal way, to find a woman taking things personally. I happen to hold certain views about this life and the next, realism and the notions of the ideologues as Napoleon called them: I also happen to think that monogamy and chastity are good things, and that most of us men are romantic enough, if only you bloody modern women . . ."

She sprang from her chair, " Now I know — but of course I've always known — what you really think in your heart! " She shot at him forked lightnings of anger and flounced through the door.

Charles Cartwright looked into the fire in a sad, puzzled way. He drank a whisky or two, and then he also went up to his bedroom. They had separate bedrooms: they had both, from the start, believed that married people ought not to interfere with each other. To such an extent had they believed this that they had not even had any children.

II

Dorothy, once more, and for the last time, despairingly, went up to her bedroom: but not to bed. She hesitated for a long time. She had really loved Charles when she first met him, and, in spite of all his maddening faults, she loved him still. But *how* could he be so lacking in understanding of women; *how* could he be so unable to compromise. She herself had no very positive knowledge about the Bolsheviks and Mr. Gandhi: as for the history of marriage, she was quite willing to believe that Charles was quite right when he said that women were damned lucky (why would he always say " damned " ?) to have imposed monogamy upon men, that marriage was invented for women's sakes, and that if she **ever** persuaded him that "affairs" didn't much matter he would go off and have a hundred of them himself. But, why would he insist on calling an affair "adultery"? Look at poor Mrs. Hawkins next door: young and pretty, with a disgusting, fat, drunken husband; why would it be wrong for her to have a lover when all she wanted was love, which she didn't get? When she first met Charles he seemed so different; and now he was so hard and set. She had been captivated by Charles at first sight; but wouldn't it have been better if, after all, she had taken the plunge and met that man, whom she had never met, and who had begged and begged her to meet him?

*　　*　　*　　*　　*

"Box XY2" it had been, in *The Times* Agony Column. Somebody had advertised out of the blue saying that he was lonely, that he only wanted correspondence, and that, as proof of his bona-fides, he would guarantee never to seek a meeting with his correspondent. She had been at home then, a very young matron to her father's prep. school; and, with her heart fluttering, she had answered. A letter had come back, so deferential, decent and inquiring; with the assurance repeated that no meeting was sought. She had replied, giving (as a young woman can, when she knows her ground) a certain measure of consolation. He had replied again thanking her from the bottom of his heart, and talking about books and the world. She, wanting to know about books and the world, had paraded her poor knowledge, and asked, catechismically, for more information. So they had gone on. He never revealed his identity. He never would. He wrote so understandingly — more understandingly than any man whom she had ever met. He talked of flowers and museums; he held before her eyes visions of their visiting museums and gardens together; he, shrinking from women, apparently, talked of what might be if only the world were different from what it was. He wrote " Oh, if . . ." and there was the implication " I dare not, lest both of us be disappointed, though both of us, ephemeral creatures, under the vast mysterious sky, hanker only after love and comfort and a mutual sinking into one another . . . and delight, also, but that as something thrown in, to which one has no claim." And then his letters had stopped. They had stopped at just the right moment. For they had stopped just when she had met Charles Cartwright. So quick, so sympathetic with women, so humorous, so interested in the beautiful, so fond of flowers, so anxious to please and to show her all the museums. If only Charles had been all that he seemed to be — or if only she had taken the extreme step and met her correspondent!

She moved from her chair and went to her desk, her whole soul crying in her, " Can't I have a second chance? Why can't women have a second chance? " It was extravagantly unlikely that he, the unknown, the perfectly sympathetic, the utterly considerate, would still be watching the columns of *The Times*. Even if he was he might have scruples about another man's wife: these men having such a dreadful sense of property. But he might, he might, and this had now got beyond bearing! Why, even this evening, Charles had recommended her to consider the first few chapters of Genesis. He had said: " It would be all right in Eden, where there was no marriage and the fruits dropped off the bough, and the lion grazed beside the lamb. But that myth means something. An even greater poet than Shakespeare wrote it. ' You shall earn your bread by the sweat of the brow,' " Charles had said; and deduced from it, in his maddening, masculine way, the whole structure of civilisation, social and sexual.

Dorothy almost screamed. She *didn't* want to be unfaithful. Besides, she *did* love Charles. But it was *awful* to listen to his theories; and it was *awful* to feel that woman must always be dependent upon man. Working herself up and up, getting more and more into a frenzy, she got to the point at which she said to herself, " I simply *won't* be tyrannised over any more. There was that nice man I corresponded with all those years ago. I've never met another man who would quite understand, but I'm *sure* that one would. Why *shouldn't* I write to him? Why *should* this silly institution of marriage preclude me? Why *should* I be bound by all these wretched vows that men have invented for a world of men? "

III

So she wrote. It was just at the time that he was looking for it. " Elaine " appeared in the Agony Column after all those years; and " Lancelot," after all those years responded. Neither had looked at that column for years; but each resumed the examination of it at the same time. There was a tentative answer and a tentative reply. Ultimately, both parties feeling guilty, and both parties (in point of fact) half resolved to get a slight " kick " out of the meeting, and no more, there was an assignation.

Charles arrived at Sloane Square Station first. He was five minutes early. He almost left. " Why," thought he, " should I be meeting this complete stranger here, probably a governess with eczema, when I've got my darling Dorothy at home, who is worth all the women in the world." Then honour crept in. " Well," thought he, " I can't let a woman down. I promised to meet her here, both wearing red carnations, and here I'll have to be, and stick it out." He became more and more nervous; and then, on the stroke of the hour, he saw walking out of the gangway, wearing another red carnation . . . good God, Dorothy!

Had he not been petrified, he would have run. He could not run. No such impulse came to Dorothy. She walked up to him, as cool as a cucumber, and said " Hallo, Charles, what are you doing here? " His mouth dry, as after a night's debauch, and his lips hardly able to separate, he whispered: " Nothing; I was just meeting a friend. Wha-a-at are you doing here? "

Dorothy replied brightly: " Oh, I thought Ena Waring would be here. She promised to meet me."

They waited for ten minutes. Then they went to tea at Rumpelmayer's. She knew, but she never spoke a word. So, after a longer delay, did he know. Nor did he speak a word. But awake that night, he murmured to himself: " Blame Adam and Eve."

A MINGLED STRAIN

By

STORM JAMESON

NOTE

In Miss Storm Jameson's *A Mingled Strain* the plot becomes submerged in a presentation of the Jew in literary London. In the plot as outlined by Mr. Fothergill there is no suggestion that the father of the hero had lost his money, that the hero himself had been at Oxford, has been politely snubbed in the army mess, wrote poetry for money, etc., etc. Likewise in the plot no such characters as Emilia Meindl, or Mrs. West are indicated. From the point of view of Mr. Fothergill's conception, such incidents and such characters are irrelevant. Yet the moment the emphasis is laid, not upon the story, but upon the character of Josef Meindl, the Jew, each factor falls into place. The main theme is that of race consciousness. Josef's grandfather had lived for fifty years in London without becoming part of it. And his grandson was also isolated. His mother made his world. He had *one* friend, killed early in the war, and one legacy, his friend's Helen. The figure is built up touch by touch of a shy, sensitive, lonely soul. So comes the futility of his life, Rose's delight in torturing him, Mrs. West's frigid culture, and the final collapse of his dream. Then the race consciousness asserts itself, and the inheritance from the long line of Siegfrieds, Josefs, and Sigmunds transforms him from Josef Meindl, romantic and selfish lover of one woman, into the Josef Meindl whose function it is to perpetuate his race. As from this angle Rose's torture and Mrs. West's culture are both non-essential, he accepts his situation and is happy in his dreams. *A Mingled Strain* is not so much a story, as it is a psychological study of a man isolated by his inheritance. The aim of the author is to make you comprehend, and by comprehending, sympathize. The limitation of this type of work is obviously that it requires a reader with an analytical turn to enjoy it, and it requires careful reading; no loitering here! But the right reader finds in it ample compensation.

A MINGLED STRAIN

By Storm Jameson

BEGIN with the man himself, with the blood — part Jewish, part German-Austrian. Josef Meindl's grandfather remembered the high flat house in the Stern-gasse, sunlight on moving water, and the light from a row of lanterns falling through leaves onto a café table. He lived in London for fifty years without acquiring any image clearer than his image of these things. He described them often, to his wife, the Cockney girl he married, and to his eldest son. When he died it seemed as though they were forgotten, since Siegfried Meindl never once spoke about them to his own son. Perhaps he was ashamed. He may have thought of the Stern-gasse as shabbier than it was, and the family had prospered. Young Josef played in Kensington Gardens under the eye of a starched Methodist nurse, whom he respected but did not like. He liked Kensington Gardens. One day in autumn he stood so long staring at a bush covered with glittering drops that she came over and stood beside him. There was nothing to see and she told him in her sharp voice to run about and keep himself warm. He obeyed her at once; he was a good-natured little boy, and handsome in his Jewish way. He was not strong and did not go away to school. His first contact with the outer world was Oxford. He had expected to be happy there, and was. He made a friend, and in his Christmas vacation he discovered London, for the first time in nineteen years. With William Dampier he dined gloriously in cheap restaurants in Soho: five courses and a pint of 'claret' for two and nine-pence (including tip). Because William was poor, and stiff about it, he pretended that his father kept him very short. They stood in a queue for the pit, admired the same actress, read the same books, and quoted the same poems. When the war broke out they presented themselves on the same day but though William was taken he was left. It took him a year, and a number of rebuffs, to persuade a sergeant of the Loamshires that he was worth shooting. By then William had been dead six months.

He had inherited from William the idea that he ought to see the war through as a private soldier, but his mother broke him of that, and he applied for and was given his commission in the Loamshires. In September 1916 he was drafted to one of the regular battalions in France. His first moments in the mess put him in his place as a Jew. Later, someone discovered that he was only three removes from a German, and the discovery did him no good. Early in the New Year he was wounded and went home. When he was ready to go out again he was posted to one of the new battalions. He was more comfortable here, found time and heart to write poetry and saw some of it in print, but made no new friend. A scar had formed over the memory of William.

The war changed him: outwardly, from a handsome youngster to a haggard man, thin and lined; inwardly, from child to poet. During the war his father died suddenly. Supposed rich, Siegfried Meindl had made so many mistakes since 1914 that his widow found herself left with two hundred a year. She sold the big house, paid his debts, and retired with an incomparable dignity (she was a Jew) to three rooms. Josef, she said, would start in business as a wool buyer with her brother. Josef agreed. He worked hard to learn a new trick, fourteen hours a day, and wrote poetry at night. His thoughts were of the war, of William, of Kensington Gardens in snow. He wrote of these different things with longing and a bitter gaiety that was quite natural to him and seemed affected. The

second small volume of *London Sonnets* made him a name
and some money, which other literary men said was due to
his being a Jew and 'traditional.'

He met Rose Evans in the restaurant where he and William
had always dined. Since then it had changed hands and name
and become fashionable, and as he stared at it he was recalling
lines he had read that morning:

> *Well, Alphonse; well, Madame; well, Marguerite,*
> *They've no more use for us in Wardour Street.*

His glance rested on the young woman at the next table. She
was looking at him with so clear an air of appeal that he went
over to her directly and she told him that she had just missed
her purse. He paid the bill for her and took her home. She
was a journalist, living in Bloomsbury. He fell in love with
her on the way there, with her eyes and her hands, both very
beautiful. Afterwards he walked about Battersea all night,
thinking of the shadow below her throat and her rounded
body. They were married within the month. His mother did
not like Rose but she accepted her at once and ordered him
to be kind to his wife. She meant faithful, and he began by
destroying the boxful of letters from William's girl. He had
not seen her and he did not know her name; he called her
Helen. Their correspondence, begun after William's death and
through his sister, had been the only outlet for all the emotions roused in him by the death of his friend and the war.
He told her everything about himself, about the French Jewess
who comforted him on his first leave, about his fears before
a raid and the agony of relief when it was over; he sent her
his first poem about the war, and wrote — to be sent to her
when he was killed — a long wild letter about her and William and himself as a triad of true lovers. Although it was
never seen by her this absurd letter heightened the physical

barrier between Helen and himself. He did not try to remove it.

In the last year of the war he reached a stage of disillusion and bitterness about it and about the waste of men and time which left marks on him. He avoided any experience that did not promise a painless and definite conclusion. It was better to think as little as possible, to work hard, and to write poetry only at night. His splendid vitality, the Jew in him, came to his help here and he found that he could live comfortably on three hours' sleep a night. He evaded Helen's invitations: after a time she ceased to offer them but the letters went on. Her deeply spiritual symphony and comprehension had become necessary to him. He had written to her about the first meeting with Rose.

He felt a sharp sense of guilt when he was burning her letters and hurried away to Rose. She let him stay the night. They would be married in a day or two, she said. He might stay if he liked. He was grateful, for her kindness, and for her calm way with him. She was calm and passionate. It was a month or more before he discovered that she was also jealous, extravagant, and lazy.

His uncle had doubled his salary when he married but it was soon inadequate to the demands she made on it. She spent recklessly. When he spoke to her about it she said she had always imagined that Jews made a great deal of money but she realised now that all they did was to save it. She would not entertain the literary men and women with whom his poetry had brought him acquainted because, she said, they were his friends, not hers. For the same reason she refused to go to their houses and was stonily jealous when he went without her. She was jealous of every woman, convinced that he would be unfaithful to her if the opportunity offered itself. To hear that he had spoken to any other woman put her in a passion of suspicion and rage. She was especially jealous of his mother, but Emilia Meindl awed her by her fine unassumed dignity, and she waited until the old lady had gone before loosing her suppressed fury on Emilia's son.

He had an immense slow patience with her. To him she seemed a child, to be treated as a child. He spoiled her. Everything she wanted he gave her, sitting down night after night, when he came home from the office, to make the extra money she asked for. He wrote articles and reviews, read for publishers, translated German novels. He never stopped. He grew thinner and more haggard, his clothes shabby, his black hair falling lankly. He did not mind the work. Some impulse in him was perfectly satisfied to go on working for a beautiful capricious child. Only he knew how beautiful she was. When he came to bed and took her in his arms she was compliant and eager, warming and comforting his tired body. And she wept when she had behaved very badly and begged him to forgive her, her slender body shaken with sobs and her face desperate, appealing. He forgave her at once. It was quite easy.

One Sunday afternoon they had been to Richmond. The grass in the Park was wet but Rose pranced over it, the fur collar of her coat pulled up round her cheeks, her long thin legs seeming to twinkle as she walked. She was gay and very happy. Meindl looked from her to the thin young birches, naked against the sky. He felt a thrill of joy and pleasure quickening in his blood, an exquisite happiness. The rhythms of a song, gay, simple, and proud, like an air by Purcell, began to form themselves in his head. He trudged beside her through the long grass, which soaked him to the shin bone, hands thrust in his pockets, head dropped.

As they walked back to the Park gates they passed Mrs. West, wife of the editor of the *Critic*: he took his hat off with a quick smile. He liked Mrs. West, and the smile changed the character of his face, from the tragic-eyed poet to the boy, the friend of William. Rose noted this, as she noted everything he said, looked, and did. Over tea, in the conscientiously seductive café in the High Street, she charged him with being in love with Mrs. West. Her eyes blazed and the hand lifting the teapot trembled. She spoke in a low voice, with a smile. Anyone watching them would have supposed a friendly if ill-assorted pair, she fresh and lovely, he stooped, an old-young man, with worn face and hands.

" Don't be foolish," he said gently.

" You smiled at that woman as though you were her lover."

" I smile at everyone in the same way. I know quite well that I have a charming smile. I use it. All these people, wives and daughters of editors, are useful to me."

" How? " she asked, in a louder voice.

" They help to make me — as a man of letters," he said patiently. " They help to keep me in the swim. You know what that is worth as well as I do. Nothing to me — when I am writing a poem. Everything, when I come to sell it."

Rose looked at him. " You put a price on everything."

" Of course I do. I write poetry because I like to, in a way because I can't help writing it, and then I take a great deal of trouble to make myself heard. Why not? Why is it proper for a novelist to want to sell his books to as many people as possible and improper for a poet to feel the very same wish? "

" You think about it like a Jew. Ikey Mo sells his poems."

" You would be surprised," he said unmoved, " how hard many writers who are Christians work to secure attention for their books."

" Is that what you are doing when you sidle up to your Mrs. West? "

" Partly. I like her. She's kind and a good sort."

" She praises your poetry," Rose said swiftly.

Meindl smiled at her. " Her husband reviews it."

" If you knew what I think of you when you show off like that —— Perhaps you don't care what I think. But your dear friend William once told you what *he* thought about literary back-scratchers. And now you're one."

His face had changed as she spoke. " Who told you what he said? "

" You told me yourself."

" I don't remember."

" Well, where else could I have heard it? "

He did not say anything. What was there to say? He supposed that he must, at one of those moments when she showed herself everything he wanted her to be, have told her more about William than he remembered. And she had remembered it especially, with that uncanny precision she had in choosing what would most hurt him. She knew him too well. No one, not even William, understood him so clearly, with so sure and delicate a sympathy. Her sympathy with him was, you may say, purely a matter of technique. What, by its means, she divined about him, she made use of to hurt and punish. There was never anything random in her thrusts. She knew perfectly how, where, and the weapon. And how to comfort him afterwards.

It is hard to say which gave her the sharper satisfaction. She would torment him with complete callousness for hours and then, as if some point of satisfaction had been reached, would melt suddenly into pity, with every emphasis of passionate love.

They finished their tea, Meindl silent under her gibes, and went home. She followed him upstairs to the door of his room. He was going in when she caught at his arm. " Josef! "

" Well? "

"I'm sorry."

He leaned against his door, and smiled a little. "Well, it doesn't matter."

"Oh it does, it does!" Tears sprang to her eyes. "I ought not to have brought your William into it. You must forgive me."

Meindl looked at her blankly. "Certainly I will," he said with a vague smile. His glance shifted from her face to some point on the wall behind her shoulder. Then he turned round and went into his room, shutting the door. She stood and stared at it, surprised and incredulous. She could scarcely believe that he had snubbed her.

She went away to think about it, and in doing so made her first serious mistake with him. For once she failed to understand him. All her suspicions fastened on the brief episode with Mrs. West. She had never seriously believed in her accusations even when she was making them. With a sense of loss and amazement she faced the thought that they might be justified. He might really be in love with Mrs. West. "He is," she said, trying the sound of it, frightened.

Real terror made her lose her head. She began telling other people that he was in love with Mrs. West. She told his mother. Emilia Meindl was very cold with her: she said that if it were true Josef was very naughty and she would speak to him, but — she shrugged her upright old back — what could you expect, with a man, and a young man? "Josef is only twenty-six," she said thoughtfully.

Rose was startled. She had forgotten her husband's real age. He looked so much older. After a time, she grew certain that he was carrying on with Mrs. West, and every evening when he came home she flew at him with taunts and questions. She really made his life unbearable at this time. And always, because the two thoughts were connected in her mind, she left off vexing him with Mrs. West only to pick up William, and behave in the same way with him. She had gathered from somewhere a very accurate account of William — how he looked and how he laughed, lifting his upper lip. She invented things he might have said, so apt and wounding that in the end Meindl was certain that William had really said them and that he himself had betrayed them to her. To escape this form of punishment — worse than any other — he began to stay away from her. He told her lies to account for himself, and because he had always told the truth she believed them, though she pretended she saw through him. He took to going straight from the office to dine with friends, certain, since Rose declined to know any of them, that she would never hear of it. Naturally he met Mrs. West at these dinners. With as much nature he became conscious of a subtle relation between them, created by Rose's words and hints and imaginings. He found himself looking closely at the woman to whom Rose had given him. The closer he looked the more and more closely he was aware of her and she, at last, of him. They drew slowly together.

She was surprised and moved by his interest in her. A woman of forty-seven, her husband a dusty lion among critics, she had rarely been without lovers. She had a reputation for beauty, created in the first place by all those young writers to whom she had given work and praise and a delicate patronage. She wrote, too, careful subtle books in which every word was beautifully selected and placed. Only it did not matter whether they were said at all. She was now more than a little faded but her long pale face, the nose slender, the eyes wide and vague, had a certain air. A trifle arrogant, even a little vacant, but still an air. She was a little short-sighted, which gave her a peering look, like a large tired bird. And she believed in herself and in her husband and in the supreme importance to literature of the *Critic* and its young men and all their works. That actually the *Critic* could not have been kept going without the money left her by her father (a hearty vulgar draper) shocked her dreadfully when she remembered it. She tried not to remember it, and by a gradual refinement of her mind contrived at last to eliminate all memory of the old man's gross cheerful face and voice. She herself had a long lean flat body, and she was never able to believe in the literary merits of a plump man. One of the first things she had noticed in Meindl was his haggard frame.

They became lovers almost by accident. A wet afternoon, Mrs. West bored and a little afraid of her reflection in a mirror, and Meindl racked by a fresh quarrel with Rose. They glided into it over China tea and rusks. He was a little surprised by her kind and experienced response and soothed by her gratitude. She was genuinely grateful. He had restored her self-confidence and she felt a familiar pride when she viewed herself and her lean lightly mottled flanks before putting on her clothes. There and then she determined to raise Meindl to a more eminent position among the reviewers of the *Critic*.

He was still innocent enough to be a little surprised by his success. Also, he was a kind creature. The ardour shown by this faded woman touched him. He guessed how it was with her and he was anxious not to hurt her. And not to spoil her vision of herself as the delicate-souled writer and woman condescending to a young man. Endymion and the moon. The moon had long melancholy limbs and a peering face. He thought she must have been rather lovely as a girl, before she acquired the slightly dusty look that comes of living always in a London room with draped windows and too much tobacco smoke and intelligent conversation. Oh those conversations, so good, so unemphatic, and so completely meaningless.

Meindl wearied terribly of them. He began to imagine William leaning against one of the windows with that comical air of impatience he wore when things bored him. William looked at him and laughed: " It smells so like death in here," he murmured. " But it's you who are dead," Meindl said sadly. At which William laughed more than ever, shaking his head: a lock of his hair fell across his face, smooth and young with laughter. " Oh no, oh no."

" Oh no," Mrs. West said gently. " I can't agree. A book should be —— "

She went on in her consciously quiet voice, with her explanation of what a book should be, not realising, or oblivious of, the fact that a book can only be what it is, if it is alive at all: there is no infallible rule. Almost everyone in the room agreed with her. Meindl, who had missed the beginning of the argument, listened in silence. Afterwards, when he was alone with her, he tried to console her for having mislaid her youth in this withering atmosphere. He was wonderfully considerate and gentle with her, trying to warm her back to life with the warmth in himself. There were immense reserves of warmth in him, from the sun beating down on the little café at the corner of the Stern-gasse. He drew her towards these, hoping to revive in her the little spark of life there might still be in the depths of her nature. But it was no use. She did not know that she needed to be revived. She still thought of herself as conferring a great gift on this haggard young Jew poet, with the tiresome wife, and hugged to herself the thought that she was still beautiful, still able to enjoy the most refined and exquisite sensations, still alive.

He was kind, honest, and inexperienced. But when the practical advantages of an affair with Mrs. West began to show themselves he was not slow to seize them. He accepted the position of literary editor of the *Critic*. The salary was not to be sneezed at, the duties were unexacting — the *Critic* was a monthly, and he could do all the work in the evenings and one or two afternoons during the month — and the authority it gave him was very useful at this stage in his career. He saw all these benefits in the moment when Lionel West, worked on by his wife, offered him the job, and gratitude to Mrs. West swelled his throat. At the same time he realised that he must establish himself on a surer basis than her special interest. That would come to an end. He could not go on for ever trying to make up to her for having died of culture. Besides, she did not know she was dead. He worked hard to make himself indispensable to Lionel West, and laid mattresses everywhere, to break his inevitable fall. Under all his real kindness and gentleness and honesty lay his profound sense of the reality of life. Nothing endures but what can be touched and grasped. Even that is dissolved by death. The final basis of his life was this deep sadness. It underlay everything else, older even than the material and sensational bases of his thought. It impregnated all he wrote, even the wit and gaiety of his early poems is tinged with this indefinable pain, the immediacy of his knowledge of death.

All this time, what did he think of Rose? He was being unfaithful to her, precisely as she had always said he was and with the very person she suspected. He did not feel guilty. He felt that she had brought it on herself, by her attitude to him. He did not want her to be unhappy. He took every precaution to keep her from finding out. If he had been compelled to choose between her and Mrs. West he would not have hesitated for a moment. He loved Rose. But, except in bed, she was an intolerable companion. He did not expect her to change. Nothing changed. An illusion of change could be produced by shifting one's own position with regard to a thing

or a person. He had shifted his with regard to Rose. He was
still in love with her, but she was no longer the only woman
in his life. She was one of two. By just that much he was free
of her.

He owed this freedom to Mrs. West. After a time he began
to realise the possibilities in his freedom. He had cut himself
off from Helen, from what had once seemed a spiritual necessity, because he felt he owed it to Rose. He wanted Rose to
possess all. She had in effect refused the gift.

It was not with any idea of punishing her that he had
turned to Mrs. West, but at the bidding of the frightful hunger he had endured ever since William died. Rose had not
tried to satisfy it. Mrs. West could not. He began to think that
the woman he had sought in both these women, in Rose first
and then in Mrs. West, was Helen herself. Whom he had
never seen. Helen. The cries of lovers, the songs made by
poets, echoed through his brain. He cleared them out and sat
down to write to her. He offered no excuse for his long silence. He told her he was married but he said nothing more
of Rose and nothing about Mrs. West. When he had finished
the letter he had time to wonder whether the old channel was
still open. It must be. He wrote " Helen " on the envelope
and put it inside another, addressed to William's sister in Scotland, and sent it off. When it had gone he felt a lightness in
his limbs like a return of youth. Poetry, which had been dor-
mant in him for many months, sprang like an unsealed fountain through all the tiny nerves of his mind. He began the
composition of the long sequence of poems on his friend
which appeared under the deliberately noncommittal title of
Songs for William. Three of them were written in the two
days when he was expecting an answer from Helen. It did not
come. There were a dozen reasons for the delay. William's
sister was away. Helen was away, doubtful of him, ill. He was

not much worried. Not for a moment did he cease to expect the answer.

On the sixth day after he had written his letter he came home from the office early in the evening. As he walked up the path to the house he glanced at the French windows of Rose's sitting-room and saw her there, seated, turned away from him. He saw the line of her hair and cheek and her lovely wrists, bent backwards. He stepped on the grass and walked towards her silently. The door of her room opened and a servant came in with letters. He saw her choose one from the pile, open it, and take out the other letter addressed to Helen. He was close enough to her now to see both the superscription and the writing. Without thought he stepped quickly aside, away from the window, and stood for a moment against the wall. Then he went away without entering the house.

He went to his club and sat down in the window to think. Outside, the buses went up and down past the Green Park. The trees were bronzed and dying, burnt by the sun. Here London smelled of dust, sun, petrol, and cigars. He stared and saw nothing.

His mind groped after explanations. William's sister knew he was married and had sent the letter to his wife in malice. Or Helen had sent it, to punish him.

Neither explanation was any use, because he had known, as soon as he saw the letter in her hands, that she was Helen. He tried saying it. " Rose is Helen."

Old Smithson, dozing by the fire, turned in his chair. " What did you say? Oh it's you, is it? Were you speaking? "

" No, sir." He got up, smiled, and went out of the room. Old Smithson watched him in drowsy annoyance. A poet and a Jew. The club was going downhill fast.

Meindl left the club. He walked quickly. His wife's face, as she looked at the letter addressed to Helen, moved closely behind his eyes. He saw every inflection on it, of surprise, recognition, and triumph. The triumph stayed. He saw the faint beginnings of a smile on her full lips. Every circumstance that related her to Helen rushed through his mind at once, leaving him bruised and conscious. In the same moment his passion for her left him. He had never wanted to take Helen into his arms. It was Rose he loved, the wasteful passionate child. Who, no more than Helen, existed, except in his mind. Emptied of passion, he saw clearly the strange subtle mind of the woman he had married, neither Rose nor Helen, but a complex meeting of both natures, of the one that punished and the one that understood him — and rejected them both. Neither of them was his woman. He would never go back there.

He had walked without thinking and now he saw that he was approaching his mother's house. His thoughts took another turn. He would never be able to tell his mother why he had left Rose. The truth would only vex and bewilder her. If he told her that Rose was an intolerable woman she would look at him fiercely and tell him to remember his duty. And so she did. She listened to his truthful account of Rose's tempers and extravagance, and told him to go home and keep her in order.

"You married Rose to please yourself," she said. "How dare you, sir, come here and tell me she is a bad woman? Be off back to her at once."

"Very well," he said submissively.

She kissed him, standing stiffly, her back as straight as a girl's, to wave him out of her room. No weakening for Emilia Meindl in anything that touched a duty.

When he left her he did not know whether he was going to obey her or not. He slouched across Battersea Park, avoiding the strolling evening couples. A thought that had been lying in wait halted him briefly at the turn of the path. He faced it without effort. He was not shocked by the thought that he had married William's girl. Someone would have married her. And it was right, certainly, that William's friend should get the children that William had not had the time to get when he was killed. A new aspect of his marriage confronted him. One of those subtle transformations, wrought upon a nature from within, took place in him. He ceased abruptly to be Josef Meindl, romantic lover, and became the mind-piece of old Franz-Josef Meindl and goodness knows how many Siegfrieds, Josefs, and Sigmunds, kind and ruthless patriarchs, to whom marriage for the poor trivial purpose of enjoying one woman rather than another was inconceivable. Marriage was for security and the perpetuation of seed. This was something he had always known and had been able to forget. He accepted it with profound and incurious satisfaction.

He knew precisely what Rose would do now. She would not confront him with the letter to Helen. She would wait, watching the growth in him of anxiety and disappointment, until the ripe moment for crying: "I was Helen, you fool. Now you know." He smiled without malice. The moment would never come. By now it was overpast and poor Rose would wait and wait, for nothing. In the end she would lose confidence and muff it. He was nearly sorry for her.

He began to run through the drifting dusk, waving his arms. The amazing truth broke on him as he ran. In the end, Rose-Helen was not his Helen. The identification was not complete. Helen had been. "Helen is," he said. Still in her own place and time, awaiting a poet. Countless images of her pressed upon his mind. Among them faintly obtruded the image of Mrs. West and of herself with her. He grinned.

> *Scaramouche et Pucinella*
> *Qu'un mauvais dessein rassembla. . . .*

He ran the faster, leaving out of sight a baffled Rose-Helen and a faded Pucinella. William's laughter, Helen's smile, possessed his imagination to the exclusion of all other sights and sounds. "William," he exclaimed. "Helen." And "How happy I am."

THEY THAT SIT IN DARKNESS
By
Rebecca West

NOTE

If *A Mingled Strain* may be considered as a psychological study of a man isolated by his inheritance, so Miss West's solution, *They that Sit in Darkness,* may be regarded as a pyschological study of a man isolated by his environment. The two stories should, therefore, be carefully compared. Since the position of the Jew is familiar, Miss Storm Jameson needs but little space to develop it; but Miss West is faced with a most difficult and delicate problem. She must make us understand how a man can both know intellectually that he is a fraud and yet emotionally believe in his own tricks. Consequently follows the long detailed account of the mediumistic household. Of the twenty-two pages, seventeen are used to give this background. Unless the reader understands that the circumstances of George Manisty's life were such that the ordinary rules do not apply, his tragedy will leave him cold. For this reason Father and Momma are elaborately presented, and George's "vocational training," and his father's pride in his skill, and his triumphs as a boy medium are clearly stated. Then the utter loneliness of his life drives him to the relief of an anonymous confession. He knows he cheats, but yet there was also " a magical transfusion of matter, a sieve-like quality of this world that let in siftings of eternity." It is the sense of this that makes him fall in love with Ivy Bentham, and it is his sense of this that brings about the catastrophe. His faith in this medium-wife makes him write the letter, and his love for his fraudulent wife keeps him from reading her answer. Without the elaborate preparation the success of the story could not have been achieved. As it is, *They that Sit in Darkness* is a triumph of construction. Each of the earlier scenes gives its quota of information to enable the reader fully to appreciate the relief of the " trapped creature that feels at last kind fingers loosening the spring on its leg." Momma's miserable life, her exposure, and her drinking are motivating forces, and almost the last words are " Poor Momma." It will repay careful analysis.

THEY THAT SIT IN DARKNESS

By REBECCA WEST

GEORGE MANISTY had a fine head, and so his father had had before him; pale, shining grey eyes which long vision made look at once blind and all-seeing, fine brown hair dusted with gold which seemed blown back from his high white forehead, a mouth which even when he felt most completely at repose was compressed as if under discipline by pain, a pointed chin which, because of this long vision, he carried high and thrust out so that he had an air of fastidiously disdaining the world. As he was chronically tubercular, his tall body was very thin and his skin glazed with a luminous pallor; and he was racked by temperatures which took him up to peaks where he sparkled and crackled with what was surely more than human vitality, and dropped him down into abysses where he lay spent and panting, virtue having gone out of him. So it had been with his father. They were alike even to the long blue-white fingers, so supple that they could all or each be pressed back till the nails lay against the sparse flesh of the wrist. And they were alike in trade. Each earned his living by communing with the dead.

It followed therefore that George Manisty had never known any but those who communed with the dead, or who desired to do so. His home had always been a villa in South London, the last of a road which a speculative builder had long ago led out to the open fields in an orgy of unjustified faith in the fecundity of Londoners. It was very quiet. Long grasses grew in the ruts outside its gates, and four out of the nine neighbouring houses lacked a tenant. It was also very dark. The round butt of a steep hill, blackened with clumps of gorse, stopped the afternoon sun; and as if that were not enough the builders had encumbered all the ground floor rooms with verandahs, and had brought the slated eaves low over the upper storey windows. Yet it was not quiet and dark enough for the Manistys. It was their habit to sit in the basement, very often with the shutters fastened to keep out the nearly imperceptible noises of this limbo between town and country.

There was a breakfast room down there which they used during the hours the daily servant was there. When the winter mornings were dark she would ask, "Shan't I bring in a candle?" but Francis Manisty always shook his head, and when Momma had been well enough to get up she used to exclaim in pious horror, "Snakes and ladders, no!" There was too much of this light, so damaging to their special talents, lying about uncageable in the open streets. They had no need of it for reading the papers for that they never did; the deeds of the living had no interest for them. But they chattered perpetually of the deeds of the dead, and a world where these were the ghostly small-talk. "Met Jenkinson in the Underground coming home. He's going to Cardiff next week, so I told him all that I was telling you about that old woman whose Father called his horse Bucephalus and goes all gooey if you fetch the old man up and get him talking about it. And when I told him I was going to York he spilt quite a lot. It seems there's a chap up there called Sprott whose wife died when he was at the war — here, George, you listen to this . . ." and George listened for probably there would be a sharp question when he got in from school in the late afternoon, "Now, George, what was I telling you this morning about a chap named Sprott? And where did he live?"

For they would still be talking about the dead, though by that time they would have moved into the kitchen to do it. It was nice there. Mother would be sitting at the table, at her elbow the bottle out of which she had to drink so often because her heart was bad, and she would be looking warm and mellow and pretty. In the house she wore her hair in fat brown sausage-curls tumbling over her shoulders, just as she had been wearing it when she and her Pop, Ira Wickett, the celebrated medium of Palmyra, New York, who had learned to make raps from the Fox Sisters themselves, had found the young English conjurer sick of a fever in a Pittsburgh hotel. Since the glow from the kitchen-range and the gas-jet disguised the puffiness under her eyes and made an agreeable flush of the bluish venous smears on her cheeks, and her bulky body was obscured by the shadows of a big basket chair, she might still have been a young woman of rich beauty.

Meanwhile Father would be cooking chops or steak or fish for high tea in a frying-pan that sent up a curling incense of onions, and little George was set to make toast and founder it with a good block of beef dripping; and usually there was a glass dish of tinned fruit in syrup. After Father and George had cleared the table they would sit down to lessons: not the lessons the boy had brought from school. Since they dealt with the world of the living they were unprofitable to him. The lessons he had to learn now were in the nature of vocational training. " That's the ticket, that's the ticket," Father would say. " You slip the wedge in between the slates and write — and talk, talk quick! Then if the pencil scratches they don't hear it. That's right — keep going — when you're at a loss cry out loud and happy — ' I can feel them! Oh, they're so close the blessed spirits! ' With a little catch in your breath. That's done already is it? Ah, whose fingers has my boy got? You won't disgrace your dad! " So the whole evening went by, all diligence and praise. Momma used to sit quietly, saying sometimes, " I heard you move then, honey," but sinking deeper and deeper into a drowse, until she no longer took any more doses

from the bottle at her elbow. For half an hour before his bed-
time the gaslight was turned out, so that he could put into
practice what he had been taught. Then his Father came into
his own, his voice became sweet and strong and charged with
ecstasy, and George glowed with a junior version of his pride.
They could feel the manual and vocal tricks cohering together
into a presentation that they laid before an invisible audience,
they knew themselves priests and creators.

It was not so nice when Father was away. Momma had only
one accomplishment, the making of raps; but that she taught
him thoroughly. They would sit in the dark kitchen together
while the tap-taps travelled round the kitchen along the skirting and up one side of the fireplace, like a question, and then
went across the mantelpiece and down the other side of the
fireplace, like an answer, or made the table quiver under the
fusilade, or even the chairs beneath them. " Make 'em ring,
honey, make 'em ring out like bells! " she would exhort him,
and cry out, " That's Momma's boy! " when he got the right
hopeful resonance. But after a certain hour she would forget to
teach him, and would pass into a delirium of tapping, rocking
to and fro in her basket chair, and making the kitchen echo till
it seemed the house must fall in on them, while in her rich yet
flat voice she sang hymn after hymn, freshening the tone every
now and then with a dose from the bottle. In the end, as always,
she fell into a drowse; and it was difficult work shaking her
awake so that she would go to bed. Sometimes, indeed, she
would not let herself be roused and would only settle herself
deeper in the basket chair, chuckling, " Run away to bed,
honey, and let Momma rest till she feels better."

It was not so nice, and it happened more and more frequently. For it was not often now that the Manistys could
work at him. Occasionally, especially on Sundays, they
mounted to the rooms above, and were very busy dusting the

aspidistras and the glass æolians that dangled at the doors, taking the pleated papers out of the grates and lighting fires, until Father looked at his watch and said, " They'll be here in five minutes if they found old Parkyns' fly at the station. Better begin." Then Momma and George would stand by the harmonium and sing " Let Us Gather by the River," while Father swayed over the keyboard, milking the melody out of the keys with his long supple fingers, until the crapey widow or the palsied old gentleman had infirmly descended at the gate. Time was when the searchers after the dead had been younger: had been comparatively young as the fathers and mothers of young men are apt to be, as pitifully young as their widows must be. But that time had not lasted long — " You'd think they'd be ashamed to forget so soon," Father used to say — and George had then been too small to be trusted in the company of believers, though he had crawled about on the floor and received instruction in the art of wire-laying. Since then the rush had dwindled year by year; and now Father had to travel about, seeking after the seekers for the dead, and would be at home for at best three days out of the week.

It was mainly the seekers for the dead he sought; though about his pursuit there was a certain delicacy. Mr. Sprott of York might have been a gold mine, particularly as dead Phyllis Sprott's maid had come into the fold of the faithful in Birmingham, and " there's nothing," as Father used to say, " they won't tell you, without having the faintest idea they've told you anything." But he always preferred to rely on the mere séance fees alone. " After all," he used to say, exchanging a nod with Momma, " we're luckier than most." Momma sighed. " Yes, poor blesséd Pop," turning up her eyes to the shadowed ceiling. " So we'll leave 'em be, we'll leave 'em be," he used to say, jerking his head over his shoulder, as if there stood behind

him hosts of the credulous bereaved; and through the half-
light one could see his fingers darting and interweaving in
some new technical trick.

For lately his technique from being his joy and pride, had
changed into an agonised preoccupation. It accounted for the
lesser but far more harrowing part of his trips about the country. First of all he would read, either in the daily papers or in
some journal of his craft, an account of some new medium,
and sit swaying his cooling cup of tea in the air and groaning
aloud, " They can't do that. No one could do that! Yet I wonder. I wonder — I wish I could see this fellow working." Then
he would get up and walk about the room saying, " I couldn't
do that, you know, I couldn't do what the papers say that
chap does. But they're all such liars." Nevertheless he would
know no rest till he had made arrangements to attend one
of the new medium's séances, and usually not even then. He
was himself again only when he was able to push open the
door into the flame-driven darkness that was his home and cry
out, " Momma! George! Are you there? Why of course you're
there! Well it was nothing, nothing at all! He did that old
trick that Herb Waterbury taught me way back in nineteen
hundred. Say, have you got sausages the way I asked you to?
Now watch me do a swell piece of cooking." And he would
have a happy time with the frying-pan, explaining to them
just how long he had been baffled and what had given the
show away. " It's all right! " he used to end up by saying;
and then, after a pause, he would add, " It's all right, up till
now."

His return was always as triumphant, though the advent of
ectoplasm sorely grieved him. A real or fancied identification
with inflated calves' lights touched his professional dignity.
" ' I'm a spiritualist medium,' I said to him, ' and a spiritualist
medium I remain, without setting up for a tripe-shop,' " he

once reported, "and me that never has any insides in the house except liver, and that I wouldn't if it weren't good for the blood." But in spite of this invariable triumph Father seemed to be suffering from these researches. Perhaps the suspense was too much for him. At any rate he lost weight, he began to cough, when he put up his hand to the gas-jet one seemed to be able to see the light through it. "For crying out loud," said Momma at breakfast one morning, "why do you want to run around the country snooping after fellows like these fellows that don't matter two hoots anyhow?" "Oh, one wants to know," said Father stirring his tea. "Oh, for the Lord's sake what is there to know?" asked Momma. But he answered her only with the resolute, weak, and apprehensive stare of a very ill man; which indeed he was now to such an extent that he could no longer conduct a séance by himself. For some time past he had fallen into the habit of taking George with him, although the boy was only sixteen, and handing the séance over to him. Shy as the boy was, this was heaven to him. He loved the feeling of sitting in the blackness facing his father, with their four perfect hands weaving unseen a web of emotion that fell on their companions and made those their subjects. He loved hearing his father's voice throb and soar in the ecstasy of the seer, and letting his own voice come jagged out of his throat, and recognising them as the same voice. He loved leaving the hot room and the tearful thanks, and the moist handshakes, and travelling home in the tube beside his wonderful father, who was insubstantial as flame, as delicate as a pointed church window.

Every day his father was looking more and more wonderful. But he had been looking very old, and the night he came back from Liverpool, where he had gone for the double reason of holding a séance and seeing a medium who claimed to get spirit writing without the slate, he looked very young. That was what struck George when he raised his eyes from his hands and saw his father standing at the open door. " I don't believe Dad's looked as young as this all the time I can remember him," he thought, and shot a glance at Momma, wondering if she would notice it too; but for some time she had been drowsing, her chin was down among her sausage-curls on her bust. Looking back at his father, he saw that the gaslight was showing crystal beads of rain on his coat, and that his draggled hat hung from his lax hand. He had not, as he always had done before, left his wet clothes in the hall above. " Why, Father, let me take your things! " he said. His father allowed it but did not help, standing quite still, and murmuring " My dear boy." When he was free of his things he went over and sat down on the floor in front of Momma, leaning back against her knees. " I'm sick, Cora," he said, " the way I was when you found me in that hotel in Pittsburgh." She stirred in her drowse and, putting out her hand to the new weight on her knee, stroked his hair. " It's grand to be back," he said, stretching back his throat, seeking her with his blazing eyes, his bright cheeks. " I know you'll look after me." Then his head slipped forward, and he sat nodding into the shadows, trouble growing in his eyes. " Maybe it was because I was sick, but I couldn't see how that chap worked his tricks. Not one of them. But maybe it was because I was sick. Cora! Cora! " he called quite loudly. " Do you think there's something in it after all? "

Momma was nearly fetched out of her drowse. She made her automatic response at that hour, her raps began to travel round the skirting, up the side of the fireplace; but sleep took her before they crossed the mantelpiece. It sounded as if a question had been asked, but the answer was not given. Father's chin dropped, his lips twitched in a desperate grimace, his hands began to practise with an invisible slate. George ran forward and knelt beside him. " Father, let me help you to bed," he begged. " I don't want to go to bed," said Father, " you'd think bed was a medicine the way some people talk. It's just something you lie down on." " Well let me get the doctor." " I don't want a doctor," said Father, " he couldn't tell me what's worrying me. That's all that's the matter with me. A bit of worry. And anyway no doctor knows as much about sickness as your Momma here. She's a grand nurse. I never would have got out of Pittsburgh alive if it hadn't been for her. Would I, dear? " " But, Father—— " " George, let me alone. Leave us alone. You mustn't come between Momma and me. We're all right together. See? " He looked up into the boy's face and his eyes changed as if a cloud of colder thought had blown across his mind. In a remote whisper he said, " Kiss me, boy." Then he went on, " We'll be all right, we'll go to bed when Momma's ready. And in the meantime I want to practise something. So good-night, son."

When George and the daily maid tiptoed into the room in the morning they found him still sitting with his head against Momma's knees; and Momma's grief at the moment of waking, and for ever afterwards, was frenzied and despairing. She offered George no help—but then for years it had been taken for granted that her relationship with the practical was tenuous in the extreme—in working out the problem of how he must live. Their position was not desperate. Ira Wickett had left some provision for his daughter. The house was theirs, and there was a little money. But it was not quite enough. There was needed exactly that sum that Father had made out of his séances. It was plain, therefore, that the problem was virtually solved: George must give the séances his father had given. It was an easy solution, and indeed there was no other. The lessons in mediumship his father had given him every evening had gravely interfered with his general education; he had no friends outside the spiritualist world whose influence he could evoke to give him employment; and, indeed, if he had been able to do so it would have been useless, for his mother's state of health would have prevented his going out to work every morning. For she was not getting over her loss, on the contrary she was every day more subject to it. She was in a perpetual state of hysteria that seemed at times to be verging on a more delusionary condition. Almost every day she would sit in her basket chair making raps, and would suddenly forget what she was doing and shriek with fear at the raps, and wonder if they were Father coming back to her, and then cry because she had been so cowardly as to be afraid of dear Father. In the evening it was better, for she fell into her drowse earlier and earlier; but it was quite impossible to think of leaving her every day.

So, though without vanity, he expected to be civilly received, as one who is properly shouldering his responsibilities, when he told his schoolmaster that he was leaving school at the end of the term and was going to be a medium. He was surprised, he was hurt, when he saw a look in the man's eye that plainly meant something very different. He had always known that all his teachers pitied him for something to do with his parentage, but he had thought this due to the preference for insipidity which is almost part of education. So far as he had seen anything of the homes of other children, their mothers were far inferior to his own in richness, their fathers far inferior to his in every conceivable quality that could be admired. But now he perceived that his parents had been blamed for a specific reason, and that now he too was going to be blamed instead of being pitied.

George did not like it, because the little man had always been very kind to him. He had an impulse to defend himself, to explain how his father's lessons in legerdemain had kept him back in his studies. But he had to bite his lip and break off the sentence. People did not understand about that. It would seem to the schoolmaster as if he was confessing that his father had been a cheat and that he was going to be one; and he could not find the words to explain that really it was not like that at all. He felt helpless and unhappy, and more than ever conscious of the coldness of the little man's eyes. He wanted to rouse his sympathies by telling him about his mother, how ill she was, how she thought that the rappings she herself had made were spirit messages, but it struck him immediately that that also would not do. He had to stand stupidly looking down at the floor till the schoolmaster, speaking to him more icily than he had ever done before, told him he could go.

That was the first time that George felt conscious of a difference between himself and other people, which consisted in his inability to be candid about many of the things concerning which they had nothing to hide. It depressed him every time he thought of it during the following winter, although his happiest moments came when he was giving his séances. He would leave the dark house, made desolate by Momma weeping and moaning, or laughing loudly over some small inexplicable joke, he would travel across London, or across England, it might be, to a room where something so delightful was to happen that at any point in his journey he could dismiss its tedium by resting his forehead on his hand and thinking how presently he would be sitting in the blackness, using his hands as his father taught him, palming the slate without a sound so quickly that it never showed a trace of the hand's heat, and letting his voice bell in his throat so that it sounded like his father's and whipped up the passions of the hidden people all about him, so that though the eye saw nothing the mind saw a circle of blazing light. There was always a point in the séance when this light grew so strong that he knew that he himself could not be responsible for it and he felt his father's spirit sitting close to him. Whatever he said then meant something to all of the sitters. The light would blaze higher, it would recede, when the poor real light flooded the room it was obvious that virtue had gone out of him. As they pressed in on him he would forget how he had spent weeks piecing together the convincing messages from the dead for which they thanked him, it would seem that the unknown dead had spoken through his lips, that the unknown dead had kissed him on the lips, and he would go out into the night dazzled and smiling and drunken. But in the third-class carriage he would remember that he had lied, and his chin would fall lower and lower inside his turned-up collar. When he got back to the silent house Momma would be lying in her bed, breathing stertorously, but as unlike herself as she had been a year or two ago as if she were dead; as unresponsive to the hand he laid on her, the mouth he pressed on her forehead as if she were dead; dumbfoundingly just a body. He would stand beside her, looking up at the ceiling, asking what that which is not the body is, and where it goes, as if he expected to find it a small moth folded somewhere on the cornice of the discoloured plaster.

George slept late after such nights; but after one such he woke early, one morning in the March following his father's death. For his mother stood by his bedside, calmer than she had been for months, and more brisk and purposeful than he had seen her since his childhood, though she was so bodily destroyed that for a second or two he looked at her in horror without listening to what she had to say. Her sausage-curls, which she now neither dyed nor brushed, were greasy, grey, soiled springs, her cheeks were purple, her stoutness was so increased that her dressing gown did not meet. He cried out in pain, " Oh, Momma, Momma! " But she hushed him with a finger and said, " Quiet now, your Dad's right nervous." The hair standing up on his head, he lay still. She went on, " You know well's I do he hasn't been home for months. And here was I thinking he was just like the ones I had before him. But he's back sitting in the kitchen, and he's looking peaked. He's got a story of having been on a long journey." She passed the lapel of her dressing gown across her lips and stared in front of her under knit brows, as if weighing evidence. " It's a queer story, but I believe it. So we'll treat him right. Come down and talk to him while I cook him some breakfast. He's looking real peaked I tell you."

George followed her down the creaking stairs into the kitchen where there was nothing but the raw morning light. She nodded to an empty chair and said, in the ironical tone of one who forgives but dreads to be laughed at for forgiving so tries to put a complexion of mockery on it all, " Well, here's the boy," and sharply bade George in an undertone, " Give your Dad a kiss." Then she turned to the kitchen-range and busied herself with a frying-pan of bacon. " Momma," said George. " Momma." Over her shoulder she said, " It's your Dad you should talk to. Make him feel at home. We've both wanted him at home, I'm sure."

He knelt down beside the empty space she kept on looking at, and whispered, " Father, Father." It might be so. But he had hardly time to drop his lids, so that in darkness he might see better, before a whimper from his mother brought him up again. She was leaning against the mantelpiece, shaking with a fever and crying out in a delirium which did not leave her until three days after, when she died. George's grief was greater than he had expected, for he had never felt much emotion about her other than a joy in the lusciousness she had had before she got so ill. He admired the doctor very much, and was puzzled and worried because he had an air of impatience and even disgust when he came into the house, and always spoke curtly to him. He was relieved when the doctor said that he would come in the day after the funeral to have a look at him. It showed there was no actual ill-feeling.

But the doctor was still curt when he said, " I thought so. Your lungs are pretty bad. Be careful of yourself, or there'll be T.B. and a sanatorium. No hard work, no indoor work." He gave brief directions for a régime, and was out in the garden on his way to his car as he gave the last. " And, above all, no drink."

" I never drink," said George.

" Not yet, perhaps, but you'd better guard against it."

" Why? " asked George. Then, as his eyes met the doctor's, he cried out indignantly, " My mother didn't drink. She took it sometimes as medicine because her heart was so bad. But she didn't drink."

The doctor was silenced. He made a step back towards the boy, and stopped; and his hands described a gesture of apology.

George bowed his head in acknowledgment and stood staring at something light on the ground that had caught his eye. Up till that moment he had always taken his mother's behaviour as just a mother's behaviour. He did not know that all mothers did not become comatose in the evening after a gradual mellowing; the very smell that hung about her he had accepted as the usual attribute of a mother. But he was suddenly and immediately convinced.

" She must have been a very remarkable woman in her youth," said the doctor uncomfortably.

" Who told you that? " asked George; and with a rush of hope he added, " Did you know my father? "

" No," said the doctor, " but I have read about her."

" Where, where? " asked George.

" Good-bye, I will look in again," flustered the doctor.

George's eye went back to the light object on the ground. He had been convinced of something else. If the doctor had read of his mother it could only be because she had at some time been exposed as a fraudulent medium. He remembered now that it had always been kept a secret that she had been Cora, that he had been told from his childhood that he must never mention Grandpop Ira in front of any of the believers.

He was conscious that the light object he was looking at was a cluster of snowdrops. Their whiteness and the innocence of their slenderness and drooping bells were to him a symbol of everything that his circumstances were not. For a minute he had a wild impulse to run through the gate and throw himself on the mercy of the doctor who was sitting in his car, having some difficulty with his clutch. But he reflected that the doctor, though plainly possessed of full affinity with success and respectability, would not help him. Did not the advice the doctor had just before given him sentence him to being a medium and nothing else?

The next six years passed slowly, miserably, successfully. George was at first known as the boy medium, and as he grew into manhood ladies often likened him to the poet Shelley. He would look like a young, dying god when they bound his hands and tied him up in the cabinet, a lock of his fine goldish-brown hair falling over his forehead, his mouth pressed as if in pain, his thin frame heaving with the deep sighs breathed in expectation of his ordeal. While they sat in darkness it was as if a living god moved among them, showering prodigies, writing messages, giving flowers, creating out of space the hands of beloveds that caressed as they had done when living, filling the air so full of spirits that some, unable to insert themselves in the sequence of materialisations, rapped the walls and furniture till it was like a bombardment. When they untied the knots at the end of the séance he was very nearly a dead god. His white skin, glazed with the most delicate conceivable form of sweat, looked like fine porcelain; he hardly breathed, but joy lingered on his lips. He would refuse all company to the station, and would sit with bent spine, and hanging head, to his journey's end. He was hungry not only for the immortality of his dear ones, but for honour, so that when he re-entered the dark house he could comfort himself with no fantasy about them. If it had been Father's step he had heard on the stairs, if suddenly Momma's raps had started in the basement below, he would have remained sitting on his bed, with his head on his hands. There were too many accusations to be made if he had opened the door; there were too few conceivable defences.

Loneliness was George's tragedy. He could make no friends among the believers, not so much because he felt he could not be friendly with people whom he cheated, as because he knew that those with whom he would much rather be friends would feel like that; and soon, too, he found himself calculating that this remoteness was of commercial value to him, in enhancing the effect of his personality. Since he was so successful he was able to afford good holidays, to stay at moderately expensive hotels in England and in Switzerland where he could come in contact with the friends he desired; but though he had the presentability that is cultivated by those who are doubtful of themselves it was cancelled by the sense of guilt that tied his tongue. It was during one such holiday that, shut in his room in the evenings, he wrote an article on the sorrows of a man who was brought up to be a fraudulent medium and could do no other work, and sent it to a London newspaper which published it over a pseudonym and sent him a few guineas for it. It relieved his feelings for a time, and he got a bitter and contemptuous kind of pleasure from seeing the article attacked as untrue in the correspondence columns by believers whom he had often cheated. It brought him a letter from a female medium, who was careful to give only a box number at a stationer's shop, confessing that she too was in a like position, having been reared to deceive and having no other means of livelihood nor relations who could help her to them. George was sorry for her, though for some reason he visualised her as being like Momma in her last stages, purplish and stout and bedressing-gowned, and he answered her kindly. But the correspondence naturally languished after a few exchanges; it could hardly consist of anything but reiterated complaints and commiserations. Perhaps the best thing his article did for him was to mitigate his sense of unimportance and isolation; for the newspaper liked to keep in touch with him, since he could supply them with possible explanations of the miracles imputed to any sensational new medium.

But often George thought that he should not have written that article, particularly while he was conducting a séance or had just given a very successful one. Was it right to make people think that there was nothing in spiritualism when night after night he felt his father close to him in the darkness? There might be tricks, and tricks again, but there was also a magical transfusion of matter, a sieve-like quality of this world that let in siftings from eternity. It was little enough when he wanted the whole of his father back again just as he used to be, but was it not something that that very night he had been certain, as the knots round his ankles fell unloosed in a second, that his hands had superhuman agility because they were not his but his father's? He was thinking that very thought as he stood putting on his overcoat after a séance at Barnet when a man he knew, one of the believers, came in and told him he would be welcome at a demonstration by a voice medium that was taking place at a private house not far distant. He said he would go, because of a hope that there his father might be also, which turned, as soon as the open air fanned his face, into a weariness that he should leave one circle of fools sitting in darkness round a cheat to go to another.

But this other séance was not in darkness. Round a large drawing-room furnished in the Victorian style with brass chandeliers, a prodigious mantelpiece crowned by a large marble presentation clock, and many gold-framed pictures representing Highland cattle, undaunted by the bright lights, undaunted by all the respectability, the medium was running about with a long trumpet in her hand. She was the most fairylike person he had ever seen. She wore a dress of accordion-pleated blue muslin, falling from a band of silk that girded a bust as flat and narrow as a child of ten's though she was perhaps eighteen; and because of her floating skirts and the way her light brown gold-dusted hair blew back from her forehead, she seemed to flutter and poise like a winged sprite as she ran about the room, holding out her trumpet to each of the dozen persons that were sitting there in turn. Her lips perpetually curved in a gentle smile; she waited till each had alternately put his ear to the trumpet and spoken into it, for perhaps three minutes, then, breaking into a freshet of nervous, high pitched yet soft laughter, she pulled the trumpet away and sped on with it to someone else. She came to George very soon after he had entered the room, but at first he did not take the end of the trumpet from her, he was marvelling so much at her extreme pallor, which suggested not that she had no blood but that her blood was more ethereal than other people's. But she remained in front of him, rising and falling slightly on her toes, and perpetually smiling, till he put his ear to the trumpet. A far whisper said, "It's

. . . ther." It must be Father; for nobody had ever called his mother anything but Momma. He said, " Is that you, Father? " The whisper answered, " Yes." He stared along the trumpet into the medium's pale shining grey eyes, which looked at once blind and farseeing, which brightly turned about and seemed to bless by not recognising the essential quality of anything on which they lay. In full faith he cried down the trumpet, " Did you help me with my hands tonight? " and the whisper answered, "Yes, my son, and in many other ways." He dropped his end of the trumpet, and stood with his jaw dropping, wishing that he had not been one of the fools he himself habitually cheated, asking questions that suggested their correct answers. But on the medium's face was a smile so sweet that it might well have been the centre and source of a halo. He shuddered, knowing that he was in the presence of a true medium; and then shuddered again, for as she stepped away from him she had laughed, and he had desired her as he had never desired any woman.

After the séance George was introduced to her; her name was Ivy Bentham. She talked to him pleasantly with that wonderful laugh coming up to the surface, sometimes merely shimmering behind her words. When somebody told her that he too was a medium he thought she looked distressed, and his heart stood still lest it had got abroad that he was a false medium, and she had heard. But she let him travel with her back to London, and leave her at the boarding-house where she lived with her mother, who at the moment was, she explained, absent in the North nursing a sister through a dangerous illness; and she told him too that he might telephone the next day. There was no question but that she liked him, and though of course he was not good enough for her he might have been her husband and her servant had he not been cursed with this heritage of fraud and trickery. When he got home to the dark and empty house that night he shouted oaths at the creaking on the stairs, the stirrings down in the basement. If they were what he had sometimes thought they were, so much the better. He told them three weeks later that it was because they had made him what they had that he was going to do this dirty trick and marry Ivy while her mother was away, and not tell her the truth till he had had one month of perfect happiness. But he did not abuse them. He felt a kinship with all evil, a need for alliance against the good, for he was haunted by a fear that one of the angels who spoke through Ivy's trumpet, who, she had shyly and even uncomfortably told him, had watched over her since she was ten years old, might tell her what he was. He even planned that he would bring her back there to make his confession. For he felt that Father with his twisting white fingers would bring a touch of legerdemain to the situation which would turn it all to the family's account; and he felt that Momma, sitting in the basement making her raps, would wear it all down, would make the angels sink into such a thick drowse as her own. He knew himself doubly a Judas for these plans because it was not until he had heard his father whispering down her trumpet, and had asked her solemnly if there was no trickery in her voices, and she had as solemnly denied it, that he had known for certain that the dead are alive and can be called on for aid according to their quality.

"You look so white!" Ivy had said to George as they left the Registry Office. They had had no difficulty in getting married, although her mother was still at Whitley Bay, and seemed from her letters frigidly displeased at the mere notion of her daughter's engagement, because, to his surprise, she was as old as he was: she was twenty-three. But that whiteness, which was indeed excessive, vanished almost as soon as they started their honeymoon at Swanage. He was delighted simply to be there, a married man, which was such an ordinary, unexceptional sort of thing to be, and had great delight in getting into conversation with people and telling them that in London he was a bank clerk; and he was amazed to find that Ivy was enjoying the same sort of pleasure. She had, it appeared, told the landlady that before her marriage she had been a private secretary. But their chief delight was their possession of each other. Ivy was magic, she was marvellous, she was worthy of these gifts which, when he thought of them, cooled him with reverence. She had everything, even a beautiful melancholy, which he thought not unnatural in one who was in touch with the secrets of eternity. Sometimes she would look wildly into his face and then dissolve into weeping that was the sad and enchanting sister of her laughter. He would comfort her until she slept, and then he would go out and walk by the sea thinking how wicked he was: the false that had seduced into union the true. He had deceived her utterly. She would look into his face sometimes and say, " You know I can't imagine your doing anything wrong."

But for the most part it was ecstasy, if they embraced, or if they did not. Perhaps George's highest ecstasy was when for three days he had spared her his passion, and he felt in tune with her purity, so that like her he was unassailable. He felt a great pity for all other human beings. He even thought of the poor fat and mottled old fraudulent medium who had written to him about his article, and routed her address out of his notebook, and sent a letter telling her not to despair, because there was some truth in spiritualism, there were mediums so holy that they could pierce the veil between the worlds and could let loose the radiance of eternity on mortal man. It was unfortunate that just after that his passion broke loose and he was her lover more urgently for a night than, he thought, any man had any right to be to his wife. He was afraid he had offended her, for she was very remote all that morning, and would not go out with him, saying she wanted to write a letter. But she had really written a letter, she had nearly finished the box of pale blue fancy stationery they had bought.

As the time for his return drew nearer his distress grew more unconcealable. He would bury his face in the pillow, groaning, " I don't want to go back! " And she, poor thing, thinking she understood, thinking merely that he meant that he had been happy here and did not want to go back to his work, was kind to him. Sometimes he even played with the idea of not telling her. But he would not let the dead that are damned master him quite to that extent; even if he invoked their aid after he did it, he must align himself with the beloved saved by that one act of confession. He must, to raise one practical point, give her the chance of leaving him, of deciding, even though she would forgive his prostitution of what was to her a holy cult, whether she could face being his wife if he was exposed as a fraud. Remembering the sickening hours he had spent in a Public Library reading up the exposure of Momma in the nineties, he felt he had to put that to her; although he meant to put it to her in the dark house, where Momma's raps under their feet might somehow turn the balance.

So she said again, " You look so white! " when the cab stopped among the grassy ruts in the road that was already shadowed by the butt of the hill in front of the afternoon sun. George smiled at her, and told her to take her time in collecting the smaller packages, and lifted out the suitcases. Very slowly he carried them up the path and rang the bell at the front door. The patterns of clear glass on the panes of frosted glass seemed to let out darkness into the day, instead of letting the day into the darkness, as it was meant. When the old daily maid came he said, " How are you, Mary? " and carried the suitcase into the hall. For a minute he stood feeling the full weight of the shadow on his shoulders. Then his eye was caught by something on the hall table, and he bent forward. Then he straightened himself again and looked down the black staircase that led down to the basement. " Poor old Father! " he said. " Poor old Momma."

He turned and went back into the garden, and called out to the cabman who was unstrapping the bigger suitcase, " No, wait a minute." He was not sure whether he would ever take Ivy into this house. He thought not. There was a nice big villa opposite the station which called itself a Private Hotel, and they could stay there till he had settled up everything. There was a nice big garden where Ivy could sit. He suspected her of needing sun and fresh air as much as he did. He went to meet her as she came through the gate, took some of her packages, and began to lead her about the garden. " Here's where a big clump of snowdrops came up every Spring," he said, and was touched to see that though nothing could be less interesting, she was interested for his sake. Abruptly he asked her if she would mind very much if they gave up being mediums, if they sold this house and went to somewhere like Swanage and kept a shop; and because he saw in her eyes the look of a trapped creature that feels at last kind fingers loosening the spring on its leg, he looked away and squeezed her arm and said, " That's what we'll do, then." Then his eyes went back to the patch of earth where the snowdrops came, and he said irrelevantly, " Poor Momma, poor Momma." He hardly knew why he said it, he was only filling in time while he wondered whether he would or would not tell her about the two pale blue envelopes, both readdressed, that he had found lying side by side on the hall table. But it did not matter, it would be all right anyway.

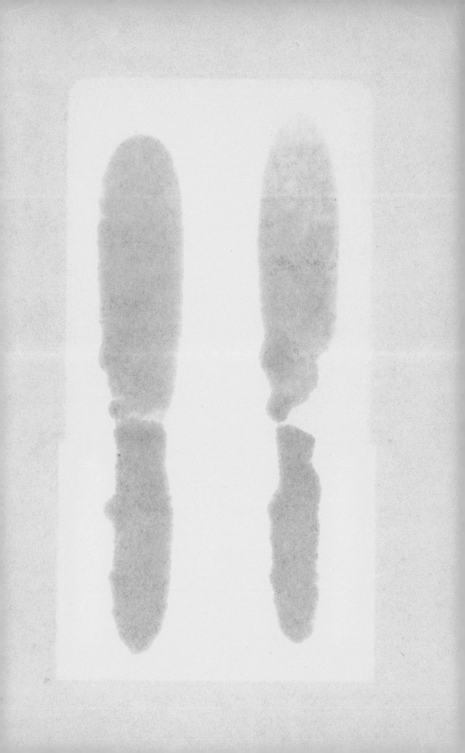

DATE DUE

GAYLORD   PRINTED IN U.S.A.